"Let your mom have some caffeine first!"

Troy passed Michelle a cup of coffee. The tree had more presents underneath it now than it had when she'd finally gone to bed last night. She glanced up at him. He met her gaze with a big grin and grabbed her free hand.

"I know you don't want charity, but I've got more money than I need and no one to spend it on. You guys have had a tough time, and I know you wanted to make this Christmas special for the kids."

His eyes were warm, and his expression sincere.

"Plus, this should get me out of doing dishes, shouldn't it?" His eyes sparkled as he broke the serious mood.

Michelle took back her hand, reluctantly. It had felt better than it should have. She'd invited Troy for Christmas, thinking she was paying him back for all he'd managed to do for them. But somehow, he'd turned things around again, and she was even more in his debt.

Dear Reader,

I'm thrilled to be here with my second Harlequin Heartwarming book, and that you're here, as well!

We met Troy in my first book, *Crossing the Goal Line*. He wasn't exactly hero material. But what if he lost some of his macho attitude? What if he got sick, and couldn't have kids? How would that affect him?

Then I considered what kind of woman could match him. She'd need to be strong. And who would be stronger than an army veteran? Enter Michelle, widowed, newly discharged, with two kids. The trio push Troy out of his comfort zone, and inspire him to be a better man.

I'd love to hear from readers. You can find me at kimfindlay.ca, on Facebook under KimFindlayAuthor or on Twitter, @missheyer74.

Kim

HEARTWARMING

Her Family's Defender

———

Kim Findlay

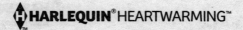

Recycling programs
for this product may
not exist in your area.

ISBN-13: 978-1-335-63363-7

Her Family's Defender

Copyright © 2018 by Kim Findlay

Printed in U.S.A.

Kim Findlay lives in Toronto, Canada, with her husband, two sons and the world's cutest dog. When she can get time away from her accounting business, she can be found sailing, reading or writing, depending on the season, time of day and her energy level. You can find her at kimfindlay.ca, on Twitter, @missheyer74, or on Facebook.

Books by Kim Findlay

Harlequin Heartwarming

A Hockey Romance

Crossing the Goal Line

Visit the Author Profile page at Harlequin.com for more titles.

To Victoria, Claire, Adrienne and Jessica,
who have made me believe I'm a writer.

CHAPTER ONE

TROY HAD NEVER realized that the carpet in the hallway of his condo building had green in the pattern. But then, he'd never had his nose shoved into it before. As he breathed in the musty odor, he tried to assess just how much trouble he was in.

A crazy fan had somehow flipped Troy over, pinned his arm behind his back and sat on him. Not good. On the other hand, he was bigger than she was, and he should be able to get free; he just didn't want to do any damage to his arm while he did so. Training camp was starting soon, and after missing all of last year, he needed to be healthy and ready to play.

Troy was a professional athlete, he was single and, in his opinion, pretty good-looking. He'd been a key part of the hockey team who'd won the Cup in a hockey-crazy city that hadn't won that prize for more than fifty years. So he had fans. But he'd never had one go so overboard that she'd snuck into his condo building, followed him into the elevator and then somehow dropped him to the floor. He'd be happy not to have another.

Why hadn't he paid more attention to the woman who'd followed him into the elevator? He'd been thinking of the day he'd spent on the water, wondering if he should get a boat for himself instead of checking her for her ranking on the crazy meter.

Which would be in the red zone.

He hadn't really noticed her until he was ready to get out on the penthouse level. There were only two condos on this floor: Troy's and Mrs. Epps's. Mrs. Epps was about eighty, Troy estimated, and she was away, so she wasn't inviting guests over. The only place this woman could be going was Troy's.

Troy enjoyed being popular with fans. He especially enjoyed being popular with female fans. A couple of them had become very popular with him. But he preferred to be the one choosing, and even if she'd been one of his leggy blondes, he didn't want a puck bunny tonight.

So when the door pinged open on the penthouse floor, and she started to exit, he put his arm across the open door to block her progress.

"Sorry, sweetheart. You're not getting out—" he told her, adding a hint of a smile to soften the blow.

The next thing he knew, he was examining the pattern on the carpet while the elevator doors softly closed behind him.

"Do you have a problem?" Troy asked, calling on his reserves of patience. He'd seen the movie *Misery*. He couldn't wait too long to get up if she was a real nutcase. But maybe he could convince her to get off him. And more important, protect his arm from any real damage.

"*I* don't have a problem now," the woman responded. "But *you* will when the police arrive."

Police? He'd welcome them, or even building security. What kind of crazy was this woman?

"I'm not the trespasser here, so you go ahead and call the cops and give yourself up," he said as assertively as he could while breathing in who knows what from the carpet. He was going to have to talk to someone about the cleaning in this building.

"I'm not trespassing," she argued, rustling

through her bag with one hand while keeping the other on his twisted arm.

"There are two people living on this floor. I'm one and an eighty-year-old woman is the other. Since she's away and not getting too many visitors right now, you're going to have trouble selling that story."

"Mrs. Epps is letting us stay in her place while she's on vacation," the woman responded. She'd stopped groping around in her purse. Troy wasn't sure if that was progress. He'd hoped she was searching for her phone to call the cops. Now she had both hands free to use on him. He wished he'd looked at her a little closer. He was starting to entertain the notion that she might be dangerous. She'd appeared harmless, but she obviously had some skills, since he was incapacitated on the floor, and she'd done enough research to have discovered not only where he lived, but also that Mrs. Epps was his neighbor and currently on vacation. It was adding up to *stalker* in his books.

"Nice try. Why don't we call security and ask them about this?" he suggested. Crap. He was going to sneeze. Would she break his arm if he did?

"How do you think I got into the building? Security let me in," she retorted.

He was going to have to talk to security, as well.

He spoke in a quiet, soothing voice as if she was a nervous dog prepared to attack. "Okay, then, if you really are staying here legitimately, and everything is on the level, why did you attack me?"

"I didn't attack you!" Her voice rose. "You attacked me and I defended myself!"

"Attacked you? I didn't touch you! I just tried to keep an unauthorized person from following me to my place!"

"You tried to keep me in the elevator using force."

"That wasn't force. You need to chill out."

"Easy for a man to say," she responded with rancor, but she released his arm and stood up. Troy carefully tested his arm and, finding it a little sore but undamaged, got carefully to his feet.

She took a few steps back and Troy got his first good look at her. She was shoulder height to him, about his age, but fit and held herself erect. Her hair was dark and long and tied back in a messy ponytail. She had no makeup on, and she was wearing a rumpled T-shirt and shorts. And she was majorly pissed at him.

She had let him go, but she was still on guard, and it bothered Troy. Wasn't he the one who'd been upended here? She looked like she'd been hiding behind a dumpster for a few days. She didn't appear to belong in his upscale building, let alone the penthouse. But he didn't attack women. Had he done something she could consider threatening?

"I wasn't trying to attack you." He tried a smile, one with a little extra charm in it. "But I think I'd know if my neighbor was letting someone stay in her place. The condo board here is pretty strict, so people don't just drop off their keys to strangers. You've got a good story, but you should just walk away now."

Apparently, the charm in his smile wasn't working on her. She narrowed her eyes and put her fists on her hips. "Do you even read your condo notices?" she said witheringly. "The board sent one out to inform residents that we were going to be staying in Mrs. Epps's place. But go ahead and call security if you want. Just do it fast. I've had a tiring day, and I don't want to be standing around any longer than I have to."

She gave him a long stare, stepped back another few feet and reached into her bag again. He tensed, but when she pulled out her hand she had only grabbed her phone. She swiped it, tapped, and started opening something on the screen. She found what she wanted and held it up to him. "This is a copy of the condo letter."

She must have decided she was either out of danger or that she could handle whatever threat he posed, because she crossed over to him and held the phone out. He reached for it, but she held on. As if he'd try to steal it.

Reading the screen, he recognized the condo logo on top and scanned enough to verify that Mrs. Epps had asked the board to let someone stay in her condo, and that the board had agreed.

The brunette stepped back once he raised his eyes. Darn, he was in the wrong. She'd nailed it when she'd guessed he never read those condo board letters. They were usually about some stupid rule, and no one expected him to follow every rule.

He should apologize, but it stuck in his throat. He was a big guy, and made his living dominating his opponents physically. This woman had dropped him to the carpet without breaking a sweat. That was troublesome. She had no idea who he was, and that made him all too aware of the year he'd missed playing, and what else he could still miss. And certainly the way she was looking at him like he was a creep wasn't helping.

But fair was fair. She did belong here, and he'd missed the memo. He probably had more paperwork about the whole deal that he'd ignored.

"Okay. I'm sorry I tried to block you from getting off the elevator. But you didn't need to pin me to the ground. Maybe say something next time."

"You think *I* overreacted?." She eyed him levelly. "Have you ever been assaulted?"

He squelched the glib response that tried to work its way up. A lot of guys came after him on the ice. He was assaulted pretty well every hockey game. But he was paid for that, and knew what he had signed up for. What she was talking about couldn't compare. And if she had been attacked herself at some point…

She continued. "I was in the Forces. I learned how to protect myself, and I don't apologize for that. I have two kids who will be staying here with me. I will protect them, as well."

And with that she turned and walked toward Mrs. Epps's door. She inserted the key and walked in without giving him another look.

TROY LOOKED AT himself in his bathroom mirror. He was dressed only in running shoes and shorts. Some might label this prolonged self-examination as narcissistic. Troy certainly would admit to vanity, but that wasn't what this was about.

He was fit; more fit than he'd ever been. And as a professional athlete, he was used to being in good shape. There was nothing to concern him in his reflection. But still he stared, trying to drill beneath the skin, down through the blood and muscles to the basic cell structure. It was useless. If the cancer was coming back, he wouldn't find it on the outside, just like he'd noticed nothing a year ago when it first attacked him.

Still, he looked at himself. He was in peak condition, but knew that as fit as he was, as well as he ate and trained and as much as he checked himself every day, he was no longer invulnerable. He never had been: he just hadn't realized. Now he did. And while he saw the same body in the mirror now that had made him one of the best defensemen in the league, he couldn't trust it anymore.

"ANGIE, THIS IS your room." Michelle paused in the doorway, letting her daughter peer inside.

"Wow!" Angie said. "This place is awesome! Way better than our old house in Winnipeg!" She pushed past her mother, eager to start pulling her belongings out of the boxes and finding places for them in this larger room.

Michelle smiled. She'd agonized over the decision to move. Leaving behind the city they'd called home for years hadn't been easy. Growing up an army brat and then joining the Forces herself, she was accustomed to moving. This, though, was the first time she'd relocated entirely on her own, leaving a support network behind without having one waiting for her. Her encounter with the man who apparently lived across the hall had made her second-guess her decision, but that had been the only negative note so far.

She'd just picked up the kids from the airport and was showing them their home for the next few months. They were going from base housing to a penthouse condo. They should be pleased.

Tommy was tight on her heels, following her to the next doorway.

"And this is your room."

Tommy paused, considering. He'd always been a quiet kid, but during the past year he'd become more so. Michelle tried not to reveal her worry: they each had to work through their grief in their own way.

"It's nice. Where's your room, Mom?" he asked.

Michelle wrapped her arm around his shoulders. He kept close tabs on her, and that was only natural. She hoped the new setting might help him come out of his shell.

She led the way to the master suite. She'd never had a room like this in her life. As an army brat, her lodgings had always been geared more to function than comfort or style. But this room had a king-size bed, walk-in closet and en-suite. Which meant she wouldn't have to share a bathroom with the kids. She couldn't remember ever having a bathroom to herself before.

Angie soon followed them in to scope out the rest of the place.

"This is wicked. How long can we stay here?" she said, running her hands over the duvet on the bed.

"We're house-sitting for Mrs. Epps until you get out of school in June. Don't get too used to it, though. We were lucky Great Aunt Agnes knew her friend was looking for a house sitter. After this we'll have to find our own place and start paying rent, and we definitely won't be able to afford anything on this scale."

Tommy had gone to the windows, providing vistas across the city. "No one could get in through these windows, could they?"

"Of course not, dork," Angie responded.

"Angie, don't call your brother names."

Tommy frowned at his sister. "Toronto is dangerous. I heard Grandma telling Mom that."

Michelle sighed. The kids had recovered enough from the tragedy in their past to resume their sibling bickering, which was good, but exasperating, as well. She gave Tommy a stern look. "You weren't supposed to be listening. Toronto is no more dangerous than Winnipeg."

According to the statistics, anyway. But it didn't feel that safe. It was big and strange compared to living on the base. For example, the way she had responded to the man in the elevator. That had been a gut reaction. She'd been attacked once, years ago, though luckily her training and fitness had prevented the attack from being more than an attempt. Since then she'd kept herself prepared, physically and mentally.

Michelle wondered if she should warn the kids about their neighbor. She hadn't run into him since that first encounter, so with any luck they wouldn't have very many encounters with him. He obviously was well-off, since he lived here and dressed the way he did. But he still made her nervous. He'd *said* he thought she was following him, but what kind of person suspected perfect strangers of following him home? She hoped her warning would be sufficient and he'd behave if the kids did run into him.

Michelle looked at Tommy, who was still eyeing up the windows for security measures. No. She wouldn't worry him further by bringing up their neighbor.

TROY WAS GLAD he didn't bump into his new neighbor when he left for his workout. He'd missed her yesterday, as well, and he hoped that indicated her schedule wouldn't sync up with his. He certainly hadn't seen Mrs. Epps much. He should read that condo letter to check how long she'd be around.

If any of the guys on the team found out

how quickly and easily this woman had dropped him to the floor, he'd never hear the end of it. He didn't think he gave off a scary vibe—at least, not off the ice—and it was unsettling to know he'd made a woman feel threatened. All in all, he would be happy to not run into her very often. He had enough to worry about getting his career back on track.

At the gym he pushed himself like always, did just a bit beyond what he had before— lifting a few pounds more, spinning the bike a little faster. Seeing those numbers rise gave him the illusion that he had his body under his control, and sometimes he needed that. He wiped the sweat off his brow and grinned at the trainer when he gave Troy a thumbs-up.

He was on such an endorphin high he almost forgot the new neighbor until he got home. Somehow, as soon as the elevator doors opened on his floor, the air was vibrating. He paused.

The stairway door pushed open and a young girl raced out then skidded to a halt and stared at him.

He recognized immediately that she was a fan. There was a look, and she had it. A little awestruck, a little overwhelmed and a lot of shock. He smiled. He liked kids, and they tended to like him. He'd been told that was because he still hadn't grown up himself, but that didn't bother him. He believed it was because he still remembered how to have fun; he hadn't lost that with whatever else the cancer had taken.

"You're Troy Green!" she said a little breathlessly.

"I am," he agreed.

"Do you live here?" she asked.

"I do. What are you doing here?" Running up from another floor, he expected.

"I live over there." She pointed at Mrs. Epps's doorway. "We just moved in. Me and my brother and my mom. I'm Angie, and my brother is Tommy and my mom's Michelle."

Ah, the new neighbors.

Just then, Michelle moved like a rocket from the condo doorway to stand in front of her daughter. A younger boy followed her and clung to her side. She was standing protectively, eyes focused on Troy. She spoke to the girl, gaze still on Troy.

"Angie, what have I told you about talking to strangers?"

Angie rolled her eyes. "He's not a stranger, Mom. That's Troy Green."

Michelle's mouth tightened, and she balled her hands into fists.

"How does she know your name? What have you been asking her?"

Troy's jaw dropped. First she thought he was attacking her, and now she thought he was a danger to her daughter?

Angie pushed past her mother with her arms crossed. "I recognized him because I don't live under a rock. He plays for the Blaze." When her mother didn't respond, Angie continued, gesticulating wildly. "The Toronto Blaze! The hockey team! They won the Cup two years ago—the first time in *forever* a Canadian team won it! I watched with Dad before—"

She blinked rapidly, then spun and raced into their condo. Michelle watched her go, one hand resting on the boy's shoulder, her expression troubled. The boy kept his gaze on Troy, but he clearly wasn't a hockey fan. He appeared to be evaluating Troy on some scale and, considering his mother, Troy knew he wouldn't be scoring well. Troy was relieved when Michelle turned back and he could look at her instead.

This time there was no anger in her voice. "I'm sorry we're a bit on edge. We don't know anyone here, and our family from home warned us about Toronto."

Troy kept silent. After the conclusions she'd jumped too, he wasn't in a rush to let her off the hook.

"I'm a little too protective of my kids—do you have any?" she asked.

A voice yelled down the hallway before he could answer.

"No, Mom! He's single, just like you. He's thirty-one, so you're two years older than he is."

Troy had to hold in a laugh. The mother might suspect he was a budding serial killer, but the daughter thought he was okay.

The woman's face flushed. She had picked up on her daughter's matchmaker vibe. "I'm sorry," she repeated. "Come on, Tommy," she said. She pulled the boy to her doorway with some speed.

Troy was glad that this time he wasn't the one feeling awkward.

He wasn't the one feeling awkward the next morning, either, when there was a knock at his door.

MICHELLE HAD HAD no intention of knocking on her neighbor's door—ever. But she had also never imagined she'd have any reason to.

Being a single mom wasn't easy. Michelle

had known moving to Toronto was going to make it more difficult, in some ways. In Winnipeg, she and the kids had a support group: grandparents, the military, friends. The problem was that everyone knew their story. They couldn't escape the pitying glances, the overwhelming sympathy and in some cases, the distance some of their friends had tried to put between her family and theirs, as if they carried a virus that could spread if there was too much contact.

The kids' paternal grandparents were still grappling with their son's death and found it easiest to blame Michelle.

Michelle's family wanted to be supportive, but since they were in the military, they were scattered across the globe. Once Mitch's funeral was over, they'd had to return to their own commitments. They kept in touch by Skype, and they could do that as well from Toronto as Winnipeg.

So here Michelle and the kids were, in a new city, making a new start.

It was the first day of school for all three of them. Last night Michelle had planned carefully so that the morning would go smoothly. Lunches had been made, clothes had been laid out. She had timed what they'd need to do and left a buffer for accidents.

Except she hadn't accounted for the stupid Ontario milk bags. What was wrong with the cartons and jugs they had in Manitoba? In Ontario, the cartons only came in small sizes, and her family went through a lot of milk. She'd picked up one of the pitchers they were supposed to put the bags of milk into, but she hadn't put the bag far enough into the jug, and it had tipped out, pouring milk all over Michelle's shirt and the counter and floor.

And it had been the last bag of milk, of course. So no cereal for the kids. She'd made sandwiches with the last of the bread last night. No toast, no time to make anything like pancakes and she didn't have milk or eggs anyway. The seconds had ticked by. She'd wanted to hit something out of sheer frustration.

She was considering picking up something for the kids' breakfast on the way to school when she heard the faint ping of the elevator and footsteps going down the hallway, followed by the sound of a door opening and closing.

Before she could think it through, she told

the kids to mop up the milk and went to ask her new neighbor for some milk.

She knocked at his door and stepped back. Should she apologize again? Grovel?

The door opened. Her neighbor stood there, but she couldn't form the words.

She understood now that he was a hockey player, and he must have just come in from a run. The weather was still warm and much more humid here than in the Prairies. That would explain why he was wearing only shorts and shoes, and his incredible body was glistening with sweat. She might be a widow with kids, but she could appreciate that.

She stared for a moment, and then suddenly her mind flashed into the past. Back to when she'd first met Mitch, in basic training. They were both young and fit. Mitch had been a runner, and she'd seen him so many times just like this—shirtless, sweaty, looking so good…

But after his last mission, Mitch had come back a changed man. He'd let himself go, along with a lot of other things. So it had been a while since she'd been around a half-naked man looking as good as Troy did right then.

If only it could have been Mitch, still with them in every way. Coming in hot and sweaty from a run and pulling her into his embrace while she squealed, and he pretended not to understand what she was squealing about…

Troy raised his eyebrows. "Hello?"

Michelle forced herself to glance up, and she saw amusement in his eyes. He thought she was tongue-tied from staring at his naked chest. As if. Yes, she was staring at him, but she could handle an attractive body. It was remembering the past that would bring her down.

"Did something happen?" he asked.

Michelle followed his gaze to her shirt and realized the wet milk was making her shirt mostly see-through. Drops were dripping from her hem onto her feet. She could only imagine how the rest of her appeared.

She took a breath. She was army, for goodness' sake. Discharged now, but she was tough. She straightened and looked him in the eyes.

"We're out of milk. Could I borrow some?" She should probably at least say *please*, if not actually grovel, but she just couldn't while he had that smug expression on his face.

He paused for a moment. "Sure," he said and invited her in.

If Michelle had bothered to imagine what a single, successful hockey player would do with his place, she would have pictured this condo. The leather furniture was tan instead of black, and the place wasn't as messy as she might have guessed, but she would wager he had someone come in to clean for him, and that it had been done recently. The big TV, gaming console and sound system, the modern furniture, it was all right out of Single Guy with Money designs.

She followed him into the kitchen, which was sleek and modern—and mostly unused, she suspected. While he opened the fridge, she pulled her shirt from her sticky torso. She'd have to take another quick shower. Reflexively, she pulled her necklace out from under her shirt as he turned to her with one of those ridiculous bags of milk in his large hands.

"Wedding ring?" Troy asked as he eyed her twisting the golden band that hung from her necklace.

Michelle followed his gaze and realized what she'd been doing. She tended to play with the ring when stressed. Before Mitch died, when she'd worn it on her finger, she'd twisted it around and around when she was upset. After he died, she'd moved it onto a necklace around her neck, but the instinct was still there.

It wasn't hard to figure out why she was stressed at that moment. Three people were starting school today, and she was going to have to start her own preparations all over while trying to get them out the door on time. That would count as stress.

But Troy had paused, waiting for an answer. "Yes," she said, taking a step closer to the milk and escape.

"Divorce?" he continued, passing the bag of milk toward her eager hands.

She shook her head. When he didn't let the milk go, she sighed, frustrated. "I'm a widow."

Surprised, he released his grip. She grabbed the needed bag and pivoted to leave.

"Cancer?" he asked. It was an interesting guess, but not unreasonable. Still, Michelle was not getting into their story with a man who was basically a stranger. They were trying to escape the past in Toronto, not drag it along with them.

She glanced over her shoulder as she headed for the door. "Sorry, long story, and I have to shower again and get the kids to school. Thank you for the milk."

She left, aware she was in his debt. She'd have to deal with that. She didn't accept charity. She stood on her own, and didn't plan to let her neighbor think otherwise.

TROY WATCHED MICHELLE LEAVE. The milk-drenched T-shirt had given him a pretty vivid picture of her shape. He'd tried to remember she was someone's mom, but he wasn't blind. And she'd obviously taken a good look at him, so turn about was fair play.

But once she'd said she was a widow, those thoughts had fled.

A presumably young man could die from many causes. But he'd done the research on this during those dark days, and outside of accidents, suicide and murder, cancer was the top cause of death for young men.

He did his best to avoid dwelling on thoughts about cancer. He had a clean bill of health now. He'd beaten it. But every story the papers ran about him now mentioned the reason he'd missed last season. Every reporter wanted to know how he felt about it, if he was over it, if he could return to where and what he'd been.

Of course he said he'd beaten it. Of course he said he was the same player he'd always been; cancer hadn't changed him. He wanted to believe it, so that was what he told everyone.

He couldn't play his game if anyone thought he was soft or weak in any way. So he acted tough, and joked about beating everyone on the ice the way he'd beaten this disease. He never spoke about those black nights. When the doctors had first said the *C* word.

He hadn't thought he was really sick. Just a minor urinary tract infection. The doctors would give him some antibiotics, and then he'd be fine. But it wasn't an infection. It was prostate cancer. There was something in his body that wanted to kill him.

It took a while to get his mind around that. So he'd acquiesced to the advice of his doctors to wait and evaluate how things progressed. He'd tried chemo and radiation, before everyone had finally agreed that surgery was the answer. In hindsight, he'd have been smarter to just have the surgery at the very beginning. The various courses of treatment had meant that he'd missed a whole season before he had a clear bill of health.

During that year—a long, difficult year he did his best to forget—there had been too many nights when he'd woken up in a panic, unable to sleep while Death lay stretched out in the bed beside him.

He was mostly over that now, but there were still nights when he'd wake up, sure he could feel the cancer in his body again, killing him from the inside. The doctors believed they'd caught it all, that it hadn't metastasized and spread elsewhere. It was worth losing his prostate for that. But there were no guarantees.

Michelle's comment about her husband only reminded him of that.

After she left he pulled out his phone and called down to the concierge and asked for the name of his new neighbor. He gave it, and Troy typed "Michelle Robertson" into the search bar of his browser. He added "army" and "widow" to narrow the results down.

He wanted to know why her husband had died. He realized she might not be happy about it, but he was willing to push some boundaries when it came to the big C. He needed to know if it was cancer, and if it was the same kind that he'd had.

Prostate cancer was rare in young men, but Troy knew only too well that didn't mean younger men couldn't get it. He wanted the cause to be anything else, so that Troy's own odds were better.

It took a bit of searching, but he found out the answer. And it was anything but what he'd expected.

CHAPTER TWO

"IT'LL BE GREAT," Michelle said, ruffling Tommy's hair. The look on his face told her that he didn't believe her, but knew she had to say it anyway. She wanted to hug him, but he was too old now for such displays of affection in front of others. So she watched him file into the school with a pang.

Michelle and the kids hadn't arrived at school with the additional time she'd hoped for, but they hadn't been late. The kids were nervous. Angie got more talkative when she was unsure of herself, while Tommy grew even quieter. Michelle was nervous, too, mostly for her kids. Angie was outgoing, and likely to make friends. Tommy had always been shy, with a smaller circle of friends than his sister, but that was even more the case since his father's death. He wouldn't make the first steps to reach out to someone, and her heart ached to force the other boys to be kind to him.

She waved the kids off and then, once they'd disappeared into the school, she headed for the nearest subway entrance.

She hadn't had a chance to familiarize herself with her route to class the way she'd have liked to do. Subways were new to her, since they only had buses back in the 'Peg. Fortunately, the Toronto Transit System was mostly one loop south and north, and one main line east and west. She had to listen carefully to the garbled transit announcements and watch the map closely, but she made her way to school without mishap.

She then followed the instructions she'd carefully printed out to get to her classes.

She'd enrolled in a one-year bookkeeping program. She didn't have an avid interest in numbers, but math had been one of her better subjects, and her years in the Forces hadn't provided her with many marketable skills outside the army. Bookkeeping seemed manageable for someone with only a high school diploma, and it also had good job prospects.

Once she found her classroom, she sat in the back and tried to be invisible as the teacher began the lesson. Since she was so new at this, and hadn't been in class for a long time, she was planning to attend a lot of the lectures in person, even though it was possible to do most of the program online. Though that would be a nice option if she needed to take time with the kids.

The first class was overwhelming. She was scribbling notes madly, even when she didn't understand what she was writing down. The matching principal almost made sense, but who decided on the boundaries for materiality? The students around her were all taking notes on their computers, while she was there with a binder and pen. She couldn't keep up. She was definitely going to have to watch this lecture again at home.

She ate her lunch alone on a bench outside. She watched the other students walk by. They were mostly in groups, and they were all younger. The students were wearing new clothes that looked old, while she was wearing old things that she hoped looked new. She felt ancient and stupid. What had she gotten herself into?

She made her way back to the kids' school for the end of the day in plenty of time and waited for them to come out. Some other parents began to gather. Michelle knew she should introduce herself but she couldn't, not now. She was tired and discouraged. She wasn't ready to answer the questions about what she did, where the children's father was, what had happened and then the inevitable response, "oh how sad."

The bell rang, and kids started spilling from the building.

Angie was the first to appear. She had another girl with her and she dragged her new friend over to her mother.

The other girl, Brittany, was a hockey player, and Michelle understood immediately how the two had bonded. Angie was hockey crazy. Her dad had started to watch games with her before his first tour. Michelle had enrolled her in skating lessons, but Angie had wanted to play hockey and it had been her passion ever since.

It was no surprise that Angie had recognized Troy Green. Angie still loved the Winnipeg Whiteout, but as soon as the move to Toronto had been broached she'd been checking out the Toronto teams and players. The other Toronto club had been around longer, but the Blaze had won the Cup a couple of years ago, and Angie had picked them as her Toronto team.

Angie was overflowing with information she wanted to share with Michelle about Brittany's hockey team. Angie had gotten all the details about when she herself could try out. She and her new friend had compared skills and were sure they would end up on the team together.

Michelle had been avoiding the *H* word. She knew Angie loved hockey, and was good at it, but her ambition of being the first woman skater in the top league had very little chance of coming to pass.

In fact, this year, playing at all might have little chance of coming to pass. Here in Toronto, without a car and with cash tight, Michelle couldn't afford the fees, the gear and the transit to the games and practices. She had learned from experience that the practice hours were early and awkward, and away games were unlikely to be on the subway lines.

So she made noncommittal responses to Angie, greeted Brittany's mother and kept one eye open for Tommy. She smiled as he finally emerged, walking slowly, head down and alone. Her smile faltered.

Michelle told Angie to say goodbye to her friend, gathered Tommy and headed home.

Michelle managed to avoid the upcoming storm with Angie about the hockey team by trying to draw Tommy out as they walked to the condo.

"So, how was school, Tommy?"

He didn't look up. "Fine."

"Do you like your teacher?"

Tommy shrugged.

"Tommy's got the strictest teacher in school. My teacher is nicer, but she gives lots of homework," Angie said.

"Were the other kids nice?" Michelle asked Tommy, voice tight with worry.

"They're okay."

Michelle told them a bit about her school, editing out all the worrisome parts, but their interest was perfunctory.

When they got to the condo building, she let the kids head up in the elevator first, while she stopped to ask at the desk about nearby grocery stores. There was a store not far away that would deliver, apparently.

She'd go get milk and bread from a convenience store tonight, and order some groceries online for tomorrow. She'd probably have to find a more economical solution going forward, but there was just too much to settle right now. They'd treat themselves to pizza tonight. She needed to get on top of things, not let things get out of hand like they had this morning.

When she got up to the top floor, Tommy was standing in the doorway of the condo, waiting, while Angie was chattering to their new neighbor, Troy Green. She was telling him all about the new hockey team she assumed she was joining, and asking him if it was a good step on her path to playing professionally.

Troy was being patient, but he was dressed to go out and Michelle was afraid Angie was holding him up. She sighed. Angie would be angry with her for breaking up her *tête-à-tête*. Then she'd have to finally tell her that she wasn't playing hockey this year. She closed her eyes for a moment, and with a mental sigh, opened them and squared her shoulders.

"It's not fair!" Angie yelled at her mother, face red.

Michelle struggled to hold on to her temper.

"I know it's not fair. But we just don't have the money."

"Dad would have let me." Angie threw the words at her.

Michelle flinched. If Angie's father was still alive, they wouldn't be here, wouldn't be having this conversation. "That's irrelevant right now," she answered.

"Is Tommy doing his Tae Kwon Do?"

"Yes. But—"

"That's so unfair. It's because he's a boy, isn't it? I hate you!" Angie spun around to run to her room.

"Angela Louise Robertson!"

Angie stopped. The full name was a sign of her mom losing it.

"I am doing *nothing* differently because Tommy is a boy. Tommy is wearing the same dobok as last year, so I don't have to buy that. The dojang is two blocks away so we can walk and the lessons are reasonable. On the other hand, you grew out of all your hockey gear last year and it costs a he—a heck of a lot more than a dobak. The arenas are all miles away, and we don't have a car. And hockey is *very* expensive.

"If you can come up with something cheaper to do, I'll sign you up tonight. We could try swimming, or soccer…and when I can afford it, we'll get you back into hockey, but I just can't right now!"

Unfortunately, the cold hard facts didn't help with Angie. She turned her nose up at Michelle's offers and wouldn't even let Michelle finish an invitation to join Tommy at Tae Kwon Do.

"I'll get a job."

"A twelve-year-old can't make enough to cover hockey costs. There's not much you can do right now anyway. You'll need to take the babysitting course to make money that way, and we don't know anyone in Toronto to baby-sit."

Angie's lip quivered. "I'll ask everyone who sends me money for Christmas to send it now instead."

Michelle explained that wouldn't be enough. It wasn't just the fees; it was equipment and transportation. Their family members weren't rich.

Michelle couldn't ask for any more favors from her family and friends. She wanted more than anything else to give her daughter what she wanted, what she dreamed of, but she simply did not have enough money. If she gave up school and got a job, maybe they could cover hockey this year. But next year, when they were no longer house-sitting and had to pay rent? Michelle had to finish these courses so she could make enough money to support them. Angie, though, could only see her dream slipping from her fingers.

Michelle finally went out for pizza, reminding the crying girl that she was in charge of her brother while her mother was gone. While she was out, she picked up milk and bread for breakfast and lunch tomorrow. The pizza she carried was no longer the big celebration she'd hoped for. It seemed as if everyone had had a crappy day.

Everyone but her neighbor. Troy Green was already inside when she walked into the elevator with her food at the lobby floor. He'd obviously driven into the garage and gotten on the elevator at one of the parking levels. He looked relaxed, carefree and rich, a shopping bag from a name-brand store in his hand.

"I ordered some milk, so I'll be able to return the bag you loaned us tomorrow," she said tersely. She only had a small carton with her now, but she felt obligated to indicate she didn't intend to freeload.

"Don't worry about it. I have more than enough."

He glanced at the flat red and green box she had balanced over her grocery bag. "Pizza, eh? Kids must be happy about that." Considering how poorly she'd treated him, he was being nice. Michelle realized she should respond in kind, but it had been a difficult day, and it was far from over yet.

She smiled perfunctorily. "That was the plan."

"Your daughter is pretty excited about playing hockey—want me to check out this league she's talking about?"

"Angie isn't playing this year," she said flatly, watching the floor numbers going by.

"Does she know that?"

"She does now. Excuse any sounds of wailing you might hear from our condo."

"Is it because of me?"

Michelle rolled her eyes. Of course, it *had* to be about Mr. Hockey Superstar.

"We don't have the money to buy her equipment. We don't have a vehicle to get to games and practices. Unlike some, we can't afford it."

Michelle was relieved when the elevator doors opened. She refused to defend herself to this spoiled man who could buy anything he wanted, while she couldn't give her daughter the one thing she dreamed about. *It must be nice to have everything go right for you*, she thought sourly.

When she knocked on the door, Tommy opened it, and she took a deep breath, preparing to deal with her world: the one where things always seemed to go wrong.

TROY WONDERED WHY his new neighbor disliked him so much. He was trying to be nice, considering what she'd gone through. He'd been making polite conversation and, *wham*, out came the guilt.

He wondered if Michelle didn't want her daughter playing hockey. But one look at the woman's eyes and he could see that it was ripping her up to not be able to give this to her child.

He didn't like that look. He'd seen too much of that the past year. People who were desperate to help but helpless. He didn't want the reminder of the bad time. Besides, it wasn't fair.

He remembered when he'd played as a kid. His dad had sacrificed a lot so he could play. He'd worn second- or third-hand hockey equipment most of the time. It had been just his dad and him, and money had been tight. Troy had shown talent from his first league games, though, and his dad had dreamed of success through his son's hockey career, so it had taken priority over anything else.

It had consumed his father. He'd take Troy to any ice they could find and drill him, working him hard to make him better. It was too bad he'd died before Troy had lifted the Cup. His dad might finally have been happy with what Troy had accomplished. Sure, he'd been happy when Troy was drafted, but he'd complained that he hadn't gone top ten, and that the Blaze was a crap team. Well, that crap team had won the Cup, and Troy had his ring.

Maybe it was just as well his dad hadn't been around when Troy got his cancer diagnosis. He didn't think the old man would have been much help with that.

He sat back on his recliner and turned on his gaming system.

He'd had a good meeting with his agent earlier, discussing a new endorsement deal that had come in for him. He should feel like he had his life back. But he couldn't stop thinking about the unhappy girl next door.

He frowned. Michelle had spoiled a good evening. She'd brought up bad memories. He tried to bury them again, forget about her and her kid.

But after learning about her husband...that was pretty horrible. It was one thing to read about suicide in the news, but another to see people struggling with the result. To see them, and not do anything. He had been able to get help on his way up, but the family across the hall were on their own, from what he could tell.

When he'd been growing up, hockey hadn't just been something he enjoyed. He and his dad had moved around, and Troy had been in hand-me-down clothes, but his talent at hockey had provided him with friends, and status at school. He had no idea how to help Tommy, but it would be so easy to help Angie by giving her that same cache...except, Michelle.

He was tempted to just go over and offer to pay for the kid's hockey. But he was sure she'd slam the door in his face.

Maybe if he could get the kid into a program that would pay for hockey He worked for a hockey team—they must have some kind of fund for underprivileged kids.

And once Angie and Michelle were happy, he could focus on regaining his own life.

The team was a few days into training camp and Troy was feeling good. He was in the best shape of his life; his skills were as sharp as they'd ever been in training camp.

Coach Parker was running drills. Troy's job as the defender was to stop the winger coming in. But as the winger approached him, Troy froze.

He'd done this hundreds—if not thousands—of times. But that had been before he got sick, when he could trust his body to be strong, invincible. Now, he didn't trust it.

So instead he tried to use some fancy stick work to steal the puck. But JP slipped past him, and buried the puck in the net.

"What the— What was that, Green?" Coach Parker yelled at him. The other players had turned at the noise. He could feel their stares.

"Trying something new," Troy said with a grin.

Coach shook his head and barked for the players to start the next drill.

Troy had always played a physical game, never afraid to throw a hit, block a shot or get into a fight.

But he was cautious now. What if he jarred something and that caused the cancer to come back? It wasn't logical, but the fear was there all the same. And he wasn't sure how long he could cover it up.

Troy rushed through the cool-down, and was in his street clothes before a lot of the players were even out of the showers. He couldn't deal with anyone else getting on his case right now.

Unfortunately, he ran into starting goalie Mike Reimer's wife, waiting for Mike to come out. She was a redhead with thick glasses. She and Troy hadn't ever gotten along that well. The first time he met her she'd reamed him out for a play on the ice. Another time she'd checked him onto his butt when he made a comment about her hockey skills.

She'd ended up helping the team during the playoff run. Following the hip check she'd given him, he'd scored a breakaway goal in the first playoff game. It had ended up becoming a good luck ritual, with players lining up for the privilege of having Bridget knock them down, but she and Troy never became friendly.

Today she studied him intently as he strode out of the locker room. Not a good sign.

"Good to see you back, Green," she said. She wasn't completely convincing. Her arms were crossed, and her eyes squinty.

"Good to be back," Troy answered.

"Feeling okay?"

Troy eyed her suspiciously. "Are you asking to be polite or is there a reason for asking?" he asked. Bridget had never been one for small talk.

Bridget grinned. "I was trying to be tactful, but I'm not very good at it. I was watching you play, and I wondered if you'd rushed back too quickly."

Troy suppressed a smile. People had been wondering about that since camp began, but they had all approached the matter delicately. Bridget had always been blunt.

"Did Mike tell you to ask me?"

Bridget squinted at him again. "Mike doesn't 'tell' me to do things. I asked him how you were doing." She paused.

Troy didn't want to play games. "And what did he say?"

"He didn't. So something was wrong."

Damn. Troy had hoped no one had noticed.

"It's just the start of camp. Guys aren't in game shape yet," he said defensively.

"I understand why the others are being a little careful checking you, but I don't understand why *you're* being so…hesitant. Everyone expected you to come out, I don't know, mad. You lost a year, but instead of taking it out on the ice, you're skating around as if you've got eggs in your pockets."

Troy took a step toward her. He was a big

guy, and when he wanted to, he could be pretty intimidating. Bridget planted her hands on her hips and set her jaw.

"I'm going to say something," she began, "and you can take it or leave it. But it's not something anyone here will tell you. I had a swimmer last year who had cancer. He got through it, but he decided against returning to swimming. There was no shame in it. He just reprioritized his life. If playing hockey isn't what you want, you can retire."

Troy gaped at her. Retire? Was she crazy? He wasn't going to retire. He was going to play. If she had wanted to anger him, mission accomplished. If they wanted him to go out and plaster someone into the boards, just get Bridget to do her motivating speech before a shift, and he'd be set.

"Are you doing psychotherapy now, Bridget? Am I supposed to break down and spill all my problems?" Troy mocked.

"Please, no. I'd need months of therapy myself if I ever got into the mind of Troy Green." She shuddered.

Troy frowned. She was looking at him with that "poor you" expression that revolted him. He wanted to divert her, quickly. And a perfect distraction popped into his head.

"I do have one problem you might be able to help me with."

"Girl trouble?" Bridget asked, a smile pulling at the corners of her mouth.

Troy wanted to refute that vehemently. He didn't have girl trouble, and if he ever did, he certainly would never discuss it with Bridget. Just the thought of it made his hair stand on end.

Then he considered. "Well, it's kind of girl trouble."

Bridget made a face.

"It's about a kid."

"*You* have a kid? Say it's not so," she said with surprise.

That jolted him. Had she found out he couldn't have kids…? No, she couldn't. That wasn't something he'd shared with anyone. Focus, Green.

"No. It's my neighbor's kid. She's a girl, and plays hockey. Well, she did before they moved here, but her mother can't afford it now and I wondered if you knew any way to get money for her to play. I asked the team's management, but they don't have anything they can set up at this point in the season."

Bridget looked puzzled. "What about her

father? And if they live near you, how can they not have enough money?"

"Father's dead—war vet. But they're keeping that news to themselves. And I don't know exactly what's going on, but I'm sure they don't have money. They're house-sitting for my neighbor. I don't think they're paying rent."

"Why don't you just pay for the kid's hockey? I heard about that endorsement you signed. Surely you can afford it."

"Of course I'd pay if I could. But the mother wouldn't go for it." Troy could imagine Michelle's reaction if he made that offer.

"How old is this girl? And what's up with you and the mother?"

"Kid's twelve, and nothing's up with me and Michelle."

"Is the girl any good? And are you sure the mother wants her to play?"

Troy remembered Michelle's eyes. "Yeah, I'm pretty sure money is the problem. And Angie, the daughter, tells me herself that she's good. According to her, she's going to be the first female skater in our league."

Bridget smiled at that, and Troy caught a glimpse of why Mike liked her so much.

"Why don't you bring her and—Michelle,

was it?—to the game on Sunday? Let me talk to them, find out what they need, and I'll try to think of something."

"Yeah, that might work. There's a boy, too."

"Do we have to get him into a league, as well?" she asked sarcastically.

Troy shook his head. "Doesn't seem to like hockey." Troy thought of the way Tommy watched him. "He's a little odd."

Luckily, Troy had succeeded in distracting Bridget enough that he was able to get away from her without any more talk about how he was playing.

And doing something for Angie made him oddly happy. For some reason he hadn't been able to shrug off the girl's situation. Maybe because when he bumped into her in the hallway, she looked like a kicked puppy. Maybe because he remembered growing up, poor, moving around…if he hadn't had hockey, it could have gone badly. He thought Angie might need hockey to give her a strong center to her life.

He remembered how he'd felt when he was afraid he'd never play hockey again. He'd been afraid cancer would take that away. And it still could…there were no guarantees. He didn't need the reminder of that in Angie's eyes.

He realized he was going to have to be more aggressive on the ice, too, if he didn't want the coaches to start asking questions like Bridget's.

Damn cancer! It had taken all it was getting from him.

MICHELLE STARED AT the results from her first bookkeeping test, fingers clenched around the ring on her necklace. She heard the other students talking around her. "Oh, I got that first question confused!" and "I had the amortization right but I really messed up the Allowance for Doubtful Accounts."

Unfortunately, she had gotten everything wrong. She felt nauseated. How could she have messed up so badly?

"Hey, Michelle, how'd you do?" Rin asked.

After two weeks of classes, Michelle had gotten to know some of the other students. She, Rin and two other students now hung around together at classes and lunch.

She thought of the four of them as the island of misfit toys. She was older, and had kids, so she wasn't the typical student, and the others weren't, either. Boni was a refugee from the Côte d'Ivoire. She was in her late twenties and still coping with learning English. She was great with numbers, though. She rarely made a mistake on her assignments. Unfortunately, the language barrier prevented her from explaining to people like Michelle how she arrived at her answers.

Khali was supposed to be taking this course to help her husband once she was married. Her mother had made it clear that she would not be working after the wedding, but understanding the books was key to keeping her future husband in line. Khali didn't worry about her results, since her future was set. Instead, class was a chance to get away from a very protective and strict family.

Michelle wasn't sure why Rin was taking the course. He understood some concepts brilliantly and flaked out completely on others. He was more interested in finding a girlfriend than learning the material. Michelle and Boni were too old for him, and Khali wouldn't consider him seriously, but he stayed with them. He called them his "pretty ladies" once. He didn't try it again.

Rin often talked about parties they should come to, but Michelle couldn't since she was home with the kids. Boni was too busy with her part-time work as well as courses, and Khali had neither the time nor inclination.

Still, it was nice to be invited, and she felt less alone when she was attending classes and tutorials with them.

Michelle shrugged at Rin's question about her test results.

"I may have to drop this course," he said. "I just don't get it." Rin shook his head.

Michelle didn't have that option. She had one year before she had to support herself and her kids in a new city, and she needed this certificate. But she didn't want anyone to know how desperate she was.

"Well, I'm going to have to go back over this material," she said. "It's just the first test, though, right?"

Rin grinned at her. "Wanna come to the bar tonight? We can drown our sorrows. Boni? Khali?"

Michelle forced a smile. "Sorry, got the kids. Have one for me."

Khali rolled her eyes at Rin, and Boni shook her head gravely. Boni slipped away, and Michelle waved goodbye to Rin and Khali as he continued to try to convince her to come out with him.

Michelle caught the subway and headed for the school. Tommy's class had taken a field trip to a conservation area today, so Angie had been allowed, after repeated persuasive arguments to Michelle, to go home on her own. She'd texted earlier that she'd made it safely.

Angie had gotten over her initial anger about missing hockey, but she was still sullen whenever she remembered it. She said she was keeping up with her homework, but Michelle was waiting for the other shoe to drop. Angie loved hockey so much...would being without it mean she'd start acting out, get failing grades, fall in with a bad crowd?

Michelle waited at the school till the bus arrived with Tommy and his classmates. Every day Michelle hoped to see Tommy with a friend, but once again, he got off on his own, head down. Michelle blinked back the tears. She wondered if this move to Toronto had been a huge mistake. What had she been thinking?

It was a quiet walk home. When they arrived at the condo, she asked Tommy if he wanted to push the button on the elevator, but he just shrugged. Michelle's shoulders bowed, and she wondered how much more she could take.

She heard Angie's voice as the doors opened. She glanced down the hallway and sighed.

Angie had taken to haunting their neighbor. He was her contact with hockey, and a star, and she cornered him every chance she got. Michelle was going to have to talk to her about it. The guy was being nice, but he probably had to be nice to fans as a member of the team. Eventually he'd get tired of it, and she couldn't afford for him to go to the condo board and complain about her and the kids.

"So who's your favorite player?" she heard Troy ask.

If Michelle had asked that question, she'd have gotten an eye roll. But for Troy...

"Bruce Anders," came the quick response. Michelle's mouth twitched. If Troy had been hoping to hear his own name, he didn't know kids, especially her daughter. Her daughter wouldn't recognize tact if it hit her with a hockey stick.

"But he's not even on the Blaze. I thought we were your team," Troy objected. Troy was standing in his doorway, undoubtedly hoping he'd be able to slip inside soon and have some privacy, while Angela hovered halfway between the two condo doors.

"The Blaze is my *Toronto* team. I'm from Winnipeg. The Whiteout is my real team."

Troy glanced up at Michelle and grinned. At least he wasn't taking it too personally.

"Angie, is your homework done?" Michelle asked. She hated being the heavy all the time, but she had to get her daughter away from the poor man she'd cornered. She wouldn't embarrass her daughter by explaining that she was bothering Troy in front of him.

Michelle got the expected eye roll. "I know the rules. I have to do my homework after dinner, before I can watch any TV."

To her surprise, Troy sided with Michelle. "You do what your mom says. Hockey players have to listen to their coaches, you know."

Unfortunately, that didn't help as much as he might have intended. The sulky expression returned to Angie's face. "I don't have a coach."

"Your mom is your coach. You go get that homework done."

He waved at Michelle, and then was able to escape into his own place.

Michelle opened the door to their condo, and the kids followed her inside. It was Friday, the night they ordered in, giving Michelle a break at the end of the week.

Michelle dropped her backpack on the

floor. Tommy switched on his video games, as he did so often after school.

Michelle could never decide if it was worse to let him handle grief on his own terms, using the games as he needed, or if she should intervene. The kid had so little in his life, it seemed. His Tae Kwon Do was his only interest outside video games. Next year, she swore, when she wasn't tied up with classes, she was going to find something for him to do. Maybe he'd like to play guitar. Or swim. Something.

"So what do we want to order tonight?" she called out, forcing a cheerful note into her voice. Thank goodness she didn't need to cook.

Angie shrugged, and draped herself over the recliner. Michelle had to call again to Tommy to get his attention, and he said pizza. Pizza was his standard choice.

Michelle was getting tired of pizza, but she didn't have the energy to come up with an alternative and talk them into it, so she called the familiar number, and placed the usual order.

"Angie, come help me empty the dishwasher," she called.

Angie dragged herself over, doing an excellent facsimile of a martyr dragging herself to the stake.

"You were talking to Troy again," Michelle said.

Angie shrugged. Michelle kept her voice level with effort.

"I hope you're not annoying him—"

Angie straightened, eyes flashing. "I'm not stupid, Mother. I'm not annoying him. And you can refuse to let me play hockey, but I'm not giving it up, and I'm not going to stop talking to Troy just so you can pretend I've forgotten about playing!"

Michelle stared at Angie.

"Hon, I know that you'd sooner give up your cell phone than hockey, but bothering Troy isn't going to help you play. If I had the money…"

"Sure. Whatever."

Angie stomped off to her room, and Michelle let her go. It was easier to put away a few dishes than fight with her daughter. She sank her head on her hands on the counter, and breathed deeply. How could she get her daughter to understand this wasn't a malicious act on Michelle's part, but necessity?

Tommy paused his game and came and

hugged her. It almost brought her to tears. "Thanks, sweetie."

"I'll help you." He started to put away the cutlery.

Michelle sighed. Tommy didn't yell at her and roll his eyes, but he still hadn't made friends. She'd really appreciate some kind of sign that this decision to come to Toronto hadn't been a complete mistake.

MICHELLE WOKE UP the next morning from dreams of endless tests where she knew none of the answers and had red X's slashed over everything she wrote. It took her a moment to realize she wasn't sitting in an exam room, but lying in her new, comfortable bed.

When she sat up and threw back the covers, the rustle of paper indicated where she'd left her test from yesterday. No surprises as to where that dream came from. She picked the test paper up from where it had drifted to the floor and stuck it in the notebook she'd been working in when she fell asleep. She hoped she might have finally worked out the right answer to question one. Or maybe that had been a dream, as well.

She stretched. It was Saturday, so for one morning she didn't have to herd everyone out the door. She could hear Tommy in the living room, but there was no sound from Angie. Michelle pulled on her ratty robe and yawned her way to the kitchen. Two cereal bowls in the sink showed her that the kids had both gotten up and eaten. But the bowls also mocked her. Saturday morning and she hadn't gotten up to make a good breakfast for her children. She wasn't doing anything right. Her shoulders slumped.

She poured water into the coffeemaker with bleary eyes. They should do something fun this weekend. She'd rather spend the time studying, but the kids needed her attention, too. She flipped the laptop toward her, and typed in "cheap things to do in Toronto" while the coffee machine gurgled.

There was a knock at the door. Michelle wished she'd had a chance to ingest some coffee before dealing with whatever new problem was waiting for her on the other side of that door. Had the kids done something? Had Troy complained about Angie?

She opened the door to find Troy standing there. He was awake, alert, showered and dressed. He had no responsibilities, no problems and enough money to satisfy every whim. He was carefree while she was almost going under. She hated him in that moment.

"Can I help you?" she asked, trying to keep as little of the door open as possible. She hadn't looked in a mirror yet; she had no idea what her hair was doing, or how bad the robe would look to him, but she would have placed a bet on "pathetic."

Troy grinned. "Not a morning person, eh? I have something for you, if it's okay." There was a dip in his confidence, perhaps as he got a better look at her.

Michelle blinked. She really required coffee before dealing with this. "What is it?"

"Tickets to the game tomorrow. It's only the preseason..."

Angie came bursting out of her room. She must have ears like a bat.

"Oh, Troy!" she squealed. "Really? Tickets?"

Michelle realized she couldn't refuse them now. She could only fight so long. It probably wouldn't help Angie resign herself to not playing this year, but she deserved a treat. They all did.

Troy eyed her questioningly. She gave him begrudging credit. He apparently had intended to get her approval first. Michelle shrugged. It was done now. And if he was giving them tickets, that gave them a weekend activity on the cheap. Unless they got some concession food…

Angie had grabbed the tickets and started drilling Troy with questions. The coffee-maker beeped. Michelle veered to the sound and asked Troy over her shoulder, "Coffee?"

She was surprised when Troy said yes, but she had no more brain cells firing until some caffeine got up there.

TROY WASN'T SURE why he said yes to the coffee. Michelle didn't look like she'd meant the invitation, but Angie had lit up.

The girl was bouncing on her toes at the news she was going to a game. He warned her it was just the preseason, but she didn't care. She had a million questions for him. He answered as best he could, since she didn't always wait for an answer. He knew she'd been having a rough go of it without any hockey to play, and he didn't want to make things harder for her. He hoped that Bridget could come up with some idea to get her to play.

He checked out the condo while Michelle poured out the coffee. This place was roughly the same size as his, but had a whole different vibe. Mrs. Epps definitely had old lady furniture. The couch was chintz, and the legs on the table were fussy, elaborately carved and curling. Troy preferred the clean lines on his stuff. Some of the old lady effect was offset by the kids' debris scattered around.

Same basic layout as his condo, totally different feel. Maybe not as calm and soothing as his place, but it had something his clean lines were missing.

Michelle had to dig around in the cupboard for sugar for his coffee. She obviously took hers without. She set it out in front of him. As he stirred the spoon, he watched her wrap her hands around the mug as if she had just come in from the cold and was warming up. Her eyes drifted closed as she held it to her lips, and he could feel her pleasure as she savored that first caffeine hit. Her eyes opened, and he was annoyed to find himself self-conscious when she found him staring at her.

He noticed Tommy playing a video game with men in uniform running around killing each other. He wondered if that was really appropriate for a kid his age, but he didn't think Michelle would appreciate his interfering. Angie wanted Tommy to switch to a hockey video game so they could all play, but Michelle looked like she was waiting for Troy to leave, and Troy didn't want the kids to start fighting, even though he was tempted to agree. Michelle would blame him, and he was trying to improve relations with this family, not make things worse time with them.

So he offered to drive them to the game tomorrow.

Michelle frowned. "Don't you have to be there early to get ready?"

"Yes! Could we go early with him and check out the arena?" Angie asked.

Troy held up his hands. "Whoa! I'm not going to be playing tomorrow."

Both Michelle and Angie had disappointed faces, but probably for different reasons.

"The regulars aren't playing tomorrow because we're checking out the rookies and wannabes. I'll get you seats for a regular season game later," he promised, hoping he wouldn't forget. Not that Angie would let him.

The girl perked up at the prospect of another game. "Are you going to be sitting with us, then?" she squeaked.

He hadn't thought much past getting them close to Bridget, but now that Angie had brought up the idea, he did want to sit with them. Troy nodded. Angie cheered, but Michelle had a dazed expression, as if someone had hit her on the head. Hard.

CHAPTER THREE

TROY KNOCKED ON their door the next day and was almost bowled over by Angie. She had on a Team Canada shirt.

"I'd have worn my jersey but it's from the Winnipeg Whiteout so Mom said that might not be polite," she blurted.

Troy saw that Tommy had a similar T-shirt. He should have gotten some Blaze jerseys for the kids, he realized. That was stupid of him. Michelle was wearing a red sweater with jeans.

"Best I could do," she said. "At least it's the right color, isn't it?"

It was. The Blaze colors were red, yellow and black. Red was definitely her color. It brought her face to life.

The sweater also hugged her figure much more closely than a jersey. And it was a pretty nice figure. With her hair flowing loose down around her shoulders, and without that stressed expression on her face, she looked good. Troy reminded himself that she wasn't his type—he preferred blondes—and that she was a mother, and he wasn't big on responsibility.

Troy took them over in his big black pickup. Michelle was in the front seat with him, but Angie was as close to a front seat passenger as was possible while being restrained by a seat belt in the backseat. Tommy was quiet, but appeared to be happy to be there.

Troy was able to park in the players' lot, and took Michelle and her family in through the players' entrance. Michelle tried to remain unimpressed, but Tommy's eyes were wide and Angie couldn't be still. Or quiet. She asked questions as if she'd been called up from the minors and was going to be playing here next week and needed to know every detail.

Troy had gotten them seats in the lower bowl so they could be close to the action, and so they'd be close to Bridget. But before they could get to their seats, he was stopped by fans, so he waved the family on. Angie looked disappointed, but Michelle shoved her forward. Troy felt oddly bereft as they left.

MICHELLE LET THE kids each hold their tickets so they could find their own seats. She was sure Troy had been getting a little over-whelmed by Angie's questions. But Michelle hadn't seen her daughter this happy since they moved to Toronto, so she had been hesitant to play the heavy again. Angie would be quiet when the game started and she was absorbed by the play on the ice.

Michelle was impressed with the seats: they were quite close to the ice. Angie was thrilled, and even Tommy was looking more interested than he had been in anything but Tae Kwon Do for a while. She was grateful to Troy for this break. It had been easier than expected to get the kids to do their chores yesterday when they had this treat to look forward to today. They'd even had a dance party last night, the first since they'd moved. She smiled as she saw Angie taking photos with her phone. She'd have something to show her friends at school Monday.

Michelle was surprised when the redheaded woman behind her said hello. She judged the woman to be just a bit younger than she was, and was with a boy about Tommy's age.

"Are you here with Troy?" the other woman asked.

Michelle nodded, cautiously. She had no idea if that was a good thing or a bad thing.

"I'm Bridget," she said, holding out a hand. "My husband is one of the goalies. Troy said he'd invited his new neighbors to the game today, so I guessed it was you."

Michelle took the proffered hand. "I'm Michelle, and these two are Angie and Tommy."

Bridget shook each of their hands. "This is my nephew, Bradley. Did I hear that someone here was a hockey player?"

Michelle wondered what Troy had been saying about them. But Angie thought it perfectly natural for people to be interested in her, and answered promptly.

"I'm going to be the first girl playing in this league—the first one not a goalie, that is." She said it pugnaciously, ready to do battle since people tended not to believe her.

Bridget nodded. "I was going to beat you to it."

"What happened?" Angie asked. Michelle moved to stop this line of talk, which might be too personal, but Bridget merely pointed to her glasses. "I don't have proper depth perception, so I couldn't play professionally."

Angie cocked her head. "So you don't think it's crazy for a girl to want to play? Most people tell me I won't because girls can't play against guys."

"That is so not true. I play with my brothers all the time," Bridget assured her.

Angie looked at her with respect. "Real hockey? On the ice? And you don't play goalie?"

"Nope. Real hockey. I play defense, like Troy."

Angie's eyes widened. "I'm a forward," Angie announced.

"Winger?" Bridget asked.

"Center."

Bridget raised her eyebrows. "You're going to have to be really good."

"I am," said Angie confidently.

Michelle marveled at her daughter's self-assurance. She couldn't remember a time when she'd felt that way. But her daughter had no doubts about her own abilities. Michelle was proud, but also afraid of what knocks life might have for her daughter.

Meanwhile, Bradley had started a conversation with Tommy. Bradley was taking on the biggest part of it, but Tommy was answering. Bradley was bragging about his uncle, and when Angie learned that Bridget was married to the team's starting goalie, Mike Reimer, Michelle could see that Bridget had become a very important person in Angie's eyes.

The kids went down to the glass, after Bridget assured Michelle that it was fine, and watched the players come out to start warming up. Michelle sat back in her seat and was pleasantly surprised when Bridget sat down beside her.

"Troy said you were a widow, and new in town." Michelle tensed, wondering what else he'd said. He had mentioned that she was a widow, and that Angie played hockey? She wasn't sure how she felt about that. She hadn't told him their story, but she also didn't want to be so reticent that it would arouse anyone's curiosity. She wanted to shut that part of their lives behind a firmly closed door.

"That's got to be tough," Bridget continued. "Mike and I have put off having a family till he retires because we didn't want one person to have to carry all of the load."

Michelle just nodded. It *was* difficult, but she wasn't used to sharing personal information with strangers.

"Are you okay with Angie playing hockey? Some people don't think it's a game for girls," Bridget asked with concern in her voice.

Michelle smiled. "Don't let Angie hear you say that. She believes she can do anything the guys can."

Bridget laughed. "I agree with her on that." She turned to Michelle. "Can I be blunt? I'm not really good at being tactful. Troy said Angie isn't playing with a team this year—" Michelle stiffened. "But next weekend Mike and I have rented out a rink for a family hockey game, and it would be great if you could come along. Angie would get a chance to play, and Tommy would, too, if he wanted. Do you play?"

Michelle shook her head. Things were moving too fast here.

"We wouldn't want to impose, and we don't have skates—"

Bridget interrupted. "It's not an imposition, I promise. There will be a ton of people, so a few more is not a problem. And we have lots of extra skates and gear."

At the mention of spare gear, Michelle sat up straight and looked directly at Bridget. "Why would you invite strangers to join you? What did Troy tell you?"

"Not much. Just that you were new here, and a widow and couldn't swing hockey this year. But I can give you three good reasons to have you come join us."

Bridget held up her hand and started counting off fingers. "First, that's just how our family is. We love having company, and the more, the merrier." Bridget nodded at the three kids at the glass. "The kids are getting along, and there's more where Bradley came from. Second, I'd love to help Angie achieve her goal. I have five older brothers, so I'm all about girl power. Thanks to Mike, we have some pull in hockey circles, so maybe we could find a way. And finally, Troy. He and I don't always get along, and inviting you to the game is probably the nicest thing I've known him to do. I'm happy to encourage that."

Michelle wondered why Troy was being this nice. It apparently wasn't his normal behavior, though she had to admit that he'd been more than kind to her kids so far. The kids came rushing to their seats as the players left the ice, so Michelle didn't get a chance to ask Bridget.

"Mom!" said Angie. "Bradley asked if we could go play hockey with him next weekend! Can we?"

Bridget raised her hands, indicating that she hadn't arranged this. Michelle looked at Angie, happy, her normal daughter, not the sullen creature she'd been living with recently. And even Tommy, behind her, seemed pleased at the prospect. Michelle didn't want pity, and had learned to be very touchy with people who only viewed her family as a charity. But it was one party, one game—she didn't have to agree to anything more. So she nodded, and was rewarded by a hug from her daughter. It felt good.

TROY CAME DOWN the aisle. He'd made a detour to pick up a gift for the kids, so he'd been gone longer than he'd expected and missed the warm-up. He saw Michelle and Bridget sitting together and talking to the kids, apparently getting along well. He should have been prepared for that. Neither woman seemed to like him much, so that gave them something in common.

Tommy noticed him first and prodded his sister. Angie turned with a big smile on her face. "Guess what, Troy? I get to play hockey next weekend!"

Bridget glanced at him. "I invited them to a birthday party. The family's rented the rink and will be having a big multigenerational hockey game. I want to see the league's first female skater-to-be in action." She gave Angie a nudge with her elbow.

Troy was glad that Bridget was working on a plan, but after her invite, his gift might seem anticlimactic. He pulled out a couple of jerseys he'd picked up in the team store. He looked at Michelle, hoping this wouldn't upset her.

She frowned.

"I couldn't have kids here without proper jerseys," he joked. "Not when they're sitting with me."

The kids didn't wait for their mom's permission. They pulled the jerseys on and looked for their mother's admiration.

She told them they looked great, but her furrowed brow gave him reason to believe she might not be completely happy with him. Too bad. It wasn't going to hurt anyone, and it made them happy.

The Blaze lost the game, which frustrated the kids more than the adults. It was just a preseason game, and very few of the men on the ice would be there for the regular season. Mike Reimer had joined Bridget, and Angie assured them that when Mike and Troy were back on the ice the team would start winning. Troy could see that Angie admired Bridget. He tried not to be bothered by that. He'd asked Bridget for help, and Bridget and Angie had a lot in common.

Mike had drawn Michelle into a conversation about prairie weather, since he had grown up in Saskatchewan, neighboring province to Michelle's home in Manitoba. The three kids were talking about the game, and Bridget took the opportunity to update Troy on what she'd worked out.

"They're coming to Brian's party next weekend. I'll see how good Angie is and then we can try to figure out the right place to get her to play and how to work that out."

This was exactly what Troy wanted, but he wanted to be a bit more involved, somehow.

"Why don't I bring them? I want to see Angie play myself. Plus, they don't have a car."

Bridget stared at him for a minute.

"What? I'm not invited?"

She smiled. "No, you're welcome to come. We can put you in goal."

Troy didn't trust that smile, but he'd gotten what he wanted, so he let it slide.

THE FOLLOWING WEEKEND Michelle tentatively walked into the local hockey arena for the party. Tommy was sticking close to her, while Angie ran ahead toward the change room. Michelle entered it behind her and was immediately bombarded by a chaos of voices and bodies, all of them strangers.

Troy soon followed her. He'd dropped them off at the door while he parked the truck. For once, Michelle was happy for his swagger. He hollered "Bridget" and one of the redheads popped up and came over.

"Michelle, Angie, Tommy, so glad you could make it!"

"And me?" Troy asked.

"Troy, I'm so glad you brought them," she answered him with a grin.

Michelle decided she had been right last week. She liked this woman.

Bridget yelled for some other people, and Angie and Tommy were led over to be sized for skates. Michelle politely refused the invitation. She was a mediocre skater, and had brought along her textbooks, hoping to get a chance to study while the kids had fun. Angie was soon rushing out to the ice, and when Michelle saw that Tommy was being taken care of by Bradley, she relaxed, waved them off and headed out to find a quiet place to review her notes.

She found a seat halfway up the stands, and watched for a few minutes to make sure the kids were all right. Angie was showing off for Troy.

Apparently, before the hockey game started,

there was some other game that involved hopping on ice, skating backward and squatting down. She was a little concerned about Tommy, but the other Blaze player, Bridget's husband, was keeping close by him and helping him. She appreciated that she'd had one bit of luck, at last. She'd met some seriously nice people.

She pulled out her notebook and read over the test again. She hadn't had a chance to go through it after last week, and she was still struggling with the amortization and allowance accounts. The teacher had given the class another assignment and more materials to read this week. It honestly seemed that the answer to every question that came up was "create a new account" and Michelle was losing track of them.

She sighed when she read her dismal grade again, and tried to follow the red X's to trace where she'd gone wrong. She was so absorbed she didn't notice someone had joined her till she was right beside her.

An attractive, self-assured woman had sat down.

"Hi. You must be Troy's friend?" she asked.

"Neighbor," she corrected. "I'm Michelle."

The woman held out her hand. "I'm Karen.

I'm one of Bridget's sisters-in-law. Not one who plays hockey. She told me you're studying bookkeeping?"

Michelle shook the other woman's hand. "Trying to." Michelle sighed. "I never thought I was an idiot in school, but maybe it's been so long my brain has dried up. I really don't get this."

"Can I have a look? I'm a CPA, so I ought to understand some of it."

Michelle's cheeks flushed. She handed over the sheets with embarrassment. "I haven't been in classes since I graduated high school."

"Don't sweat it. I'm happy to help. I get some sloppy work come across my desk, so if I can help you it might be good for me someday."

She took a moment to read over the questions and Michelle's answers. "Hmmm. Did you go over T accounts?"

"I missed that class, so I've been trying to figure out if they're on the balance sheet or the income statement."

Karen nodded her head. "Neither and both. Got some paper?"

Michelle pulled out a pad and forgot where she was as Karen went over what a T account was and how it helped. Either she was an excellent teacher, or Michelle did better studying near ice, because it finally began to make sense. They went over the amortization question Michelle had messed up on, and she was able to locate exactly where she went wrong and how to get to the right answer.

Karen nudged her to look up. There was some cheering on the ice, and Angie was doing her scoring celebration. Michelle stood up and cheered, hoping someone would give her the details on the goal before Angie grilled her on it. Michelle felt bad that she'd missed her daughter's goal, but she was finally starting to understand bookkeeping, and that lifted a huge weight off her shoulders. Sometimes it seemed she had to pay for anything good with something bad. Some kind of karma scale perhaps?

She turned to the woman who had dropped out of nowhere to help her. "Thanks so much, Karen."

"No problem. And I see Jee down there taking video on her phone. I'll ask her to show you your daughter's goal."

Michelle would have been content to leave as soon as the game ended, but the group moved en masse to another room where there was a huge spread of food. Michelle was embarrassed that she hadn't brought anything, and she didn't even know the person whose party it was. But Troy was her ride, and she couldn't leave till he did. As well, she'd lost Angie in the crowd, and found Tommy hanging close to Bradley. She was so happy to see Tommy with a friend that she thought she'd find a little corner where she was out of the way.

A pretty, very pregnant woman came over and introduced herself as Jee. She showed Michelle Angie's goal and promised to email a copy of the video. Michelle thanked her. Jee's husband, who turned out to be the birthday boy, called over to her, hoisting a toddler and then rubbing his hand on Jee's protruding belly when she neared him.

Michelle grabbed her necklace. She could remember so well. Mitch, holding a toddler-aged Angie in his arms, listening to her babble away while he caressed a pregnant Michelle's abdomen. That was when Mitch had still been her Mitch, before he went overseas. He'd been so handsome, so vital, the center of any group he was in.

They'd gotten married when she found out she was pregnant with Angie. It hadn't been their plan, but Mitch had been thrilled with the baby, and with Tommy, too, when he was born. Michelle had been worried about swollen ankles and how she'd cope with a toddler and a baby, as well, but Mitch had always been a rock, helping out in any way he could. His parents hadn't been pleased about the rushed wedding, but they'd loved their grandkids.

"You okay?" Troy was standing in front of her, holding a heaped plate of food. Michelle shook off her memories. She couldn't afford nostalgia now.

"I'm fine. My mind just wandered."

"If you need to leave…" he continued.

Michelle checked on the kids, still enjoying themselves. But they couldn't impose any more on Troy than they already had.

"Do you want to go? I'll get the kids. But I'm fine if you'd like to stay," she said.

He grinned suddenly. "It's kind of fun. I was an only child. I never had parties like this."

Michelle smiled. "I have three siblings. It wasn't quite this crazy, but pretty close."

"Are they still in Winnipeg?"

Michelle's smile faded. "No, scattered around the globe." She answered his inquiring look. "Military."

"Family trait?" he asked.

She nodded and then excused herself to find Bridget. She didn't want to talk about her family, or her past.

TROY LET MICHELLE ESCAPE. He was pretty sure that was what she was doing. She didn't like talking about anything very personal, or about her past. He understood, given what he'd found out about her husband's death. Though he didn't think she'd be happy to know how much of her past he'd uncovered.

She was prickly, and he wasn't sure how to handle that. His relationships with women were mostly simple. They knew what he wanted, he knew what they wanted and they made each other happy for a while. His dad had drilled caution into his head—he'd said there would be people who would try to take advantage of him once he made it to the pros, so he was always careful. Of course with Michelle, this wasn't a romantic kind of thing. He just felt sorry for her and wanted to help a bit.

With that thought, he looked for Bridget. Normally it wasn't that hard to find a redhead in a crowd, but half the people here had bright red hair. He'd met Bridget's dad, who also had red hair, and apparently she had five brothers supposedly all here somewhere in the crowd. He'd stopped trying to keep track. If they were anything like Bridget, their family must be bedlam all the time.

He finally tracked her down, standing near Mike. Troy hadn't been happy when Mike was first traded to Toronto, but after that Cup run, well, you couldn't go through something like that and not have a bond.

"Bridget, Mike. Nice party," he said.

Bridget eyed him skeptically. Troy doubted she would ever get past their first meeting.

"So, Bridget, what did you think of Angie?" After all, he'd never been invited to any of Mike and Bridget's social events. This whole thing was in aid of Angie.

"She's good," Bridget said. Mike nodded from behind her, arms wrapped around her waist.

"She's really good, in fact," Bridget continued. "But what exactly are you thinking of? Do you have any ideas? Or did you just want to pass it on to us?" Bridget asked.

Troy paused. He wasn't quite sure. He'd hoped Bridget would have an idea. But he wasn't going to dump everything on her lap. In fact, he wanted to follow how the girl did. He was responsible now.

"I didn't expect to leave it all to you. They're

my neighbors. I want to make sure Angie can play the game she loves. It's not fair that she can't just because they don't have the cash. I've got more than enough money, and I want to help out."

Bridget glanced over at Michelle, talking to Bridget's mother.

"Are you just going to offer it to her?"

Troy sighed. That would be the easiest thing, but...he was pretty sure Michelle wouldn't take it. And if Angie ever found out her mother had refused it, things would be pretty ugly across the hallway. He wasn't trying to make things worse for them.

"She won't just take it. I was in trouble just for buying the kids those jerseys last week. I wondered if I could give them the money and say it was from the club."

Mike and Bridget stared at him.

"The club?"

"Yeah, the team's a hockey club. Her husband was in the military, and so was she. I asked if the club had some kind of program to help vets and their families. They don't, but Michelle doesn't know that. I can tell her I pulled some strings and got Angie sponsored."

Bridget looked at him as if he was a little dim. "So you're going to pay Angie's fees but tell her mother that the Blaze is paying for it. What about Angie's gear? Michelle said she didn't even have skates. Are you going to cover that, too? You can't give her a check, or transfer money to her from your account. She'd realize it was all from you."

Troy sighed again. This shouldn't be so difficult.

"I haven't worked that all out yet. Maybe I'll say there's a credit at the store or something."

Troy didn't appreciate the pitying glance Bridget gave him.

He snapped his fingers. "A gift card, that's what I'll do. That could come from the club."

Bridget crossed her arms. "Assuming you can pull this off, and that's a big *if*, how are Michelle and Angie going to get to practices and games?"

"What do you mean?"

"You drove them here today because they don't have a car. It would be pretty hard for the three of them to take public transit to games, and taxis would be expensive. Or are you thinking of another gift card to cover that, 'from the club.'" Her sarcasm was obvious, but Troy wasn't giving up.

Troy set his jaw. "I'll find a way."

Mike glanced over at Michelle then the kids, who were talking to Bradley.

"You really like these people?" he asked Troy.

Troy shrugged. "Michelle's struggling. She won't admit it, but Angie's let things slip. I feel bad that she's working so hard and having such a tough time. It's tough for a kid when they have only one parent and not much money. Besides, she's a vet, so we should help out, right?"

Bridget sighed. "Well, I won't tell her what you're up to, but don't be surprised if it all blows up on you."

MICHELLE RELAXED AGAINST the seat cushions as Troy drove them home. The kids were watching the video of the game on Michelle's phone. Angie dissected her every move, making sure she still had her skills.

"Thank you," Michelle said to Troy.

He gave her a strange look. "What for?"

"For taking us to the game. Introducing us to Bridget, giving us a ride today. The kids had a really good afternoon."

Troy seemed to relax. Michelle wondered what he'd been worried about.

"I'm glad. Did you enjoy it?"

"It was good to watch the kids having fun, being kids. And Karen, one of Bridget's sisters-in-law, helped me with some homework. So yes, I enjoyed it."

"Then that's good. The O'Reillys are nice," Troy said agreeably.

"Do you spend a lot of time with the guys on your team?"

Troy shrugged. "Not Mike. The married guys are usually busy with family stuff when they're not at games or team events. I hang out with the single guys."

"I appreciate you giving up some of your weekend for us. That was more than generous. We don't want to intrude, though. Tell me if Angie starts to become a nuisance."

There was quiet for a moment, and Michelle tensed. Was he trying to find a tactful way to admit that Angie was bothering him?

"Don't worry," Troy said finally. "I'll speak up if she becomes a problem."

Michelle sensed that there was something going on here that she didn't understand. But they were entering the condo garage and there wasn't any more opportunity to press him further.

TROY TOOK ADVANTAGE of Angie's openness to find out when he might be able to speak to Michelle privately. Angie was still young enough to think it was perfectly normal for a relative stranger to be curious about her family's schedule. She'd mentioned there was a window of time after she and Tommy went to bed when Michelle studied.

So tonight he'd skipped out on going to the bar with some of the guys after the game and headed to her condo.

He rapped quietly on the door. He waited a moment, impatiently, and was about to knock again when she opened the door.

She had her hair knotted up on her head, and some glasses on. She was wearing a shirt and pants that looked comfortable and worn— probably pajamas. There were shadows under her eyes, and he hoped he could make this work to take away some of her worry. If his plan failed, she probably wouldn't want anything more to do with him. He tried not to acknowledge how much that idea bothered him.

"Anything wrong?" she asked.

"Can I talk to you for a moment?"

She paused and then pulled the door all the way open.

There were textbooks on the island and a glass of wine, mostly empty. The kids' stuff was strewn around, too, in contrast to his condo, which the cleaners kept in pretty good shape. Troy decided that he appreciated a bit of disorder. It was relaxing; it felt like a real family home, not a magazine spread or a show home.

Michelle picked up her glass and lifted it toward him. He shook his head. He wasn't a wine drinker. His dad had always called wine a woman's drink, and the attitude had survived. He could drink wine at a dinner, but his preference was beer, or bourbon. He doubted Michelle would have either on hand, though. He had plenty stocked up at his place, and if this conversation didn't go his way, he'd need some once he slunk home.

Michelle carried her glass over to the couch and curled up. She took a sip of wine and waited for him to join her.

Troy sat in an easy chair and leaned forward. He took a moment to marshal his arguments.

"I don't want you to get mad, but after I saw how well Angie did last week, playing hockey, I talked to the team's management."

That was mostly true, except that he'd talked to them before he saw Angie play.

Michelle put her glass down. She looked like she might get mad anyway, so Troy rushed on.

"I thought it was a shame that she had to give up playing. So I asked if the team's club had any kind of program for kids. It turns out they do have something for vet's kids. Angie told me both you and her dad were in the Forces. It's some kind of bequest thing, and they don't publicize it, but there's some money there. So I talked to them about Angie, and they can help."

Michelle didn't yell at him, or throw anything. So far, so good.

"I know this wasn't really my place, but I talked to the coach of that team Angie wanted to play for, and he'll allow her a tryout. I know she can make it—she's a good little skater.

"The team gave me this card." He reached into his pocket and pulled out the gift card for the hockey store he'd been told was most reasonable price-wise. He tossed the gift card onto the coffee table in front of her.

"This bequest covers equipment and fees with the team. I'll let the club know if she makes the cut, and they'll send the money directly to the team. The coach wants Angie there Saturday morning."

Michelle stared at the card, and then back at him. Troy figured he'd go for broke.

"Now, here's where I got a little pushy, I'm

afraid. I just landed a sponsorship deal that includes a new truck. I don't want to sell my old truck, 'cause I like it, but I'm supposed to drive this other one till spring for the publicity. Mrs. Epps always let me use her extra parking stall for this kind of thing, so I thought, if I was parking that truck in her spot all winter, well, you could use it for hockey. Keep it from sitting cold, battery dying, that kind of thing.

"I'm sorry if that was presumptuous, and if you insist, I'll go back and tell the club you need transit passes to get to the games. But I'd be a little embarrassed, so I'd rather not, if you don't mind."

Troy could feel sweat trickling down his back. He hadn't been this nervous since his last oncology visit. Michelle was sitting very still, staring down at the card. He couldn't tell what she was thinking. He'd thought it was a pretty good story, but would she buy it?

"You've gone to a lot of trouble for us," Michelle said, quietly.

Troy took a breath. "My father always had a lot of respect for the military. He was always buying coffee for soldiers, things like that. I guess I just want to keep that up, in his memory."

Troy's father had never had that much concern for things that didn't directly affect him, but there was no way Michelle could know that. He had to try to make her think he didn't pity her because he was sure that was something she could never swallow.

Michelle opened her mouth, either to accept or reject, when a voice came around the corner.

"Mom? Can we do that? I promise I'll do all my homework and all my chores and never disobey you ever, ever, ever..."

Angie was at the corner, hair stuck up on one side, face pleading.

"Why aren't you asleep?" Michelle asked.

"I heard Troy's voice and wanted to know why he was here," she said, matter-of-factly. "Please, Mom? Please, please... I'll never ask for anything again."

Troy had decided it wouldn't be right to bring his offer up in front of Angie. If Michelle said no, Angie would be heartbroken. But he'd done his best to play fair, and now Angie was probably his ace in the hole. He wouldn't be able to say no to her now, and she wasn't even his kid. Michelle would have to cave.

Michelle hesitated for a moment. Her brow creased as she tried to work out if this was on the level, or if it was some kind of charity. But when she looked at her daughter, he knew the balance had tipped in Troy's favor.

"I guess. If Troy has gone to this much trouble for us."

Angie raced across the room and hugged her mom. "I promise I'll be perfect, Mom. If I can play hockey, nothing else matters." Then she ran to Troy and wrapped her arms around him. "Thank you, Troy. You're my favorite player now!"

Troy felt the warmth of her arms around his neck, and the smell of her shampoo filled his nostrils. Kids were easy. For a moment he remembered that he wouldn't ever have a child, but he pushed that thought aside with practiced ease and hugged her back.

Michelle stood up and gave her daughter's ponytail a tug.

"You need to get back to bed, young lady. I'll work out the details with Troy, but you have school in the morning."

Angie thanked Troy profusely, hugged her mother again and ran back down the hallway.

"How can I thank you?" Michelle asked with a wan smile.

Troy had a quick image of Michelle giving him a hug. He liked it more than he should.

He shook his head. Michelle came with kids, and that was something he always avoided.

"Hey, it's a club thing. I just did the research. I figured Angie deserved her chance."

He left quickly after that. He'd succeeded in convincing Michelle to take the money and the truck, and he didn't want to mess anything up now.

CHAPTER FOUR

"YOU'RE LUCKY SHE still wants to play," the guy at the hockey store said. "My sister gave up at about that age. She started getting interested in boys and was afraid they wouldn't like her if she played sports."

Michelle was handing over the gift card to pay for Angie's hockey gear—a *huge pile* of gear. Angie had grown out of her equipment from playing last winter in Winnipeg so Michelle had left it behind. There had been no point in bringing anything that was too small in the U-Haul: it had been hard enough to pack up stuff from three lives. Angie had assumed they'd buy more, and Michelle hadn't said anything to disabuse her of that assumption then.

In Winnipeg they'd mostly found second-hand gear online, or at hockey equipment sales at the rink. It had been pretty exciting for Angie to go to a store and buy everything new. Troy had insisted on coming with them, and while Michelle had had some reservations, it had turned out for the best. Sure, Michelle had handled most things while Mitch was overseas, but when it came to hockey gear, Mitch had either helped while he was home, or some of the other dads had pitched in. Michelle had never played hockey. She could tick necessary items off a list of equipment, but she didn't know why one piece cost more than another, or what variations were available, and if it was worth it or necessary. A stick was a stick, right? Apparently not.

Troy had helped Angie pick out her equipment, and the two of them had debated the pros and cons of almost every piece extensively. Michelle had left them to it, and played solitaire on her phone.

"Yes, I am lucky," Michelle said to the cashier. She followed the clerk's gaze to where Troy and Angie, apparently indefatigable, were looking at what Blaze merchandise was available at the shop.

"Do you think he'd mind signing something for me?"

Michelle shrugged and watched the cashier head over to Troy as she put the sales slip in her purse.

She'd been surprised by the clerk's comment about her daughter's possible interest in boys, but she should have realized Angie was getting to that age. It was possible: Michelle hadn't been much older than her daughter was now when she had her first boyfriend. The thought made her shudder. She glanced over at Angie, still clutching her new skates to her chest as if someone might steal them away. Okay, Michelle had time yet.

She saw Troy nod at the clerk and sign the hat the young man proffered. She smiled. She wasn't just lucky that Angie still wanted to play hockey. She was lucky to have Troy help them. Almost every good thing that had happened here in Toronto could be traced back to him: meeting the O'Reilly family, Karen's help with her classes, and now, a chance for Angie to play hockey. It was nice to share the burden— But she caught herself. The burden was hers, and she couldn't let herself rely on anyone else. Troy looked up and caught her eye and she flushed.

Saturday was Angie's tryout, and she was looking forward to it, without any apparent nerves. Michelle wondered again at her boundless confidence. Maybe it was that first-child thing, but Michelle had never had a fraction of her belief in herself at that age.

They schlepped Angie's big bag of hockey gear into the elevator. Tommy had his video game to keep him busy. Michelle thanked her lucky stars that he didn't object to coming along since he was too young to stay on his own. Michelle knew from experience that this trip to the arena wasn't going to be short and sweet. She might not be familiar with hockey gear, but she'd sat through a lot of hockey practices. She'd brought some textbooks along so that she could try to get something accomplished while waiting, as well.

This was her first foray driving Troy's truck on her own, and she was nervous, even though he insisted it was just his winter vehicle. It might be just a winter vehicle, but it was obviously expensive.

He had taken her down to the garage to show her how it worked. Michelle could drive, but this was a city she didn't know, especially by car. Troy had talked her through the navigation system, the radio and numerous other bells and whistles, and then had had her drive round the garage and back to Mrs. Epps's parking spot. He said his new truck was arriving any day, and in the meantime, he'd keep driving the Ferrari.

Michelle had held her breath when she'd

parked the big truck into the slot beside that. It was shiny, red, pristine and looked almost like a toy. An incredibly expensive toy.

At least Troy's truck wasn't such a big change from the vehicle she'd driven in Winnipeg. It had been an SUV: practical for a cold, windy city, with lots of room for passengers or gear.

She took a breath before putting the truck in reverse. The Ferrari was gone: Troy must be at his own practice. Angie had helped her punch the location of the rink into the navigation system, and the computer voice gave them their first directions. Troy was organized with his things, and the truck was tidy, but it still seemed to smell, to feel like Troy. But Troy was elsewhere, and Michelle was doing this on her own.

Michelle had allowed lots of time to get there, as usual. Early on a Saturday morning, the streets were fairly deserted anyway. They arrived with time to spare, and Michelle saw Angie into the change room. Her offer of assistance was rejected, so Michelle and Tommy headed up into the stands.

Michelle had planned to read through a couple of chapters, and maybe start on some of her assignment questions, so she pulled out a book while Tommy started up his video game.

When the girls skated onto the ice, though, she found her glance wandering toward the workout. Angie was with her friend from school when she skated out, but when the coaches arrived the girls became one big group. She soon gave up on the book to watch Angie. She thought Angie was doing well, but she also recognized that she was a biased observer, and not one with a lot of hockey knowledge.

Michelle glanced over at the other parents in the stands. They were talking together, but she and Tommy sat a little apart. Eventually she'd get to know them if Angie made the team…if they weren't too upset about her daughter crashing in so late. With any luck she could set up some car-pooling.

Practice was wrapping up when someone sat down beside Michelle. She glanced up, surprised to see Troy.

"How's she doing?" he asked.

"Good, I think," Michelle answered, eyeing him suspiciously. "I didn't realize you were planning to come."

Troy shrugged. "Our practice ended early, so I thought I'd swing by to cheer Angie on."

She noticed the other parents were staring and pointing at them now. Obviously, it wasn't Michelle and Tommy attracting the eyeballs; it was Troy. A man from a couple of rows away came over hesitantly.

"Troy Green?" he asked, disbelief written large in his voice.

Michelle found that she and Tommy were subtly pushed out as more people began to crowd around Troy. She slid out of the way, relieved to have a bit of breathing room. Just like in the truck, his competence wrapped around them and she had to resist the urge to let someone else take over. She couldn't do that.

Tommy grinned up at her at the end of his game and leaned in to say, "I guess Angie was right. He's famous."

Michelle smiled at him. "I guess so. Maybe we should have asked him for his autograph."

Tommy considered that seriously. "Well, if you want, we could ask him when we see him at the condo."

"Ask what?"

Troy had managed to dismiss his admirers and was looking down on them with a smug expression.

"For your autograph," Tommy said seriously.

"Why, Michelle, I had no idea you were such a big fan." Troy had a glint in his eye. Michelle would have liked to call him out on it, but since he'd just been the center of a crowd of fans, she couldn't. As much as it would have been satisfying.

Troy grinned as if he could read her mind. He leaned over and ruffled Tommy's hair and said, "Sure, Tiger, anytime. But right now I want to go ask the coach how your sister did."

The girls were skating off the ice, and the parents were scheduled to talk with the coach one-on-one after, as per the paperwork Troy had given her. Troy bounced down to ice level and commandeered the coach.

Michelle knew that if anyone else had monopolized him, the other parents would have protested, but Troy was obviously able to get away with things the other hockey parents couldn't. She noticed how the other parents glanced her way, wondering why Troy was with them. They might not have believed her if she admitted she wasn't sure herself. She was worried about how easily it was happening.

Troy came back with the order of interviews with the coaches. Angie was the last one, since she was the newest. Troy passed Michelle the list and leaned back next to her. He crossed his arms and gave them a discreet thumbs-up under his elbow.

The parents made their way out of the stands toward the coaches' office. There was some tension in the crowd as one by one, the girls went in with their parents.

Troy continued to stay with Michelle and Tommy, which unnerved her. He spent some time relaying to Michelle what the coach had told him about Angie's skill level between having his picture taken with the prospective team candidates and their parents. Troy assured her that Angie had made the team. Michelle couldn't help but be pleased at the information, but she wondered how much influence Troy had had on all this. She thought Angie looked as good as the others out there, but was the coach allowing her to play just because of Troy?

She gave the kids some money to get some hot chocolate, and asked Troy to talk in private.

"Maybe we should wait till the kids are occupied elsewhere," he said with a glint, following her around the corner.

Michelle had her own agenda and ignored his flirtation. "Troy, I need to know. If Angie makes the team, will it be on her own merits, or will it have been a favor to you?" For Troy this might be fun, a novelty, but not for Angie, and therefore, not for Michelle, either.

Troy held his hands up, indicating his complete and utter innocence. Michelle raised a skeptical eyebrow.

"I pulled strings to get her to try out late. That's all."

"And did the coach understand that, as well?" Michelle continued, with a mother's ability to sniff out prevarication.

"Why are you complaining? She's gonna be on the team!" he said.

Michelle stood in front of him, speaking softly but forcefully. "Because this is important to her. She has to know she made it on her own. You're not always going to be around to pull strings."

Troy made an X on his chest with one finger. "Cross my heart, I just got her a tryout. She's good, and the coach was happy to have her."

Michelle searched his face. His expression was too innocent. But she didn't think he'd tell her any more even if she kept pushing, so she decided to accept it for now. She'd speak to the coach later, if Troy was right that Angie was in. Troy might believe he was doing them a favor, but false hopes were cruel. It was better for her daughter to have her feet firmly on the ground.

Finally, Angie was called in. Michelle started to follow her, but found Angie glaring at her.

"What?" Michelle asked.

"I don't need a babysitter," Angie hissed, opening the door.

The coach invited Michelle in, and introduced himself as Jack Albee. She bit back an urge to stick her tongue out at Angie. Since this move, Angie had been aggressively asserting her independence. Michelle wasn't ready to let her go yet. As well, legally she had another year before she could do these interviews on her own.

In front of Angie, Michelle couldn't ask the coach how much Troy had influenced the decision, but as Troy had indicated, Angie had made the team. The coach noted that Angie needed to work on her passing and teamwork. Angie soaked up every suggestion in a way she'd never accept criticism from her mother.

Troy had stayed with Tommy outside the

room. When Angie raced out, full of her big news, he reacted with as much pleasure as someone invested in Angie's career. Michelle wondered why.

"Come on. This is something to celebrate!" Troy said. He high-fived Angie and then Tommy and held his hand up to Michelle, a grin on his face. Michelle glared at him, but slapped his palm, perhaps a little harder than was necessary.

ONCE TROY HAD SHEPHERDED Michelle and her family out of the arena, he offered to take them to a place close to the rink with great burgers.

"Why don't we all go over in the truck together, since there's more parking here? You can bring me back, and I'll head home in the Ferrari." It was a practical suggestion and pleased him for some reason.

"Are you sure your car will be safe if you leave it here?" Michelle asked, looking at the expensive toy, which stood out among the other vehicles in the arena parking lot. There were people gathered nearby, staring at the shiny red vehicle. "Would anyone vandalize it?"

Troy shrugged. "It's insured." He worried

a lot less about his car since he'd been sick. You could always get another car.

The burger joint had a laid-back atmosphere, but as it turned out, the restaurant catered more to adults than kids. Troy realized this when Michelle picked one burger for the two kids to share, since the sizes were so large. There were no acceptable drink options other than water, unless you considered that beer had some nutritional benefits. Troy would have argued for that, but of course, that wasn't something you'd offer kids. Michelle vetoed soft drinks, and stuck to water herself. He had a lot to learn, he noted. The kids liked the fries and the milkshakes, at least.

Angie was talking nonstop about what she'd done on the ice and what her friend had done and what everyone else had done. Then she wanted to repeat what the coach had said about her skills on the ice and what she needed to work on.

Troy listened, amused. Had he sounded the same when he was her age? Michelle and Tommy were content to sit back and let Troy bear the brunt of it.

When the burgers were mostly consumed, and Troy had speared the last few fries from

Michelle's abandoned plate, he asked, "What are you guys doing with the rest of your day?"

"We are doing homework," Michelle said firmly.

The kids sighed but didn't argue.

"What? On a Saturday?" said Troy.

Michelle glared at him. He came close to flinching.

"I always did my homework Sunday night," he added. When he did it.

Angie spoke first. "I promised Mom I'd do my homework when she says since I've got hockey now. And we're going to be spending Sunday with the O'Reillys anyway."

Troy raised his eyebrows. They were getting mighty chummy with Reimer's family. He felt left out. Not that he didn't have things to do, but...

Michelle continued the explanation. "Bridget's sister-in-law Karen is going to help me with my homework again. And the kids want to hang out. Apparently, there's a lot of road hockey going on over there," Michelle explained. "Thanks for introducing us to Mike and Bridget. They've been great."

Yeah, Troy thought, but he'd only set that up to get Angie into hockey. He closed his mouth on the words, though. If he told Mi-

chelle that, the whole deception would be
exposed, and Michelle would flip. And honestly, why *should* he feel left out? Playing road
hockey with a bunch of kids? That couldn't
be any fun. Not when they weren't your kids,
right? So he said he was happy they'd all become friends and tried not to feel like someone had just stripped him of the puck when
he wasn't looking.

When the bill came, Michelle insisted on
paying. Troy tried to argue. Most people
feigned reluctance, but often expected him
to pick up the tab. Honestly, it made him feel
good to know that he could.

But Michelle wouldn't give. She insisted
that Troy had already done too much for them,
so this was the least she could do. She gave
him the same glare he'd seen her give the kids
when she thought they had gotten out of line.
Troy got the sense she might drop him to the
floor again if he pushed it any further, and
he was wearing an expensive leather jacket
that wouldn't mesh well with the spilled beer
and peanut shells on the floor. It frustrated
him. He hadn't really thought how much the
meal would cost, since he planned to drop his
Visa down, but he was pretty sure it was a big
amount for Michelle.

His dad had always harped on the idea that women would take you for all the money they could get. Obviously, his dad had never met anyone like Michelle. Troy had to admit he hadn't, either. His last girlfriend had had pretty expensive expectations of what dating a hockey player was like. Surprisingly, it had been easier to deal with her.

Maybe he felt guilty for causing Michelle to spend money she didn't have. Maybe he felt left out since the family had their own plans that didn't include him. In any case, he heard himself saying, "Are you guys busy with the O'Reillys next Sunday, too?"

Michelle shook her head. She had that stubborn set to her jaw, and he figured she didn't want to take advantage of the O'Reillys, either. Prickly woman.

"There's a club event next Sunday afternoon. It's for kids—maybe you guys would like to come along?" Troy blurted out.

Troy kept his surprise at the offer to himself. It was true that there was an event, but Troy had never attended any club activity that was family oriented.

Michelle looked at him with narrowed eyes. The kids, fueled by fries and milkshakes, were already bouncing up and down with excitement. Troy realized he'd committed a faux pas. He should have asked Michelle first, but it was too late now.

"We'll have to see how things go with homework," Michelle warned.

As they stood to go, Troy leaned down to Michelle's ear. "Sorry. I spoke without thinking."

Michelle pulled back and stared at him for a moment. Then she nodded. "I appreciate the offer, but next time, remember I should approve things first."

Troy nodded. "Got it. But you know, even when I try..." He shrugged. He thought he glimpsed a ghost of a smile on her face before it disappeared.

Michelle drove them all back to the rink, dropping Troy off at his fortunately untouched Ferrari. Then she took the kids home.

Angie's eyes were shining, and she was wound up with excitement. Today had been more than she could have dreamed. Even Tommy was more involved with them than he often was.

Michelle was happy, but she didn't want the kids to start expecting that Troy was part of their lives. For some reason he was enjoying helping them right now, but that might change at any time. Michelle had learned not to rely on anyone else. Even those closest to you could let you down, and if you weren't prepared, it could be devastating.

Still, thanks to Troy's intervention, life had changed for Michelle and the kids. Angie was no longer sullen and lifeless. For the next while she would do anything she was asked, promptly and without complaint. It wouldn't last, but Michelle would enjoy the respite while it lasted. As well, her classes were going better thanks to Karen's assistance, and she'd only met Karen because of Troy.

Yet Michelle hated being indebted to Troy. And she knew he was hiding something; she could sense it. Maybe it was her mom-radar, but something was off. She suspected Troy had pulled strings to get Angie on the team. She hoped not. Angie would be devastated if she learned she hadn't made the team on ability. He claimed he hadn't been responsible, but they'd all find out soon when the team started playing games. Troy couldn't pull enough strings to affect Angie's play on the ice.

SINCE THE KIDS had been there when Troy mentioned the outing for Sunday, there wasn't really much doubt, but Michelle did finally officially approve it. Both kids were so excited that they did everything she asked over the week without complaint or hesitation. It had been a good week: the kids were cooperating, and Michelle was finally feeling like she understood what she'd missed on her first test. Maybe she was getting the hang of this.

But then she discovered that the event was for players' families. Troy hadn't mentioned that little tidbit until they arrived. Michelle was surprised by that, and a little concerned. She wasn't the only one surprised: there was a suspicious silence when Troy walked in with them.

He introduced Michelle to a couple of the wives nearby. Olivia Sandusky was the wife of the team captain, and a pleasant, friendly woman. Troy took the kids off to play some games and Olivia sat beside Michelle.

"Have you been seeing Troy for long?" she asked.

Michelle was alarmed. "Oh, we're not dating. Troy is just our neighbor. He's been nice to the kids. My daughter is hockey crazy."

"Oh, I'm so sorry," said Olivia. "I just assumed. Troy has never been at the family events before."

"Should we not have come?" Michelle asked bluntly, feeling awkward.

"No, of course you're welcome," said Olivia with embarrassment. "Players are welcome to invite whomever they wish. You see Mike Reimer over there? He brought his wife's nephew with him, since they don't have children of their own. Other players have done the same, so it's not a problem, it's just that, well, Troy hasn't ever done that in the past. He's been playing for the Blaze since he came up, so we thought he was avoiding the family events."

"Are you sure it's okay?" Michelle insisted.

"Please," said Olivia. "I would be upset if you were uncomfortable because of something stupid I said. Troy's just been such a…well, he normally has a different date for every event. We were taken by surprise when he signed up for this affair last week. I'd have been happy to think he'd found someone and settled down a bit. I'm pleased that he's looking out for your family. You must be pretty special."

This confirmed Michelle's suspicion. Something was going on.

Mike Reimer joined her at one point, while Tommy and Bradley were hanging out together, and Troy was introducing Angie to the other players. Michelle smiled—whatever Troy's motivation might be, her daughter was having the time of her life.

"Nice to see you again, Michelle," said Mike.

"Thanks. Are you also surprised Troy invited us?" Michelle asked, brows risen.

Mike paused, and then nodded. "To be honest, I am. Troy hasn't been at any family events before."

"So I keep hearing. I've had to explain that we're not dating."

"Sure about that?" Mike asked.

Michelle shook her head. "I haven't dated for a while, but I haven't forgotten how it works. Troy is not interested in me romantically." She frowned, creasing her brow.

"A problem?" Mike asked.

Michelle looked at him. "Is it really so odd that Troy brought us here?"

Mike glanced at Troy with Angie hanging on his arm.

Mike spoke slowly, picking his words carefully. "Troy was off last year, so I've really only played the one year with him. And after what he went through, he could have changed. But it is out of character for the guy I played with two years ago, and for the guy I thought he still was."

Michelle's brow furrowed. What had he gone through? "Does he have some agenda I should be worried about?"

Mike looked again at the man and girl. "I can't think of one. Maybe you're just a special family and bring out the best in him."

Michelle considered that *special* label. They *were* a special family, but she'd been working very hard to make sure no one realized that. She was becoming convinced that Troy had discovered their secret. Maybe as a result of this whole bequest at the club. Come to think of it, how had the club verified that she was a veteran? If they'd contacted the military about her, they might have discovered the story. Troy could have learned it that way. Michelle wondered how many other people might know. She found the thought depressing. She realized she'd indulged the hope that Troy might like spending time with her—them—just for themselves.

MICHELLE WAS QUIET on the way to the condo, but Troy didn't notice because Angie was talking nonstop. She'd had a great day. Troy was surprised by how much he'd enjoyed it himself. He'd never gone to the family events since he didn't have one and wasn't looking for one. He liked his life as a single, successful and footloose guy, and avoided anything that had the whiff of responsibility attached to it. He'd always assumed these family things would be boring. But it had been kind of nice.

He remembered that he'd promised them tickets to a regular season game. Maybe he'd get them all jerseys with his name on it—he'd have the cutest little fan section.

When they got off the elevator, Michelle told the kids to go ahead into their home. She asked Troy if she could talk to him, in private. Troy glanced at her face, and realized she wasn't wearing a happy expression. He couldn't think of anything he'd done. Well, unless she'd found out he'd paid for Angie's hockey. Yeah, that would do it. He sighed.

He asked her to come to his place, rather than talking in the hall. He remembered that Angie had a habit of hearing things she shouldn't. He tried to think of who might have spilled the beans. Mike and Bridget were the only ones who knew, and they'd promised… Maybe Michelle had said something about the fictional bequest to someone today and learned it didn't exist? He should have considered that, had a cover story prepared.

Inside his condo Troy kicked off his boots and offered Michelle a drink. She said no, so he grabbed a beer from the fridge for himself. He could see this wasn't going to be Michelle expressing her gratitude and asking to nominate him for sainthood. He wanted to be fortified.

"Have a seat," he offered, sitting in his own favorite chair.

Michelle sat on the couch, resting on the edge rather than relaxing. She'd found him out for sure. He'd known she wouldn't like it, but he hoped she wouldn't insist on pulling Angie out. It would be devastating for Angie.

Michelle stared at the floor for a moment, then raised her eyes to his. They were pretty eyes, but they were glaring disapprovingly at him, and her mouth was set. How could he talk her into accepting this?

"How did you find out?" Michelle asked.

Troy was speechless for a moment. He had wondered how *she'd* found out about *his* secret. What was he supposed to have discovered?

She grew impatient with his silence. "I

know you discovered what happened with Mitch's death," she said. "How?"

Troy felt a wave of relief. This was easy. His conscience was clear on this one.

"I looked him up online," Troy said.

Michelle paused for another moment. "Why?"

Troy cocked his head. "You said he'd died, and I thought he must have been pretty young. I was curious." He didn't mention the cancer thing. He didn't want anyone to know how much that still bothered him.

"What exactly did you find out?" Michelle asked.

Troy took a swig of his beer. He'd thought he was off the hook, but Michelle still looked upset. He remembered how she'd deflected the issue the one time it had come up, when she borrowed the milk. Yeah, she wouldn't appreciate his detective work.

"He was a soldier. He served in Afghanistan, came home with PTSD and then was discharged. A little more than a year ago he committed suicide."

Troy remembered how that had hit him in the gut. He'd felt rather small. He'd been upset that he'd lost a year of playing hockey thanks to cancer, while this guy had served his country and returned with such serious problems. He'd ended up losing so much more than Troy had done. He hadn't realized PTSD could be that damaging, and he'd been surprised to find out how extensive that particular issue was among soldiers. Troy didn't look at much but the sporting news. And cancer stories.

"Have you told anyone?" Michelle asked. "I assume the team knows since they gave the bequest to Angie."

Troy thought fast. "No, I didn't tell anyone. If the team found out anything, they didn't mention it to me." That at least was honest. The Robertsons weren't on the team's radar at all.

"How did you know I'd found out?" he asked. He'd been pretty careful, but if he'd slipped up on this, he might slip up about Angie's hockey, as well.

Michelle stood up and folded her arms, closing herself off.

"Do you know why we left Winnipeg?" she asked.

Troy paused mid-swig. He shook his head. He'd just assumed anyone would prefer Toronto. He'd been to Winnipeg for games and it got cold there in the winter. Cold enough to freeze…well, cold.

"After Mitch...died, everyone looked at the kids with pity. Family, friends, even people who'd just seen the pictures in the paper. 'Poor things,' they'd say. Some looked at me the same way. Others would have this expression of condemnation—why hadn't I known? Why hadn't I done something, stopped him somehow? Was I the reason he did it? Everything we said or did was being examined as a result of what Mitch had done. People were suffocating us with kindness, or in some cases keeping a distance as if we carried a disease. We weren't a mom and two kids, we were 'the survivors.'

"Do you understand what that's like? Everyone staring, watching, pointing us out? I wanted a clean start. For all of us. I wanted people to meet us and get to know us as we are, not as characters in a news story.

"How did I know? Because you treated us differently. You've bent over backward to be nice to us, and there's no other reason for it. Today people kept saying to me that you never went to these family things. They assumed you and I were dating. 'You and your family must be special' they kept repeating. And they were right. But we don't want to be special. We want to be ordinary.

"I'd appreciate it if you would keep the information you learned quiet. And please don't do anything else for us. You've been very kind, but from now on, treat us like you would if you didn't know our story. We don't want to be special."

Michelle nodded, and then headed for the door. She'd left before Troy could figure out what he wanted to say.

He still wasn't sure what that was, but he knew what he was feeling: angry. He *had* been nice to them. He had bent over backward so that Angie could play hockey without getting her mom all riled up. This kind of philanthropic gesture was new to him. Michelle reacted as if that was a bad thing. He'd gone out of his way for the family, and she was throwing it back in his face, making out somehow that he was the bad guy.

She'd said he didn't understand what it was like to be the center of people's attention and pity. Actually, he understood exactly what it was like. No one had forgotten that he'd missed playing last year because of cancer. They watched him, too.

But if she wanted to be left alone, that was just fine. He had a good life, and had just been taking a bit of time out of it to be nice to a neighbor who'd had a rough go of it. He could live without that. He'd done it before, after all. He'd go back to his regular lifestyle quite happily.

Troy finished his beer and went for another.

"ANGIE! ARE YOU READY?" Michelle yelled. It was early Saturday morning. No sleeping in these days. They had hockey.

Tommy was dressed and ready, with his portable game system in hand. Michelle was considering again whether it was time to start limiting his gaming. It had seemed to help him work through his dad's death, but that had been more than a year ago at this point. She might have to cut the cord soon. However, Tommy never complained about these early, and often long, trips to the rink, and since Michelle usually spent her time reading her course material, it was a godsend that he was so happy to sit and play his game. Michelle insisted that every half hour they take a break and walk around the rink. She hoped it helped him as much as it did her.

"Angie! If we don't leave now—"

But Angie was pulling on her jacket, finally, dragging her bag of gear. They spilled out the doorway. Michelle held her breath, but Troy wasn't around, so they were good. Michelle was surprised at how little they saw Troy since she'd talked to him. They did have schedules that differed, but accidental meetings no longer occurred. She knew Troy had been upset, but she also was sure she'd been right.

It's not like they were dating. No. She had no plans to date again, and if that somehow happened, she wouldn't put the kids into the mix until she was confident her date was going to be around permanently. She wasn't sure exactly when one reached that point, but since she was staying single for the foreseeable future, it wasn't a worry. She'd had enough messiness in her life. Things might be difficult right now, but she had control over what was happening to them. It could be lonely after the kids went to bed, but it was calm. She could relax. The kids were relaxed. They needed that, and they needed it to continue into the future.

She and the kids were a unit on their own now. They had to learn to function without outside assistance. And they had to earn things, not be given things out of pity. Michelle had grown up an army brat, so she understood being tough. Her kids would have to be tough, too. Life was not easy.

They made it to the rink and, after sending Angie to the change room, she and Tommy settled in. Michelle greeted some of the other parents. They were now on first-name terms, but she didn't have the free time to chat during practices. Angie's practices lasted for hours, and then she had to attend Tae Kwon Do with Tommy. Michelle took a class with him so that she kept herself in shape. Angie had started complaining about the time she had to spend at the dojang, which was really unfair considering how long they all spent at her hockey practices. Still, Michelle thought she might start letting Angie stay home.

Then, when she wasn't doing activities with the kids, or groceries, or laundry or corralling them to help clean up, she had her own classes and homework.

She really was grateful to Troy, whatever his motives might have been. Angie was on this team, and from what Michelle could see, she was one of the better players. Thanks to him, she'd met Bridget, and through her, Karen, and the other woman's help with Michelle's classes had been monumental. She still had to work pretty hard at her courses, but it didn't feel like they were being taught in a different language. She preferred to attend classes when she could so that she could ask questions, but didn't panic if something came up and she had to follow the class on-line. She was hoping for better results on the midterms coming up.

"Okay, Tommy, time to do a lap!"

"One sec, Mom," he said. Michelle marked her place in her text and threw her bag over her shoulder. She always nudged Tommy a couple of minutes before starting, since it was never the right moment in his game.

The two of them had to make a circuitous route around the waiting parents. The first few practices people had looked up question-ingly at them, but now their odd behavior was accepted. This particular day, another mom asked if she could join them.

"I'd never do this on my own, but you're smart. Any exercise is good, and it's a great way to break up the monotony."

Michelle smiled. "You aren't fascinated by watching drills?"

The other woman laughed. "You're lucky your son isn't playing, too. My husband is watching our son practice right now. When my husband travels, I have to cover the activi-ties of two kids, and sometimes I swear I need a clone just to keep up with the practices, the games, the meetings, the fund-raisers."

Michelle glanced at Tommy, who was scrambling along a row ahead of them. He looked around as if expecting to discover someone in the corners. When she'd asked him about this, he'd just shrugged. Maybe he was imitating behavior from his games. Again, she wasn't sure if she should be probing more, or leaving him to work things out.

"Speaking of which, can you and Angie sell programs at the next Bobcats game?"

Michelle paused, working to keep her expression neutral. She hadn't signed up for that, hoping no one would notice. No such luck.

"Sure. Everyone has to do their part, right?"

She hoped she looked happier than she felt. It was difficult enough to get to Angie's team's games. These additional activities to fund raise at games for other teams were just another time waster for Michelle. The Bobcats' game was this coming Friday night. Karen had offered to come over and help her prepare for midterms. She'd have to cancel that, and get someone to come and stay with Tommy. Khali had a sister who'd offered to babysit, but that she would expect to be paid.

The conversation continued past their usual

lap. Tommy went back to his game when they sat down, but Michelle knew it would be rude for her to pull out her book. She started to panic, thinking of the time she was wasting, time she needed to study, but she fought it down. She gripped the ring hanging around her neck, twisting it to keep the frustration buried. She worked hard to keep her face pleasant and maintain her part of the conversation.

Practice wrapped up, and the group broke up to get their kids. Michelle blinked back tears. It wasn't fair. Mitch should be here, sharing the workload. But not the Mitch who'd returned from his tour. That Mitch hadn't been able to help, since he was in so much pain himself.

No, it was better when she relied on herself. She'd get through it. Somehow.

TROY HEARD THE whistle and cursed. Another penalty. Coach was going to be reaming him out again. He didn't dare look toward the bench as he followed the ref to the penalty box. He ignored the cheers of the LA fans as he sat down behind the glass.

He was angry. Angry with the doofus in the LA uniform who'd been chirping at him.

Angry at himself for poking the guy with his stick, leading to the penalty and leaving his team down a man. Since Troy was one of the top penalty killers for the Blaze, this was even harder on the team. If LA scored a goal as a result of his penalty, he was going to be even more angry. He found he was angry a lot now.

There was a groan from the crowd. Mike Reimer had just sprawled over to block what the fans had hoped would be a goal. Troy owed him—Mike was saving his butt. When the refs whistled to stop play, they called a commercial break for the broadcast. Troy leaned back, doing his best to ignore the taunts from the LA fans behind him.

He had to do something about this. When he'd had that first run-in with Bridget, he'd known he had to be more aggressive in his play. He'd worked on that, but now he'd flipped a switch too far in the other direction. Coach Parker had warned him last game about taking too many penalties. And Troy knew better. But there was a pool of anger inside that boiled over into action before he even realized he was responding. He had to find a way to overcome that.

He noticed one of the LA team's ice crew. It was hard not to notice them. Officially the women were shoveling up the shaved ice that accumulated on the rink surface, but the bared midriffs, tight pants and low-cut tops indicated that part of their job was to provide some eye candy for the fans. The woman who'd caught his eye had long, dark hair, reminding him of Michelle. His jaw clenched. He'd tried to ignore it, but part of this whole anger problem was his neighbor.

After that little chat they'd had about how Michelle didn't want to be special, Troy had done his best to avoid her. That meant spending less time at his place. When he was invited out to a club after a game, he shrugged off his strict training regimen and agreed to go. He got home later at night, and that meant he got up later in the mornings—but he could only sleep in so late. He had practice. Which meant he was increasingly tired, and his temper shortened.

At first, his lack of attention to his training regimen had helped him be more aggressive. When someone cut him off, he was too tired to worry about getting jarred. Instead, he got mad and hit them. Hard. It felt good.

But it didn't stay good. He was going out at night to avoid meeting anyone in the hallway at the condo. He used to go out just for fun, but somehow, now, he wasn't enjoying it as much. And when he was at his place, going down the hallway, he'd hear Michelle and the kids doing something behind their door and he knew he wasn't welcome.

It was frustrating. He found himself wanting to yell at her, and that was bad, so he'd stay out even later to make sure he'd miss her. Then he'd worry about his cancer coming back because he wasn't getting enough sleep. Then he'd stay in more, but he'd see Angie in the hallway, and she'd look hurt that he was never around. It wasn't fair. He needed to find a balance, but wasn't sure how. Road trips were a relief.

Until now. The commercial break ended. Troy sat up again, following the play, watching the clock count down the seconds till he could get back on the ice. Ten seconds before his penalty expired, the home team scored. The arena roared with approval. Troy was released from the box, but he felt like crap. He'd let down his team. That goal was on him.

"COMING WITH US, TROY?"

He turned and realized it was two of the youngest players who had asked. Troy had been one of those young guys, but after a season off, he'd crossed the thirty-year line, and now he was one of the old guys. At least he was cool enough to be asked to go with these two younger players. The married players, like Reimer, or the ones with kids, like Sandusky, were always heading to the hotel right after the games when they were on the road.

Troy had just received the expected dressing down from his coach, and he had had nothing to say to defend himself. One more misstep and he would be benched. He hated that. He hated that he was in this position.

He needed some way to get this horrible game out of his system. So the offer from the rookies sounded good, and he agreed to go.

These two had been brought up when injuries had left the team roster short. They hadn't played much, but were getting a taste of what it was like in the big league. Troy thought they might want him to show them around in LA, but they had a place already figured out. Troy relaxed in the cab, fine with whatever they had in mind.

They had some kind of deal set up at this particular club, because their group was ushered in ahead of the line. Troy was used to that kind of perk at home in Toronto, but on the road, especially in SoCal where hockey wasn't as big as other sports, he wasn't always recognized and usually had to be with someone local to cut lines. He shrugged. Maybe the bouncers here were big hockey fans.

It was a typical club: packed, loud and overpriced. Troy flagged down a beer and looked to see what his teammates were doing.

They were heading to a back room. Troy frowned. He had a feeling they weren't doing anything the team would approve of, but they were adults and he wasn't their babysitter. He let them go.

When a blonde asked him to dance, he was happy to oblige her. In LA, the women were all attractive, especially in club lighting. And they liked him. No one here objected to him helping them out. Troy danced with her again, since he enjoyed dancing, and it was taking the taste of the game away. The woman indicated she was willing to extend the evening, but Troy left on his own. He wasn't sure what had happened to the two rookies, but he needed to get back to the hotel to make curfew. They were old enough to take care of themselves.

TROY HAD FINALLY enjoyed a good sleep, so he got down to the bus just in time for the trip to

Anaheim for the next game. When the coach asked to talk to him at the arena once they arrived there, he had no choice but to agree. He hoped this wasn't going to be a continuation of the dressing down.

He noticed the two rookies hadn't made the bus. Maybe Coach wanted to know what they'd done last night. Troy couldn't say for sure, but he could guess.

He'd been flabbergasted when he was presented with a plastic cup.

"You want me to do what? I didn't do anything!"

The coach spun his laptop around. On it was a picture of Troy dancing with the blonde from the previous night. Troy shrugged. There were no rules against going to a club and dancing. He'd had two drinks, total, and taken a cab to the hotel.

The coach then clicked another tab on his browser. There was a picture of the two rookies snorting coke in a private room of the same club. Troy shook his head mentally at their sheer stupidity. Especially since the pictures were on the front page of a tabloid website. The Blaze was trying hard to present a family-friendly image, and this was going to play badly with management. Troy understood the cup now. He'd been there, so now he had to prove he hadn't consumed any illegal substances.

That was bad enough. But there was more.

Coach Parker told him off because apparently he really was their damned babysitter.

"You're one of the senior members of the team now. You need to grow up, settle down. Be a leader," said the coach. Troy felt the anger again. He didn't want to be a leader; he didn't want to be responsible. He wanted to enjoy himself. He'd had almost no fun growing up because everything had to be hockey first. His dad had made it obvious how much the responsibility of parenting ate into his freedom. Even now, he had to follow the team rules and keep himself in shape. Outside of that, he should be able to do what he wanted. What was the point of succeeding, making money, getting some fame, if you couldn't enjoy it?

THE TESTS PROVED there was nothing but alcohol in his system. The two idiots, meanwhile, were suspended. He'd hoped that was the end of it. Unfortunately, not.

The story had been picked up, especially in Toronto, and Troy was tainted by association. He'd been advised to keep his nose clean for the next while. And told off, again, for not being a better example.

It was all echoes of his father. He'd thought he was finally rid of all that nagging. He was in a surly mood as he headed back to his place for another nice early night. He heard Michelle and the kids laughing behind their condo door, and that only made him feel even more alone.

CHAPTER FIVE

"YOU NEED TO loosen up. Let your hair down, literally. Come on, my sister will babysit. You deserve a break."

Michelle looked at Khali. It was the last tutorial, and afterward, she stayed to chat with the other "misfits." They had exams coming up in the next couple of weeks, and then the Christmas break. It had been a long, hard slog.

Michelle was still working harder than the others. She'd passed her midterms, but by the slimmest of margins. Homework, hockey with Angie, Tae Kwon Do with Tommy, housework, laundry, meals, groceries, classes—these took up her entire life. She hadn't had fun for so long she couldn't even remember her last night out. Her ragtag group of fellow students was going out to celebrate Saturday night; even Boni had agreed for once. Michelle knew she should start studying for exams, but she was so tempted by this night out. One night for her. Then she'd go back to being responsible for her family.

"Okay," she finally agreed, asking if Khali's sister could babysit.

Angie would be upset. The euphoria over playing hockey had passed, and Angie was again a twelve-year-old girl, not an angel.

Angie thought she was old enough to baby-sit her brother. Michelle was fine leaving her with Tommy while she ran an errand, but she wasn't comfortable yet leaving the two alone, at night, till quite late. Especially when the only neighbor on their floor was either traveling or out clubbing most nights, according to the papers. Not that Michelle was keeping track, really, but this last LA story had been headline news, so she couldn't miss it. Sometimes, when she was up late studying, she'd hear the muted ping of the elevator announcing that Troy had come home. Yes, she'd admit, she had looked out the peephole at him. She'd wanted to make sure it wasn't an unauthorized stranger on their floor. She wasn't being nosy, just responsible.

Angie would have to put up with a babysitter for one night. One night, so that Michelle could relax and enjoy herself.

It took a lot of planning. It wasn't just the

night out itself, but the next day. Luckily, one of the other hockey parents had agreed to pick Angie up for the game Sunday morning. Michelle promised to do the same for another game. Angie usually had her bag packed the night before, so it should be easy to get her out the door. Tommy was going to a birthday party for someone in his Tae Kwon Do class. Michelle would need to pick up Tommy and another kid after the party, but the other parents would pick up Tommy and get both partygoers over there for the start of laser tag. Once Michelle got her two out the door, then she could catch a couple more hours of sleep. She'd probably still feel like crap the rest of the day, but she should be ready to go again on Monday. She hoped it was worth it, but the thought of a night out, dancing, unencumbered...she was sure it would be.

Saturday evening she found herself looking in her closet for something to wear. She'd been living in jeans and yoga pants for so long it was difficult to remember what other clothes she'd brought to Toronto. Anything dressy was buried in the back.

She'd had good intentions to select an outfit earlier, but after hockey practice and Tae Kwon Do, Tommy had remembered he needed poster board for a project due Monday, and once they got to the dollar store, nothing there was the right color. It had taken a while to track down what he insisted he had to have.

Michelle was only too aware that it would have saved time to take Troy's truck, but after she'd spoken to him about treating them normally she was determined to only drive it to hockey. She wished she could have avoided using it altogether, but there was no way to get Angie to hockey on time using the subway, and she couldn't afford endless cab fares. She wouldn't dare ask Troy to get the promised transit passes. She hadn't meant to be ungrateful, but she'd been incredibly disappointed to know she was a pity case again. She'd almost started to believe that he enjoyed their company, and she didn't like how disappointed she'd felt when she found out the truth. She'd probably been harsher than she'd meant to in response.

She finally found a dress: she hoped it still fit. She showered, took time to dry her hair and left it down and put on makeup. She clipped on some earrings Mitch had given her for her birthday one year. The dress fit, but more tightly than it had the last time she'd worn it. Still, with heels on, she thought she didn't look bad for a thirty-three-year-old mother of two. She smiled at herself in the mirror.

Her necklace with her wedding ring was on the dresser. She usually put it on just as she was leaving. Tonight she paused a moment, considered. She shook her head and left it there.

With a last glance at herself, she picked up her phone and went out to show herself to the kids.

She twirled for them.

"Wow, Mom. You almost look hot!" said Angie. Tommy smiled at her, but his brow was creased as if he was worried.

Her phone buzzed and Michelle glanced at the phone, not sure she really wanted to deal with anything before leaving. She read the text message and her stomach fell. Her babysitter had canceled.

Michelle knew Angie would insist she could babysit, but Michelle also knew she couldn't relax in the same way if Angie was on her own, and she wouldn't dare stay out as late. Was a shorter, less relaxing night out better than none?

"What's wrong, Mom?" Angie asked.

Michelle took a breath. "The babysitter can't make it."

Angie shrugged. "So? I can take care of us."

"I'm sure that you can, Angie, but…"

Angie's eyes rolled. "You're not going to stay in, then, are you? Honestly, Mom, give us a break. No one can get in the building, and we aren't stupid enough to let anyone in the door. I won't fight with Tommy, and he won't fight with me. Right, Tommy?"

Tommy nodded, but slowly. Being alone didn't appear to appeal to him.

Michelle looked at her daughter. "Maybe… If I don't stay late."

Angie crossed her arms. "We're not babies."

"I know," Michelle said.

She felt deflated. She had really been looking forward to this night out. She'd probably blown it up into something much bigger in her imagination than it would ever live up to in reality, but still, it had been her reward for a long, hard semester. Having a curfew was going to put a damper on the whole thing. She'd have to keep checking the time, worry about how things were going…maybe she should just cancel.

She headed back to her room. She'd been happy with her appearance just minutes before. Now, well, it seemed a waste of time and effort. She heard the condo door open, and for a second, thought that maybe the text was a mistake, or a joke, and the girl had arrived to stay with Angie and Tommy, but when she ran back down the hallway, there wasn't anyone new inside the condo. Tommy was there, but Angie was gone.

"Where's your sister?" Michelle asked.

Tommy pointed at the door and shrugged.

Michelle felt her anger rise. Yes, Angie was growing up and, yes, legally she could be responsible for herself and her brother, but Angie was not an adult, and she couldn't run counter to her mother's rules. She stalked over to the door and opened it. Her own disappointment was making her angrier, but still…

She looked toward the elevator, but there was no sign of Angie there. She glanced the other way, and there was Angie, in Troy's doorway, talking to the man himself.

TROY WAS BORED. He'd spent the last week doing exactly as he was supposed to, and he was climbing the walls. He turned off the basketball game. He'd never really gotten that sport. Half the time the players were walking. It was just too slow for him.

He was debating getting up to get a beer when there was a knock on the door.

Knocks on his door were pretty rare. It was a secure building, so the concierge would call if someone was coming up. But the Robertsons across the hall… Troy jumped up. Maybe someone was in trouble.

Angie was at the door, but not in the kind of trouble he'd imagined.

"Troy, are you going to be home tonight?"

Angie was upset. Was she mad at him? For being home?

"I didn't have any plans to go out," he answered, angry at himself about that.

"Would you be my responsible adult?"

Troy tried to understand just what she was asking. He understood the words individually but he wasn't normally considered a responsible adult. Wasn't that exactly why the team was on his case right now? And he had no idea why Angie needed one when she had Michelle, the poster definition of responsibility.

Then Michelle appeared in her doorway, and all thought fled.

If Michelle had looked like this the first day they'd met in the elevator, he'd definitely have noticed. Her hair was down and tumbled over her shoulders almost to her waist. She had obviously spent time on her appearance and it hadn't been wasted. She was wearing makeup: her eyes were smoky, and her lips…she'd put on bright red lipstick. He loved bright red lipstick. She was wearing a dress that hugged every curve, cut low enough in front to show some cleavage, and short enough to show that she had great legs with a nice curvy butt. Troy had never imagined this woman was living inside his neighbor. He swallowed. And stared.

"What do you think you're doing, Angela?" Michelle asked with dangerous control.

Ah, Troy thought. That was why Angie was angry.

Angie turned and put her hands on her hips. "I was just asking if Troy was going to be home tonight. He is, so we can call him if we need help. You can still go out."

Troy was rapidly forming a picture of what was going on. Michelle had planned an evening without the kids—that was obvious, based on how she looked. But she didn't want to leave the kids alone. Troy wasn't really a babysitter, but he was bored, and maybe he could work this out to his advantage. Staying in to take care of the kids would make the team happy, and he liked Angie and Tommy. He could babysit them for a bit.

"Sure, I could babysit," he said.

Both females looked at him. The four narrowed eyes, the two sets of compressed lips—apparently his picture had been wrong somehow.

"I don't need a babysitter," Angie spat out, giving her mom the side eye. "But Mom's afraid to leave us completely alone at night." For twelve the kid could really give attitude.

"If you don't want a babysitter, what are you doing here?" Troy asked.

Angie sighed, burdened by these slow-witted adults. "Mom doesn't trust us. She got someone to come for the night, just as if we were babies, but that person canceled. I can take care of my brother. I just need a responsible adult I can call if anything happens," Angie retorted.

"Am I responsible enough?" Troy asked with a grin.

Angie obviously thought so. Michelle was considering.

Then he remembered that stupid thing in LA. His grin faded as Michelle examined him. She'd never trust him now.

MICHELLE STARED AT TROY.

Could this work?

He'd been in the headlines lately for something that had happened in California, but from what she'd read, he hadn't done any drugs himself. He apparently didn't know how to choose his friends, but she wasn't asking him to talk to the kids about life choices. If the kids needed physical protection he was big enough, and if they needed to go to the hospital, he had a fast vehicle on tap. This might be a good first step—it would allow Angie to feel like she was independent, but an adult would still have the ultimate responsibility if something went wrong.

And she had to confess, she really wanted her night out. She'd been looking forward to it. But was she compromising her own standards because she wanted to go out so badly?

She debated and didn't notice Troy losing his smile.

Khali's sister was only seventeen. He had to be at least as responsible as a high school senior, she concluded. He paid his bills and kept a job. So if she'd been willing to let the kids stay with a teenager, she could leave them with Troy. And this shouldn't inconvenience him—he had been planning to spend the night at home anyway, and he'd probably never even hear from the kids. As long as she warned Angie.

"Okay," she said finally, and noticed both Troy and Angie looked relieved.

"Angie, go get the list I made for the baby-sitter."

Angie ran off, happy again.

"Thank you, Troy. I'll ask the kids not to bother you unless it's an emergency, so with any luck you won't even hear from them. This list has all the info you need if anything happens."

Troy shrugged. "No problem. I didn't have anything going on tonight."

Angie bounced back, handing the list to Troy.

"Angie!" Michelle said.

Angie turned to her mom warily.

"Let's be clear. A question about hockey is not an emergency."

"Mom! I'm not a moron," Angie responded, mortified.

"We're not going to put Troy out any more than we have to. He's doing us a big favor."

Just then Michelle's phone beeped.

"My ride's here. Same rules about snacks. Be safe, and call me if you need to."

She reached to give her daughter a hug, but

Angie had slipped away back to the door of their condo.

"Tommy, Troy's going to take care of us and Mom is leaving."

Michelle got her coat, and Tommy came and gave her a big hug.

"I'll be fine, sweetie." Michelle hugged him. "You have fun, and go to bed on time."

She headed for the elevator with a worried look over her shoulder. Troy was still in his doorway.

"It'll be fine. Have fun," Troy said.

Michelle thought he sounded wistful. He'd probably prefer to be the one going out. Well, for one night it was Michelle's turn. She smiled, perhaps a little smugly…she'd seen the way his eyes had widened when she came out of the condo, and it gave her a little extra boost of confidence. Watch out, Toronto. Michelle was going out.

TROY WATCHED MICHELLE make her way down the hallway to the elevator to catch her ride. She was more comfortable in heels than he'd have expected, and he enjoyed watching her. She looked like a different woman than the neighbor he knew. Did she like to dance? Did that uptight personality ever unwind?

He glanced over to see Angie watching him watch her mom. He felt his cheeks warming and wondered how mature girls her age really were.

Tommy turned to Troy once the elevator doors closed behind Michelle.

"Do you want to play video games with us?"

Troy was surprised at the offer. Tommy hadn't warmed up to him the way Angie had, but maybe the kid was nervous about being alone. He kept pretty close tabs on his mom.

"Whatcha playing?" Troy asked. "What system?"

When he heard the response, Troy mentally rolled his eyes. Yeah, they obviously didn't have a lot of money.

That system was ancient.

"Why don't you come over to my place and play with me?" he offered.

Angie stared at him. "For real?"

Tommy didn't say anything, but after a minute, nodded his head.

Troy wondered if this was the right thing to do.

"Hey, were you supposed to do homework?"

Angie cocked her head. "It's Saturday night."

"Don't you do your homework on Saturday night?"

Angie sighed. "Only when we're out all day Sunday."

Oh, of course. How did he not know that? Angie assumed their plans were published for general consumption, he guessed.

He knew Michelle had planned for the kids to stay in their own condo, and only contact him in the case of an emergency. That had been the plan. But he was the responsible adult, right? So having the kids over should be okay. Plus, he'd missed them. He wanted to know how Angie was doing with her hockey. Tommy had been playing games on that old system they had. He'd like to see if he was good on a better system. If the kids bothered him, he could send them back home, but right now, he'd like to spend some time with them.

He thought about his fridge full of beer and sports drinks.

"Bring your snacks."

THE KIDS WERE better at the games than he'd expected, even on the new system. They made him feel old. Well, older. They were also a lot more fun than he'd expected, too. Tommy was reserved, but he had warmed up to Troy, and they had a couple of good battles. Troy was pleased with himself when he was the one that remembered the kids had to get to bed.

"It's not time yet," said Angie.

Troy got up and looked at the notes for the babysitter that Michelle had left. He read the line about bedtimes, and raised his eyebrows.

"I thought you could tell time by twelve," he said.

Angie sighed. "It's Saturday!" she complained.

"Have you got hockey in the morning?"

Angie shrugged and started moving. Tommy followed her.

"Thank you, Mr. Green," Tommy said.

"Troy's fine."

After a moment he started to follow them. Angie looked at him in surprise.

"Just making sure you really go to bed."

Angie huffed, but kept going. Tommy actually grinned.

"She sometimes keeps her phone on late," he confided.

"And how would you know, nosy?" Angie challenged him.

"I see the light," Tommy answered.

Troy might be an old guy to these kids, but he wasn't so old that he couldn't remember when he was young and never wanted to go to bed. He figured he should stay at their place till he was sure they were actually asleep. That was what a responsible adult would do. Angie might not realize it, but sleep was vital if she was going to play her best. He also didn't want Michelle mad at him again. She owed him after tonight, and he preferred it when they were on good terms. Not because he knew her history, but because he liked her—as a neighbor, of course.

The kids took way longer than they should to get themselves in bed. Tommy was actually pretty good, but Angie was no longer starstruck by the hockey player across the hall. And she was mad that an adult wasn't allowing her to make her own decisions. But the more she dragged, the more determined Troy became. He wasn't going to be outsmarted by a twelve-year-old.

He remembered what Tommy said, and after finally getting to the point where he thought they were down for the night, he went to the condo door, opened it, shut it again and then tiptoed back down the hallway to the bedrooms.

"Gotcha!" he said, catching Angie with her phone in her hands.

Angie almost fell out of bed.

"I was just—"

"Settle down, or I'm taking that phone." Troy couldn't believe he was saying that. He *did* sound like a responsible adult.

"I expected that you'd be more fun," Angie complained.

Troy figured he was plenty fun. But if Angie was serious about hockey, she had to be just as serious about the off-ice preparation as the on-ice play.

"Do you want to play hockey for fun, or do you want to play professionally?"

Angie looked up at him from under her eyelids, lips pouting.

"When I was a kid, my dad was always yelling at me about getting to sleep on time," Troy continued. "I didn't like it, but when I got older, I realized that extra rest had helped. Sometimes you need every little bit of an edge you can get."

Troy hoped that would make her less resistant. Her response wasn't what he'd expected.

"Do all dads yell?" she asked.

Troy hesitated. This was an issue that could get him in big trouble. Did he say all dads yelled so he didn't sound like he was dissing Angie's dad? Did he tell her some dads didn't know how to say things any other way?

"Not all dads," he said, deciding to give her the truth as he had learned it, without trying to figure out what he was supposed to say, since he didn't know what that was. "My dad was a yeller. But when I started playing junior, I stayed with other families, and those dads didn't yell—at least, not as much."

Angie didn't reply. She lay down in her bed quietly.

Troy wanted to trust her, but he'd been a kid himself, and he knew adults could be conned. He finally settled on the Robertsons' couch. He turned on the stereo, low, and pulled out his own phone for amusement, keeping an eye on the open doorways. He only had to yell down the hallway once, and then things stayed dark. He stretched out on the couch where he could see down to the kids' rooms, and waited. He wasn't sure how long, but he must have dozed off himself.

MICHELLE SAT on her stool at the table at the club, smiling at her posse. Sure, they were younger and didn't have kids, but she was keeping up with them and she was enjoying herself. She was flushed from the heat, the dancing and the excitement. For a few hours, she was just a woman having fun. How long since she had been able to say that?

"Drink for you from the guy over there," Khali said, pushing a Cosmo across the table. Michelle wrinkled her nose. She was more of a wine drinker.

"Truly. It was for you!" Boni insisted. Boni was drinking only nonalcoholic drinks, but she was with them, and for once looked almost relaxed.

Michelle started to shake her head. She was married—and then she realized, again, that she wasn't, not anymore. Her smile faded. Mitch was missing nights out like this. Before the kids, they'd loved to spend a night out dancing. Mitch was also missing the kids growing up. There was so much Mitch would never see. She took a breath.

Mitch wasn't here, but she was. And while people often claimed their partners would want them to move on after they were gone, Michelle knew. Before Mitch went overseas, while he'd still been Mitch, he'd told her that if anything happened she was to keep living her life. She was to find another guy, but not some wuss.

Her smile returned. Mitch wouldn't approve of anyone who sent Cosmos, but she wasn't planning on marrying that guy, or anyone else. Ignoring the pink drink, she took her glass of wine, raised it for a moment in a silent toast and when someone asked her to dance, went without another thought.

Michelle was late getting home. Her feet were killing her, and she knew she'd pay for the late hour when she had to wake up early the next morning. But she was still a little buzzed from the alcohol and the dancing and feeling like just Michelle again, so she didn't care. She was humming a song when she unlocked her door and made her way into the condo. The stereo was on, low, and she twirled, stumbling a bit as she kicked off her shoes and struggled out of her coat. She recovered and saw someone moving on the couch and almost screamed out loud. She was frantically trying to remember where her best weapon was and how quickly she could grab her phone when the figure turned on a light, and she realized it was Troy.

"HAVE A NICE TIME?" he asked a little sleepily.

"What are you doing here?" she asked sharply.

"Angie kept playing on her phone, so I wanted to keep an eye on her. I was being responsible." He was pleased with himself, honestly, and hoped Michelle was impressed.

"How did you— Did something happen that the kids needed you?" Michelle started to check her phone.

"No, no problems. We hung out and played video games till I had to send them to bed. Angie tried to lie about her bedtime." Troy was still surprised by that.

Michelle tried to stifle a laugh.

"She's twelve. She didn't want a babysitter. What did you expect?"

"She has hockey in the morning. She needs her rest."

Michelle laughed out loud at that. "I bet you fought going to bed, too, at twelve," she answered.

Troy grinned. "Yeah, I did. That's why I'm here. So, did you have a good time?"

Michelle smiled widely. "Great. My feet are killing me from dancing in these shoes, and I'll have a monster headache in the morning, but it was worth it."

Troy could see that she still was a bit buzzed. She didn't look anything like his neighbor. Part of it was the makeup and the dress, but a lot of it was her expression. She was having fun. And that transformed her. If both their situations had been different...

"I didn't know you were a dancer," he teased.

Michelle walked over to the sitting area. She shrugged her shoulders, the movement making the hem of the dress slide up a bit, Troy noticed.

"There's a lot you don't know about me," Michelle responded. Troy blinked. Was that an actual flirty voice?

"I've only danced with the kids lately, but I love dancing." The music on the stereo changed to an upbeat song. "They played this tonight," Michelle said. She raised her arms and started swiveling her hips, and Troy almost fell off the couch.

Michelle was relaxed, hugged by that form-fitting dress, hair down, no frown, just a dreamy expression as if she was mentally miles away. And she could dance. Much better than he'd have expected. He'd never expected a shimmy like that...and when she flipped her hair—

Troy was a good dancer himself. It was his claim to fame on the team. He swore it helped his balance on the ice. He watched Michelle for a few moments, and after she flipped her hair again, he accepted the unspoken invitation.

She didn't notice him come up to her at first, but as he began to sync his movements to hers, he gently grasped her hand and pulled her into a spin. Instead of fighting him, as he half expected, she smiled and pivoted to him so that they were moving together. When the song changed to something slow, they moved into an embrace, following the music.

She fit against him perfectly, and they moved in harmony. Troy wondered where her mind was. How did this sexy woman who was currently in his arms mesh with the defensive woman he usually encountered in the hallway?

The song ended. With a sigh, Michelle drew away.

"I should call it a night," she said, reluctantly. "I've got the kids to deal with in the morning—and the morning is coming way too early."

"Why don't you sleep in, let them do their own thing for a bit? They're old enough, aren't they?" Troy knew he understood little about kids, but surely that wasn't unreasonable once in a while.

Michelle fell onto the couch. "If only. Angie has a hockey game in the morning. Another family is picking her up, but I have to get her up and fed and out the door. Tommy's going to a birthday party, so same goes for him. Then I can go back to sleep… until it's time to pick everyone up." She sighed.

Inwardly, Troy shuddered. He couldn't imagine that kind of headache, juggling schedules to get a bit more sleep. Not having responsibility like that meant that he could do what he wanted. And he did. After years of work to get where he was, he thought he was due. Did Michelle ever wish she had that freedom?

Troy asked, curiously, "That's a lot of work. You ever regret having kids?"

He half expected her to jump on him for the comment. Instead, she answered him seriously.

"I can't regret them. I love them, and I'm a better person for having been their mother. But I got pregnant pretty young. I sometimes think I missed a lot. I didn't have a lot of fun before I had to be responsible. Mitch was a great dad, but when he was deployed, I was on my own."

Troy sat down beside her, intrigued by this

glimpse of a different, and honestly, very attractive, woman. If she'd been single, free of kids, able to spend nights out dancing like this...he'd want to be with her. But she'd given up on all that.

And Troy...he'd had lots of fun over the years. Was that all he wanted? Was responsibility always a bad thing?

"Ever think of getting married again? Maybe having more kids?"

Michelle shook her head sharply, then flinched as if the movement had hurt.

"Nope. When the kids are out on their own, I'm going to take some time just for me. You know I've never gone on spring break? I'd like to have a spring break. Go south, away from the cold, party, get a suntan, dance all night..." Her voice faded.

Troy realized he'd never had a spring break, either. Hockey had kept him busy every winter for as long as he could remember. But he'd certainly had that kind of vacation. He tried to picture her hanging out with college kids on the sand, and he thought maybe this woman from tonight would do that. Whether she could really shake off that sense of responsibility she usually wore for longer than one evening was another question.

Troy glanced over and realized Michelle had fallen asleep. She might have been a party girl tonight, but she was still a responsible single parent, and she didn't have the fortitude for long nights.

"Michelle?" he said softly. She didn't budge.

"Michelle?" He paused. His conscience had been bothering him, so he figured he'd test out just how asleep she really was.

"Michelle, I'm the one paying for Angie's hockey," he confessed quietly.

No response. Okay, she must be really out of it. Troy stood and reached carefully under her to lift her up. She was slighter than he'd expected for someone so tough. He knew which rooms the kids were in, so he was able to find her bedroom easily. He laid her down on the bed. He noticed that she wasn't wearing the necklace, the one with her wedding ring.

The dress didn't look comfortable for sleeping, but he had no doubt that if he took it off, the woman who woke up in the morning wouldn't be the one he'd just danced with, but the one who'd rubbed his nose in the carpet when they first met. Still, he had an idea…

MICHELLE WOKE UP with a pounding head. Her mouth felt dry and gritty, and her feet ached.

She was not a young woman who could handle being out all night anymore.

She shoved off the covers, and realized she was still in her dress and hose, her hair tangled and undoubtedly makeup smudged over her face. She tried to remember how she'd made it to her bed, but couldn't remember anything past dancing with Troy…

Troy! What had happened last night?

She sat up quickly and grabbed her head when that movement started a symphony of hammers knocking at her skull. She leaned forward slowly, hands on her temples, and tried to remember. She'd danced with Troy, they'd talked, then…either she'd blacked out, or he'd carried her to bed. That must have been all—she was still fully dressed.

She remembered coming home, hearing the music…starting to dance. Then Troy had joined her. She hadn't known he could dance so well. When the music had slowed…

Her cheeks flushed. When the music slowed she'd moved into his embrace as if…as if she'd belonged there. She hadn't danced with a man like that since Mitch. Would Troy think she'd read too much into a dance? It had just been so long, and it had felt so good…

But she wasn't a woman who went dancing every night. She didn't hang out in clubs and party. Last night was a one-off. She was a single mom. Speaking of that...

She stood, carefully, listening but not hearing any sound from the kids. After a hesitant but necessary trip to the bathroom, she dragged herself to the kitchen. She had to get the kids off to their activities, and then she could...

The condo was empty. No kids. There was a carafe of coffee on the counter. And a note. She didn't recognize the handwriting but it was signed Troy. He'd gotten the kids off to hockey and laser tag, and made coffee. And he'd even left some Tylenol on the counter with a glass of water.

Michelle knew she'd have to figure out if this was okay or not later. If the kids were gone, and a look at the clock convinced her they must be, then she needed to get herself together. It would be time to get them all picked up soon.

Half an hour later she felt more like herself. The hammers were still working in her head, but after the Tylenol, there was less force behind them. Her face was clean, her hair pulled back, and she had a sweater and jeans on. She was Michelle, single mom, again. Party Michelle had been returned with the dress and heels to the closet.

There was a knock at the door. Michelle thought it was a little early for Angie to be back, but she opened the door—and had to look up. It was Troy, with a bag that contained something that smelled delicious.

"Hangover cure," he said, holding up the bag.

Michelle flushed. "I'm sorry. Did I fall asleep while you were here last night? Did you carry me to bed?"

Troy held up his hand. "Yes, but I behaved myself. Don't worry about it. Have some food. I wanted to talk to you anyway."

Michelle hated to think what he might want to talk about, but her stomach was grumbling at the aromas wafting from that bag. She wanted to talk to him, as well. She wanted to find out more about why he'd been at their place last night when she got home. He'd said there hadn't been any problems, so he should have stayed in his own condo. Something must have happened, and she needed to know what. She'd also like to hear why he'd apparently maneuvered the kids out the door this morning.

She stepped back to let him in.

TROY RECOGNIZED THAT it was everyday Michelle who answered the door, but she was feeling the effects of party Michelle from the night before. He set out the greasy breakfast sandwiches and hash browns from the bag and watched her dig in.

She moaned as she took her first bite. "This is perfect. I won't ask how you know so much about hangover cures."

Troy grinned.

As the coffee and food kicked in, and the Tylenol finally finished its job, her expression became more focused, and she turned to Troy, who was leaning against the counter.

"So, why were you here last night? Did the kids get into trouble?"

"No, they were good. We played games for a while, and then I came back here with them to make sure they settled down okay."

"You came back with them?" Michelle repeated.

Troy wondered if he'd made a misstep. He was becoming painfully aware that he didn't know anything about parenting.

"Is that a problem? Your gaming system is pretty crap, so we played at my place. I promise, I've got nothing more dangerous than beer and some bourbon over there, and I didn't offer them any. I didn't even drink myself."

Michelle considered for a moment. "No, that's not a problem, but I didn't want them to put you out."

Troy seized his moment.

"That's why I wanted to talk to you."

Michelle nodded and then winced. "I'll talk to them. They won't bother you again."

"No, that's not it," he answered. "Did you hear about what happened in LA, with those guys at the club?"

Michelle's brow creased. "I assumed you weren't in trouble about that. It was the other guys who did the drugs, right? You were just there?"

"Right," Troy reassured her. "I didn't do anything, but I was at the club with them. The team is really trying to market themselves as good, wholesome entertainment. That story blew that image up in their faces, and the team is doing damage control. I'm viewed as a potential problem."

Michelle was watching him intently. He'd better make sure he didn't oversell himself as a troublemaker or this idea of his would go nowhere fast.

"I don't do drugs. I just have a history of

partying. So, at least until this whole mess settles down, I've been asked to stay out of clubs. That's why I was home last night, and I was glad to hang with the kids." He wouldn't mention that he'd enjoyed meeting the other side of Michelle last night, too.

"I know you asked me to keep my distance from you and the kids because you didn't want any pity. Which, by the way, isn't what I feel for you. You've had a rough go and I admire how you're handling it. But I was hoping you'd reconsider spending time together. You'd be doing me a favor. I enjoy being with you guys, and I can tell the club I'm being a good boy. That way they'll also be less inclined to start trade talks."

Michelle looked surprised. "They wouldn't really trade you, would they?"

Troy shrugged. "I'm not cheap, and I'm getting older. I was off all last year. I don't think anyone is untouchable except Reimer. If they tried to move him, he'd just retire. So, anything is possible."

Troy hoped he'd have to get into a little more trouble than this before the team traded him, but it was true that no one was safe. Those two rookies wouldn't be around much longer for sure.

Michelle crossed her arms. She was obviously feeling better. Maybe he should have gotten this settled while she was still feeling the effects of last night. Or asked her while they were dancing. He remembered the beautiful woman who'd been in his arms. That Michelle would have agreed.

"What exactly do you have in mind?" So she wasn't saying no right away. Good.

Troy tried his most winning smile. "Maybe I could take Angie to some of her games or practices. We could all go out for dinner once in a while. Apparently, the aquarium is supposed to be pretty incredible, and I'd rather go with the kids than by myself. But to be honest, I hadn't worked out all the details."

Michelle seemed to be considering.

"And I pay," Troy said. Michelle opened her mouth to object and he forestalled her. "You're helping me out here, and I don't want you to say you can't go because of money. It makes me feel good to pick up the tab. And I might be able to write some of it off on my taxes. My agent is always asking me to keep receipts for things. I get a lot of stuff for free anyway."

Troy stopped, sensing that he'd pushed enough. He'd told her the truth. Just not all of it.

He'd really liked the Michelle he'd danced with last night. That was the Michelle she was meant to be, he thought, not burdened with handling things alone. He wanted to see more of that Michelle. If he could just convince her she was helping *him*, not the other way around, he might be able to do that. She was awfully prickly about anything like charity.

And it wasn't as if they'd be dating. She was an attractive woman, and he was having a hard time forgetting the image of her in that dress. But he wasn't ready to take on the responsibility of kids.

What if the cancer came back?

His mother had left him behind, and he wasn't going to do that to another kid.

But Michelle could use some help, as much as she hated to ask for it. And he enjoyed spending time with her and the kids. Right now he was finding his feet, somewhere between his carefree past and the post-cancer present. Michelle and the kids were more fun to be with than he'd expected, and hanging out with them more just seemed like a good idea.

"We can give it a try," she said finally. "You seem to have done well with the kids last night, and I appreciate that you stepped in this morning. But if it starts to interfere with your life, or we overstep, you have to promise you'll say something immediately."

Troy controlled his grin. He'd gotten what he wanted.

"So when are the kids back? Maybe we could all do lunch?" He held his breath, wondering if he'd pushed his luck too far.

Michelle shrugged. "Okay. Just remember, anytime you want to call it quits…"

Troy just grinned.

After meeting Angie and picking up Tommy, they'd gone out to a casual restaurant. Troy had done a bit of homework this time, and the restaurant had a kids' menu.

After they ate, Troy had insisted they go to the Hockey Hall of Fame and see his name on the Cup. Troy had tried to play it cool, but she'd noticed him blink rapidly when he read his name.

Their tour of the building took a while, since so many people recognized Troy, and ended at the gift shop. For a hockey fan, it had almost everything imaginable. Troy bought everyone a Blaze hat, even though Michelle had wanted to argue. He'd leaned over and whispered in her ear, "I'm paying and that's not negotiable." So she'd bit her lip. It could have been worse. She thought she'd seen him eyeing the personalized jerseys. She'd been taken aback at the price tag on those.

Now they were home, Troy was in his own condo, and it was time to return to reality. The kids settled at the table to do homework. Michelle had her own books out. They finished long before she did, as usual. Before they took off to their rooms, Michelle said she wanted to talk to them.

"You had fun with Troy today?" she asked.

They nodded.

"Troy asked if he could spend some time with us, so we'll probably do a few more things like this with him. He's pretty busy with hockey, and he travels a lot, but he asked if we could hang out when he's available."

"Why did he ask you that? Are you, like, dating?" Angie queried. Michelle was jolted. She didn't want the kids to get the wrong idea.

She shook her head vehemently. "No, we're not dating. You remember he was in the news last week because he went to a bar with some other hockey players who got in trouble for doing drugs?" It had certainly been a good teaching opportunity for her with the kids.

"Drugs are bad," said Tommy.

"Illegal drugs are bad. There are good drugs," argued Angie.

Michelle interrupted before they got into one of those familiar sibling arguments. "We already talked about that, you two. Troy got in trouble just for being at the club with the other players, so remember that when you're hanging out with friends who do things they shouldn't. Anyway, Troy's supposed to stay away from the clubs for a while, so he thought it would be nice to spend some time with us."

Angie nodded. "We're good PR, huh?"

"Well, yes," Michelle responded. "But I just wanted you guys to know it might not last very long. I don't want you to get any ideas about this."

"He might get bored with us?" Angie asked.

Michelle hadn't expected that level of insight.

"Maybe," Michelle said. "Or he might become busy with other things. But he helped us a lot with your hockey, and we're still getting to use his truck, so I thought we should do him this favor."

Once she was satisfied that the kids understood that this was a temporary, mutually beneficial arrangement, she let them start on their fun time.

It was important all three of them were quite clear about what they could expect from their neighbor. This wasn't long-term. It wasn't dating. It was just...being neighborly. Being neighborly with an attractive, single, successful man who could dance like...

Michelle gave herself a mental shake. Troy wasn't looking for a date; he'd specifically said he wanted to spend time with the *three* of them. And she was not going down that road again.

TROY WAS SURPRISED that he was reluctant to say goodbye to the Robertsons. He'd actually felt excluded when they went into their condo and left him to go alone to his.

He was also surprised how much fun he'd had today. He was amazed at how enthusiastic—and knowledgeable—Angie was about hockey. He always got a little choked up when he saw his name on the Cup. He could tell Angie was planning to read her name there someday. The kid was gutsy. Not many kids were that committed.

Tommy was a tougher nut to crack. Kid stuck close to his mother in a crowd. Hard to believe he was apparently super focused on Tae Kwan Do. Troy could hear his father's voice in his head, saying the kid was a momma's boy and needed to be toughened up. It was what his dad had said when Troy had cried after his mother left. His dad had not been anyone's definition of a nice guy. Troy certainly didn't think his dad had a great handle on people, but he wondered if maybe Tommy did need a male role model, someone to help him be a bit tougher. He was surprised when he pictured himself as that role model. No one had ever called him that before. And, surprisingly, it seemed to fit.

CHAPTER SIX

"GOOD PRACTICE."

Coach Parker wasn't exactly gushing, but he never did. When he went out of his way to say something, it meant you were doing pretty well. Troy grinned. Things *were* going well for him.

The team had picked up lately. Mike Reimer was playing like this really was his last season, though Troy couldn't believe Mike was just going to walk away. The Blaze was in a playoff position, which hadn't been the norm while Troy was with this team. And Troy was playing well. Fewer late nights had undoubtedly been good for him. He hated to face it, but he was thirty-one. He wasn't the young guy anymore.

He wasn't being cautious, either, always worried about the cancer starting up again. And he'd gotten a handle on his anger. In short, he was playing the way he should be playing.

And he was feeling something new: contentment. He was happy with where he was.

So, after another good checkup with his doctor, he was pleased with his world as he rode up the elevator. Michelle and Tommy were coming out of their place as he exited. It was nice to not be avoiding the family any longer. He hadn't seen much of them this past week, since the team had been down in Florida to play. He noticed they were both wearing white pants under their jackets.

"Hey, Tommy. Where are you going in those fancy pants?" Troy asked Tommy with a grin.

"It's my dobok," Tommy answered seriously. "We've got Tae Kwon Do."

"Can I tag along?" Troy asked. He'd actually forgotten about his rehab plan when he offered: he was just curious to see Tommy in his element, since it was rare for Troy. He wouldn't mind watching Michelle do her thing, either.

Tommy looked up at his mom. She smiled and shrugged.

"Okay," Tommy said.

He joined them as they walked the couple of blocks to the dojang. Tommy was uncharacteristically chatty, telling Troy the name of the moves Tommy had learned and trying to demonstrate as they proceeded.

Troy wasn't sure what to expect, but he was impressed. There were a range of ages in the class, and a range of abilities. But the participants were fit. They stretched, did jumping jacks, push-ups, sit-ups, squats and leg raises. They did their special moves and started kicking.

Troy was surprised by Tommy's commitment, and what he could do on the mat. He wasn't the biggest in his class, but he kept up. Michelle participated, as well, and he understood why she'd looked so good in that dress the other night. She had to be pretty fit to participate in this sport.

It also made him feel a little better about their initial meeting. After seeing what the participants did in this class, it wasn't surprising that she'd been able to flip him to the floor.

Troy still didn't really understand a boy who didn't want to play hockey, but it was probably just as well that Tommy didn't play. Michelle was only one person, and if she had two kids playing hockey all over the city, she wouldn't be able to cover it. Maybe he should follow through on taking Angie to one of her games, like he'd said he would. She'd been good, and he wanted to see how she was doing.

On their way home Tommy was still explaining a particular kick to Troy when the elevator doors pinged open on their floor. Angie popped out of the condo. Her eyes rounded when she realized that Troy was with her mother and brother.

"You went to Tae Kwon Do?" she asked Troy accusingly.

"Yes. He was there for the whole class," Tommy bragged. "He said we should stop for some hot chocolate after, but Mom was worried you'd be scared on your own."

"I wasn't scared," Angie denied quickly. "I was just checking who was coming off the elevator."

Tommy got a mulish expression on his face. He looked ready to debate the matter. Troy held out a carrier with hot chocolate and donuts and gave it a shake. That diverted the argument. Angie ran back into the condo and Tommy went to his room to change.

Michelle smiled at Troy. "That was a professional-level move to head off an argument. Honestly, sometimes they can't breathe the same air without fighting. Mind you, I was the same with some of my siblings."

"How many do you have again?" Troy asked as he pulled out the fragrant, warm cups.

"Two brothers, one sister. You?"

"Only child."

"That's right, you mentioned that before. Did you get spoiled?" Michelle asked.

Troy paused. Spoiled? Hardly.

Michelle also stilled. "I'm sorry, was that the wrong question?"

"My mom left when I was pretty small. My dad was old school. Nothing touchy-feely. He had one goal in life, and that was to have his son win the Cup."

Michelle was looking at him intently as if connecting some dots.

"Was he happy when you won?"

"He died the year before we won the Cup. But if his ghost had been around, he probably would have been asking why I had to wait till he was dead."

Troy's tone was more bitter than he'd intended. He busied himself with the donuts instead of looking at Michelle. He didn't need pity from anyone. Sure, his dad had been an SOB, but he'd gotten Troy to the top level of professional hockey, and his life was pretty good now. Except for the cancer thing, but he couldn't blame that on his dad.

"Got a favorite donut you want to grab before the kids start on them?" Michelle asked.

He glanced up, grateful that she'd given him space to move on and hadn't offered unwanted pity. She understood that shielding process well.

The kids came out, wanting their hot chocolate and donuts. Conversation became general. He stayed in the background as much as he could, watching Michelle with her kids. That was how a mom was supposed to be. These kids had been given a rough deal with their dad, but fate had certainly offset that by giving them Michelle as a mom. He felt a pang. He wondered, as he did from time to time, if his mother was still alive, if she approved of how well he'd done. Why she'd left him behind when she'd gone. He'd probably never know. But he wasn't going to repeat that with any other kids, which was another good reason not to date mothers. This friends thing with the Robertsons was a much better idea.

MICHELLE SAT AT the table, books spread in front of her. Karen was perched beside her, explaining another concept that just didn't come easily to Michelle.

"Coffee?" Michelle asked when they'd made their way to the end of the problem.

Karen stretched. "Sure. How did you get time to study this afternoon without the kids?"

Michelle pulled out the coffee and filters. "Troy took them out to skate."

Karen looked surprised. "That was nice of him. I don't really know any of the players on the Blaze other than Bridget's husband, but I thought Troy was more the party type, not the enjoying-outings-with-kids guy."

Michelle felt herself flush, but kept her back to Karen while she poured water into the coffeemaker's chamber.

"I'm not sure that he really is. But Angie is a fan, and she's pretty persistent. Also, we've made a deal. He'll spend time with us to try to redeem his public reputation. He got some bad press a while back, so..."

Karen didn't ask any more. She'd told Michelle she didn't care much about hockey. Michelle didn't mind getting off the topic. Mitch had loved hockey, so it had been on a lot when he was around. After he'd gone overseas, Michelle had had to keep up on the sport because of Angie. Michelle couldn't really remember when Angie had caught the hockey bug—perhaps when she was still an infant and her dad would watch games with Angie snuggled on his chest.

Michelle poured the grounds into the filter. "Dark roast good?"

"Anything is fine. You should taste what they serve at the office." Karen stood and looked out the windows. "Awesome place."

"Yeah, I was really lucky that my aunt was friends with the owner, and that Mrs. Epps was willing to take a risk and let us stay here."

"How long are you here for?" Karen asked.

"Mrs. Epps is scheduled to return this summer. I've been saving what I can for a deposit on a place after that. I'll have to start hunting in the spring."

"You'll be job hunting then, too?" Karen asked.

"I'm sure it will be a lot easier with a bookkeeping certificate than it is now."

"Why did you decide on bookkeeping, if you don't mind me asking?"

The coffeemaker beeped and Michelle set out cups with milk and sweetener.

Michelle and Karen returned to the table. She shrugged. "I didn't have any really marketable skills. There are lots of want ads for bookkeepers, and I read a few articles listing finance as a high-demand industry in the future. I haven't been in school since I got my high school diploma, but math was one of my best subjects. Do you think I won't be able to be a bookkeeper?" she asked anxiously.

Karen responded carefully. "I think you'll get there. But you don't seem to enjoy it very much."

Michelle nodded. "It's not that exciting, but I don't have a lot of choices right now."

"Are you sure?" Karen asked. "I'm not trying to discourage you, but it would be nice if you could enjoy your work. Believe it or not, I like what I do."

Michelle bit her lip. "Maybe I'll like it more when I'm doing real work, not just solving problems in a book. But unless you need help with Morse code, I don't have a lot of other skills."

"If you could do anything you wanted, what would it be?" Karen asked with curiosity. "Pretend you had enough money and time to train for anything you want."

Michelle looked at her, perplexed. "I'm not sure."

"What did you dream about being when you were a kid?"

Michelle shook her head. "I grew up an

army brat. I never thought about being anything else."

Karen nodded. "You were in the army, right? Do you wish you'd stayed?"

Michelle felt a chill.

She'd barely survived what being in the military had done to Mitch. She couldn't risk that happening to her, not when she had her children. No, staying in the military had not been an option. But that wasn't information she shared with others, so she forced herself to shrug, her face to remain neutral, her voice to stay steady.

"No, I'd gotten to a point where the army wasn't a good fit anymore."

She stood and took her coffee mug over to the sink. "Would you mind looking at question eight with me? I'm stuck on that one."

"Sure," said Karen, recognizing a diversion when it was offered.

"I can't tell you how much I appreciate this, Karen."

"I'm happy to help," the other woman responded. "My husband is out with his brothers, and the sisters-in-law are just a little too baby-focused right now. I'm glad for a break."

Michelle smiled. She *was* really grateful. She still had a hard time with her coursework, and that often made her panic. What if she couldn't get this certificate and a good job? There was a lot riding on her shoulders.

Luckily, Karen took the hint and didn't press any further about her time in the Forces. Too much baggage there. So far there was no indication that anyone but Troy had cared to look up their past, and she wanted to keep it that way.

MICHELLE STARED UP at Troy, mouth open.

"Hey, I'd promised you tickets to a real game."

"Okay, but we don't need seats this expensive. And jerseys..." She trailed off. The kids were already wearing theirs, and Angie was currently taking a selfie.

"I asked the team for seats, and I wasn't going to ask for the cheap ones. I mean, I have a reputation to uphold. And I would rather have you wearing my jersey than someone else's."

"The kids already have the jerseys you got them last time. And I thought my red sweater was good enough."

"You're my guests. I want you to wear my jersey. I also get a cut of any jersey sold with my name on it, so I'm profiting from this."

Troy's eyes were dancing as he teased her. She knew Troy's generosity was getting out of hand, but it was hard to fight it. For one thing, the kids were on Troy's side. For another, she was tired of always being the tough guy. Troy seemed to get as big a kick out of all this as the kids did. And honestly, there was a part of her that was enjoying it, too.

That was what worried her. Everyone was getting too into him being a part of their lives. She'd been fussing with her hair and makeup as if this was a date. But it wasn't. Troy was trying to repair his reputation, and she and the kids were helping out to thank him for what he'd already done. But her debt to him only seemed to be getting bigger.

Eventually, Troy would get tired of playing uncle. He was a single guy. It was fun for now, but he didn't have to be the responsible one. When things got tough, or he got bored, he'd be on his way. He hadn't made any promises. Even if he had, Michelle knew men couldn't always keep their promises.

She'd depended on Mitch. And why not? When she got pregnant, he'd stepped up and taken the lead for their family. He'd been a natural leader, and both she and the other soldiers had taken that for granted and let him take that responsibility. But in the long run, that had led to his downfall. Michelle had learned the hard way that at the end of the day, you should only rely on yourself.

Since he was playing in this regular season game, Troy had to get to the arena long before Michelle and the kids, even though Angie was willing to head out as early as possible to spend as much time as she could there. Troy told them there was a player pass in the truck, but Michelle decided they'd take transit. Angie started to complain, but stopped when she saw the determined look on her mother's face. She asked to go on her own, ahead of Michelle and Tommy, and had sulked when her mother told her she was too young.

Angie was wearing her new jersey with "Green" stitched on the back, and a Winnipeg Whiteout hat. The Blaze was playing Winnipeg tonight, and Angie was torn.

Winnipeg was the team she'd grown up with. She'd watched games with her dad from babyhood, and though Michelle was sure Angie couldn't possibly remember the details, love for the Whiteout had seeped in through her onesies.

Angie would not readily have transferred her loyalty to Toronto, but the time she'd spent with Troy gave her a serious reason to support his team. Since she couldn't very well wear her Winnipeg jersey after getting a new one from Troy, she wore her Winnipeg hat with her new jersey.

Tommy didn't have the same problem. He was in full Blaze gear. Michelle wore her jersey, as well, a little self-consciously. It was one thing for a kid to wear a player's jersey. For an adult, it made more of a statement, and Michelle wasn't sure exactly what statement she was making. But to not wear it would be rude.

When they found their seats, Michelle was happy to find Bridget already there with her nephew, Bradley. Bridget was in a jersey, as well: hers said "Reimer." Since she was married to Mike, that was only right.

They rearranged seats so that Bradley was between Michelle's two kids, and Angie was beside Bridget.

"You must get here early," Michelle said. Angie had nagged them into arriving as soon as possible.

"I'm like your Angie. I'm happy to watch as much hockey as I can, even if it's just warm-ups."

The two teams were each on one end of the ice, doing some kind of drill. Angie was watching intently. The warm-ups were almost over, though, and the players started to exit the ice.

Troy came skating over to the kids. Troy pointed to his head, and then to Angie's hat, and then mimicked a dagger to the heart. Angie giggled. Tommy pointed to his own Blaze hat, and Troy gave a thumbs-up. Then his gaze ran over Michelle, and he smiled broadly. Michelle couldn't help responding, though she could see Bridget watching with birdlike curiosity.

"You guys spending a lot of time with Troy?" Bridget asked. "Sorry if I'm being nosy, but, yeah, I'm nosy."

Michelle had to laugh. She appreciated that Bridget was a straightforward person. She was sure if she told Bridget she preferred not to talk about it that the other woman would leave the topic alone. But Bridget had introduced her to Karen, who had really made it possible for Michelle to keep up in her courses. She owed her big time.

On the other hand, she didn't want word getting back to Troy that she was telling people they were dating. Troy had never indicated that he wanted anything more than to spend time with the family. When that eventually stopped, Michelle didn't want pitying glances.

"We have a deal. Troy says he needs to work on his image after what happened in LA. And we owe him for his help in getting Angie into hockey and using his truck."

"Befriending a widow and her kids is certainly a new one for Troy," Bridget agreed.

Michelle decided to express some of her concerns to Bridget. "But somehow, even though we're supposed to be helping Troy, I've ended up feeling like I'm more in his debt. He bought us these jerseys for the game, for example, and I know they don't come cheap."

"It's probably good for his character," responded Bridget. "It certainly won't hurt him. From what I've heard, team management is relieved that he's avoided…problems lately."

Michelle relaxed a bit. "Good. I don't want to be a charity case."

Bridget looked at her steadily. "I don't want to rain on your parade, but I should warn you that this thing with Troy may not last. I mean, Troy isn't a bad guy, but he's not known for being the steadiest man around. I wouldn't want you all—" she said, glancing at the kids "—to get hurt."

Michelle blushed, but she met Bridget's gaze. "I'm not counting on anything, believe me."

"Oh crap, now I feel bad. Maybe I'm all wrong and Troy—"

Michelle shook her head. "No, there's nothing to feel bad about. I've warned the kids it's a short-term thing." She'd had to remind herself, as well.

Bridget sighed. "I have a bad habit of speaking before I think it through."

Just then an usher stopped at the end of their row. He cleared his throat until he got their attention.

"May I have the Winnipeg hat, please?"

Michelle looked at the oblivious Angie, and then around the arena. Noticing other people with Whiteout gear on, she went into mama bear mode. "Is there a rule against wearing the visiting team's hat?"

The usher shuffled his feet and shook his head. "It's not that—Troy Green asked if he could have it." The usher smiled tightly. "He said to reassure you it was only temporary and he would return it."

Michelle waved to get Angie's attention. It was Angie's hat; it was her decision. The usher repeated his story.

Angie narrowed her eyes and asked the

usher, "Troy wants it? And promised to give it back?"

The usher nodded.

Angie took off the hat and handed it over.

The usher nodded his thanks and left.

"What was that for, Mom?" Angie asked.

Michelle shrugged. "I don't know."

Then the soloist came out to sing the Canadian anthem. Only one would be sung tonight, since both teams were from Canada.

The kids belted out the anthem with fervor, and then the teams were introduced. Angie cheered loudly for the visitors, and then again for the Blaze. Michelle wondered which team she most wanted to win tonight.

Michelle had never been a big hockey fan. The preseason game they'd attended had been her first experience of live, professional-level hockey, but she'd been distracted that day.

This game was faster and harder, and there wasn't any distraction. She didn't always understand why the ref blew the whistle, but she just had to follow the lead of the people around her, standing and cheering when they did. Bridget looked amused as Angie kept her informed, talking over the plays in the timeouts. Michelle watched for Troy.

It was a strange dichotomy. She knew in her

head that this was her neighbor, but he was a different man on the ice, skating so fast, hitting and being hit so hard. She flinched when someone on the Winnipeg team slammed him into the boards hard enough for them to rattle, but he shook it off and kept going.

At the end of the third period, when the game should wrap up, the teams were tied, so they went into overtime. That ended with neither team scoring. Bridget explained to Michelle that that meant they'd have a shootout. Basically, the teams would take turns shooting at the other team's net until someone got the puck in past the goalie—which for the Blaze was Mike, Bridget's husband.

Michelle could see the tension in Bridget as she watched her husband. Somehow Mike managed to stop every one. Unfortunately for the Blaze and their fans in the arena, the Winnipeg goalie was doing just as well.

Then it was Troy's turn to take a shot. Michelle could have sworn he smiled at her and the kids before he went to the center of the ice and grabbed the puck with his hockey stick. Michelle forgot to breathe as he skated to the Winnipeg goalie, made some kind of feint and finally slammed the puck past the goalie.

The arena erupted, and Troy raised his arms

in victory, swarmed by his teammates. The crowd was also on its feet, cheering, the Robertsons part of the noise.

"That's it?" Michelle asked, wondering if it was time to leave.

"Stars of the game first," Angie responded, attention still firmly fixed on the ice.

People were starting to make their way out of the arena, but Angie was obviously not going anywhere. Bridget wasn't making any signs of leaving, either, so Michelle sat and waited.

Mike was announced as the second star, and skated back out onto the ice. Bridget and Angie cheered loudly. Then Troy was named first star, and Michelle found herself standing and cheering, with Angie and Tommy hugging her in excitement.

Bridget raised her eyebrows, and Michelle flushed. Then the usher returned with Angie's hat.

Angie reached for it but froze in mid-thank-you. The usher grinned and left. Tommy and Bradley looked at the hat in Angie's hands and said, "Wow!"

"What is it?" Michelle asked.

Angie stared at her with wide eyes. "Bruce Anders signed it."

"The Winnipeg forward? You a fan?" Bridget asked.

"He's my favorite player. I told Troy that. He must have gotten him to sign it."

Angie was holding the hat like it was made of gold. Michelle felt a warmth fill her. This wasn't a huge gesture on Troy's part— hockey players signed things all the time. But Troy had remembered her daughter's favorite player, and taken the effort to get the hat signed. In doing so, he'd made Angie's day— probably her week—and Michelle could easily kiss—

Whoa! No kissing. She needed to nip that kind of thought in the bud.

The kids started up the steps, Angie gripping the hat tightly and the boys discussing it. Michelle and Bridget fell into step behind them.

Bridget glanced at Angie, still looking starstruck. "Forget everything I said about Troy. That was an incredibly nice thing to do."

Michelle nodded. But her concern deepened. The Robertson family was now even more in debt to their reputably unreliable neighbor.

CHAPTER SEVEN

TROY WAS IN a good mood when he hit the elevator button for his floor later that evening. First star of the game. As a defenseman, he didn't get plaudits for scoring like the forwards often did. Goalies also got a lot of attention, especially someone as skilled as Mike Reimer. But tonight it had been his turn. Troy had been kept late after the game by reporters wanting interviews, and it had been good to get asked questions he wanted to answer for once.

He'd liked having his own fan section, too. He hoped Angie had appreciated that hat. It had taken some doing.

His mood took an uptick when Michelle opened her door as he was getting off the elevator. She still had her hair tied up, but she looked more relaxed tonight. She smiled, and he felt something ease inside him.

"I have to say thanks for the autograph on the hat. That was…amazing," she said.

Troy smiled back. Excellent.

"She's got it on her bedside table so she'll see it first thing in the morning," Michelle continued.

Troy paused at the doorway to her condo, looking down at Michelle. He didn't want to head to his place alone. He hadn't wanted to go out with the other single guys, either. What he did want was to prolong this moment.

"To be honest, I had Reimer make the request. Anders and I, well, we have some history."

Michelle tilted her head. "Should I ask?"

"How long do you have?" he replied.

"I was taking a break from studying anyway. Want to come in?"

She looked as surprised by her offer as he was to get it, but he answered, "Sure." Michelle offered him a drink. While she got it, he asked, "Did you enjoy the game?"

She paused for a moment. "I think I did. I'm not a big hockey fan." Troy rolled his eyes a bit. "But it was really interesting to experience it that close. It was different from that other game we went to, wasn't it? The one you didn't play in? More intense. On TV, you don't realize how fast you guys are going. Or how hard you're hitting each other."

Troy accepted his drink and shrugged off her comment. "That's the game. We have equipment to keep us safe."

"Oh, and congratulations on being first star. That's a big thing, right?"

Troy flashed his grin again. "For me it is. Reimer might be getting bored with it, but guys in my position don't get it as much."

Michelle waved a hand toward the living room, and they sat down. Troy relaxed in a recliner, and Michelle curled up on the couch.

"Got much more to study?" Troy asked.

Michelle grimaced. "The last exam of the semester is Wednesday. Then we get a break for Christmas. I promised the kids that on Thursday we could get a tree. They're excited to start decorating."

Troy paused. That was right; they were into December now. Christmas was coming.

Michelle had noticed his reaction. "I suppose you have someone do all that for you, the tree and the decorating."

Troy shook his head. "Never bother with decorating. I'm not usually around. I used to go visit my dad, but…" He shrugged.

Michelle gave him a sympathetic look. "Is this your first Christmas without him?" she asked.

Troy felt his face stiffen as it was wiped of all humor. "No, he wasn't here last year."

"Was it tough, being on your own?" Michelle asked gently.

Troy froze for a moment, then decided to go all in. "I wasn't exactly alone. I was undergoing treatments then."

Michelle looked puzzled. "Treatments?"

"Cancer. I figured you might have read about it since they like to drag it into almost everything they write about me."

Michelle put her hand to her mouth. "I'm sorry, I had no idea. Oh, now I feel bad."

Troy shrugged, wanting to lighten the mood. Talking about the *C* word was never good.

Michelle seemed upset. "If I'd known…"

"If you'd known what?" he asked, puzzled. He'd only met the family recently, so they certainly couldn't have done anything for him while he was going through chemo.

She sighed. "I had assumed you had an easy life with no problems. That was stupid of me. I apologize."

"What for?"

Michelle glanced down. "I'm afraid I wasn't very nice to you sometimes. I had a few moments when things weren't going well for us here, and it looked like everything was going perfectly for you. It was a little hard to take."

Troy was happy to have that mystery solved. "I knew it," he said. "I knew you didn't want to like me for some reason."

Michelle was shaking her head. "I can't believe I missed the hints. People mentioned you'd been through a lot, but I assumed that was just losing your dad." She grimaced. "Listen to me, 'just losing your dad.' I'm terrible."

Troy didn't think Michelle was terrible, but he was enjoying being the good guy for once.

"You certainly are a sorry excuse for a human being," he agreed.

Her head snapped up at that, but when she saw he was laughing, she frowned at him.

"Maybe I can ask Santa to bring me something to help with that," she teased.

That brought things back to Christmas. Troy wondered if she would let him buy her and the kids Christmas presents. Michelle was feeling in the wrong for the moment... Maybe he could work up to presents. He had some ideas in his head.

He led with, "What are you and the kids doing for the holidays? Going back to Winnipeg?"

It was Michelle's turn to pause. She shook her head. "No, we're staying here."

Troy was surprised. Michelle had talked about her family. They seemed close. He thought she'd want to be around family for the kids at least. This would be their second Christmas without their dad, he figured.

"Is your family coming here?" There was room in the condo for more people, and he could even put someone up in his spare room if that would help.

But Michelle was shaking her head again. "My parents are stationed overseas, so they can't make it. My siblings are scattered and have their own family gatherings. They offered to have us come stay with them, but I thought it would be nice to have a chance to celebrate without everyone tiptoeing around the topic of Mitch."

"Was it difficult last year?" Troy asked softly. He did his best to forget what his life had been like when his mother left, but he was sure this family hadn't built up enough scar tissue for that yet.

He shifted in his chair. He'd rather make a joke and move on to a more comfortable topic, but Michelle didn't seem to have many friends. She might not have anyone to talk to about this. Surely he could at least be a sounding board for her.

Michelle blinked her eyes and swallowed. "It was horrible. It had all been pretty recent at that point. And the house had so many memories of Mitch, good and bad. His parents broke down in tears when they visited, and everyone was so careful with us. It was truly…horrible. So this year I want everything to be fresh."

"What are you planning? Going out for a big turkey dinner?" Troy asked. Maybe they could go out together. He liked that idea. He had nowhere to go this year yet.

Michelle stared at him, brow creased.

"Go out? Where? No, we're making dinner here."

"Oh, yeah," Troy responded. That was what regular families did. He couldn't remember the last Christmas he ate at home.

"You don't go out for Christmas dinner, do you?" Michelle asked, making it sound like the last resort of the desperate.

"Well, yeah." Troy shrugged again. "That was our family tradition. After my mom left, my dad wasn't about to make a roast turkey for the two of us. And as I got older, there was always something hockey related going on, so we didn't have a turkey kind of dinner. Christmas was never a big deal."

Michelle stared at him thoughtfully. "Have you made plans this year?"

Troy shook his head. He expected he'd find out if anyone on the team was going to be around on the day, and they'd go to a hotel for dinner, then maybe come back to his place, watch a basketball game, play video games, something like that. There was often a good movie on if they wanted to go to the theater. There were options.

When he told Michelle that, she asked hesitantly, "Do you want to join us? You don't have to. But I'm sure the kids would be glad to see you. Having someone new around might be good. In fact, if you know some other people without plans, we could make a big meal. It could be nice."

Troy watched her face. He could almost see her making lists in her head to get ready for this, and her expression had lightened. He guessed that this Christmas was going to be tough for her and the kids. And the idea of joining a family dinner, having some kids around…he felt nostalgia for the kind of holiday he'd never known. And if he was coming for Christmas, he could buy some presents and Michelle wouldn't be able to complain. She'd almost turned down those jerseys today, he could tell.

He glanced up and found her watching him suspiciously. "You looked a little too happy about something," she said.

Troy tried his most innocent smile. "I was just thinking it would be nice to spend Christmas with your family. What can I bring?"

CHRISTMAS EVE. THE kids were wound up, and it was hard to get them to do their usual chores when they were so distracted. She hadn't been able to get too upset with them, because this was so different from last Christmas.

Last year they'd been in their old house, but their dad was gone. Not deployed overseas when at least they'd been able to talk to him on Skype. Gone in the worst way possible. They had still been in mourning, but also a little excited over Christmas and the mix made for a horrible holiday.

Michelle had arranged for them to do their Skype calls with family today, since working around schedules and time zones would be almost impossible tomorrow. It was difficult sometimes to have her family be so far apart, but that was the way it had always been for

Michelle and her family. She was grateful for the technology that allowed them to reach out and see each other this way at least.

After they'd shared their last "Merry Christmas!" with Michelle's parents, she closed the Skype window. She looked at her kids, smiling, excitement sparkling in their eyes. It was good to see.

They'd called Mitch's parents first. That call had been more difficult, so she'd planned it first. Speaking with her family afterward had revived the Christmas excitement for the kids and the adults, as well. Since Tommy and Angie were on the call, it meant that her parents and siblings couldn't revive the topic of whether Michelle was doing the right thing by staying in Toronto for the holidays. They'd been offered airfare to come visit various families, but Michelle still believed her idea was best.

Michelle was planning to make the whole meal herself, so she'd be busy. Troy was bringing a couple of other players for most of the day, so there would be distractions, and no opportunity to dwell on past Christmases. She needed that, and she thought the kids did, too.

But it also wouldn't be right to try to forget the past. After she put away the laptop, Michelle asked the kids to join her at the table. She went to her room and brought out a box she'd prepared.

"What's that?" Angie asked. "A present we forgot to wrap?" The tree still had room underneath it. Michelle had a lot of wrapping to do before she would be able to sleep tonight.

"No, it's not really a present." She opened it up. Inside she'd gathered pictures, mementos and the ribbons Mitch had earned during his time in service.

She looked up and saw their faces crumple. She closed her eyes for a moment and then exhaled, straightening her shoulders and opening her eyes.

"We moved here to make a fresh start." Michelle was aware the jury was still out as to whether that had been the right decision. "But that doesn't mean we forget the past. I want to remember your dad, and I want you to remember him, too.

"He was sick at the end, in his mind, and he was in a lot of pain. He said and did things I know he didn't mean. The person I want you to think of is the man he was before he was deployed. I don't ever want you to forget that your father was a brave, strong soldier, and he loved you both more than you'll ever know."

Michelle could feel her throat tightening up and her eyes watering.

She sorted through the pictures till she found one from their wedding.

"See how happy he was? I was pregnant with you, Angie, and your dad couldn't wait to meet you."

Michelle found a picture from when Angie was a baby, wrapped in Mitch's arms, sleeping on his stomach.

Angie examined the picture. "He was watching hockey, wasn't he?"

Michelle nodded. "He loved hockey—you got that from him."

She found another shot. Michelle was holding Angie, conspicuously pregnant. Mitch was resting his head on her belly.

"Your dad started talking to you before you were born, Tommy. He'd been told by someone that babies recognize voices they hear in the womb, so he wanted to be sure you would know him."

Tommy took the picture. Michelle found another, just after Tommy was born, of Mitch holding him, an expression of such love on his face that Michelle had to bite her lip to keep from crying.

Tommy examined them carefully. Of the

three of them, Tommy had the fewest memories of the true Mitch. She pulled out more photos, giving the kids a visual record of a man who was patient, loving and proud of his family. It wouldn't remove the later memories, and shouldn't, but they deserved the complete picture.

Then she started to lay out the medals and ribbons.

"Earning these, serving our country, cost your dad everything. He lost friends in battle, he lost his mental health there and he ended up losing everything in the end. But he served because he loved us, and he loved his country. Don't ever forget that."

Michelle got up and went to the kitchen, opening the fridge as if she needed to check on something. She took deep breaths, trying to control her emotions. She felt Tommy's arms wrap around her waist.

"I wish he was still here, too, Mom."

Michelle wrapped him in a hug. Angie ran over to join them.

"He was a hero, right, Mom?" She sniffled.

"He was, hon. He really was a hero." Michelle broke down, and for a while the three let their sorrow and regrets flow. When they were under control again, Michelle held a chin in each hand.

"Before your dad went overseas the first time, he told me that if anything happened to him, we were to keep living our lives. We were to enjoy ourselves. So we're going to do that. We're going to have a good Christmas tomorrow. But we don't forget him, ever."

The kids nodded seriously. Michelle let them go. They wandered to the table, touching Mitch's hard-won ribbons, looking at the pictures of the man they remembered so differently.

Michelle breathed a prayer, for her kids, and for the man who was no longer there with them.

MICHELLE WOKE UP knowing both that she'd slept in, and that something good was happening.

Then she remembered. It was Christmas.

She'd slept in because she'd been up late wrapping presents after the kids finally settled down to sleep. Thankfully, they were old enough now that they didn't wake up at 5:00 a.m., wanting to see what Santa had brought, but they were still wound up.

She could hear them moving around and

smelled coffee. She smiled to herself, and stretched luxuriously under Mrs. Epps's expensive sheets. She wasn't sure the coffee would be drinkable, but she loved them for trying.

A glance at the clock confirmed that they'd been patient far longer than she'd expected, letting her sleep in. She swung her legs out of bed and reached for her robe. They'd want to open presents, then she would make them waffles for a special breakfast. Once she had the turkey in, she'd have a quick shower and get to work on the rest of the dinner. She was mentally reviewing her list of things still to be done. She had hopes for a good day, a different day.

She halted as she came to the end of the hallway. The kids were there, as expected, bouncing with excitement, but they weren't alone. Troy was there, and once again he was ready for the day while she was a mess. It really wasn't fair.

"Merry Christmas, Mom!" Angie shouted. Tommy ran over and gave her an excited hug. "Can we open our presents now, pleeeeeease?"

"Let her have some caffeine first!" Troy interrupted. Michelle had to agree. She needed the stimulant before she could come to terms with this: Troy Green in her kitchen first thing. On Christmas morning.

Troy passed her a cup of coffee while the kids dragged her to the couch. The tree had more presents underneath than it had when she'd finally gone to bed last night. She glanced over at Troy and realized he was stirring a bowl in the kitchen. He looked up and met her gaze with a big grin.

"You don't mind, do you? You left out this recipe for waffles, and since you insist on taking care of the dinner all on your own I wanted to help out a bit. The elves over there," he said, nodding at the kids, "promised to help."

Michelle looked at her elves. They were clearly pleased with themselves. She still had some questions about this, but she didn't want to spoil anything for them today, so she smiled and let them dig under the tree.

Troy set the batter aside and came and sat in the recliner. Angie used to call dibs on that, but it was becoming Troy's seat, and Angie didn't make a peep about it. The kids pulled out gifts and delivered them to the recipients, in a long-standing tradition. Troy got a couple of packages. Michelle was quite curious about what the kids had gotten for him, but they had insisted it was a surprise.

Michelle had a few things from relatives, and she mentally crossed her fingers that no one had sent anything that would embarrass her to open in front of her neighbor. She hadn't expected him to be here for the great unwrapping.

The kids had the biggest piles, and each of them had a present that she hadn't placed there. One that was large enough for her to notice amongst the others. There was also an intriguing present in her pile, one that she hadn't seen previously. She took a casual look at the tag. It was from Angie, Tommy...and Troy. That made her blink.

"Go on, Mom! Open it!" Angie said. Michelle was surprised. She usually liked to sit and watch the kids open their gifts and leave her presents to the end.

"Come on, Mom. This is a good one!" Tommy echoed.

Michelle eyed Troy. He had an awfully smug expression on his face, but that could be because he was wearing more of that expensive clothing he lived in while she was in her ratty robe. And her hair... She started to reach up to straighten it, but his knowing grin made her stop. She was not going to preen for him.

The kids were almost jumping up and down. She was wary, but again, she wanted so badly to make this a good day for them. She set down her coffee, hoping enough caffeine had been absorbed to get her through this, and picked up the parcel.

The kids had obviously been involved in wrapping it as there was enough tape to hold the *Titanic* together, and the seams of the paper didn't quite meet. She started carefully undoing the ends, while the kids groaned. Then she grinned at them and ripped the paper off in one swoop.

They'd wrapped the present in a computer box. That was sneaky. She opened the end of the box and realized it wasn't just a computer box; it was a new laptop. Her mouth dropped. There was no way her children could have purchased that. Her eyes shot to Troy.

"Do you like it, Mom? Do you like it?" the kids were asking, but she was asking something else of Troy.

"We went in on it together," he said. "They chipped in and helped pick it out. I thought a Mac would be better, but they said you needed a PC for your classes."

Michelle glared at him for a moment. He'd cornered her, but good. How could she turn down something that the kids had chipped in on? She'd have to talk to him later, but for now she turned to her kids, watching her so intently, and told them it was perfect.

She pulled it out of its box and started it up. She wasn't sure exactly what kind of computer it was, but she was sure with Troy involved it would have been expensive.

The kids were almost on her lap. "There's a number pad. I remembered you needed that," said Angie, sounding proud. Tommy listed a series of numbers about the processer speed and RAM. Troy sat back, that smug grin on his face. Michelle would deal with him later.

Michelle gave her kids a hug. Troy might have been very much involved, but her kids had thought carefully about this, and she appreciated that.

With her gift out of the way, the kids tore into their piles. Troy had gotten each child an expensive present, and Michelle couldn't say a thing. She gave him a look that spoke volumes, though. Once he'd breached her defenses with the computer from the kids, she couldn't complain about the new gaming system he'd gotten for Tommy, or the hockey skates he'd bought for Angie.

She understood Tommy's excitement with the new game system. She was pretty sure it was the same one Troy had, and she'd heard the kids talking about how good it was. But Angie was staring at the skates, speechless.

Michelle had purchased Angie's hockey gear using the card Troy had given them. She remembered how expensive everything had been. But the expression on Angie's face told her that these skates weren't anything like what they'd bought in the fall. Knowing Troy, they probably cost as much as the gaming system had. How expensive could skates be? She was afraid to imagine.

The rest of their gifts paled in comparison, but the kids were unspoiled enough that they reacted enthusiastically to everything else. Most of the kids' relatives sent her money to shop for the kids herself. She'd gotten a new dobok for Tommy, since he was growing out of his old one, and a pair of boots for Angie that the clerk had assured her "everyone was wearing." There were books, clothing, candy—all welcomed.

Michelle didn't have anything embarrassing in her pile, fortunately. Her family tended to go for practical gifts, and the closest she came to blushing was over some flannel pajamas from her sister with hearts all over them.

Troy had been a spectator while the Robertsons opened their gifts. But having ripped open all their own presents, the kids gathered around Troy and wanted to see him open his.

Michelle was grateful when he picked up the less carefully wrapped package first—the one from the kids. He opened it with the same lack of care the kids had used. The kids were obviously pleased with whatever they had selected, and wanted to see him open it as soon as possible. Inside was a cheap picture frame with a picture of Angie and Tommy in it. It looked like a selfie shot from Angie's phone.

"You don't have any pictures in your place," Angie said. "So we thought you'd like a picture of us, so you have someone." Tommy was behind her, nodding.

Michelle froze. Where had they got this idea? And how would Troy take it?

"This is awesome," Troy said. "Bruce Anders can eat his heart out."

Angie laughed, and Michelle relaxed. She smiled at Troy.

"Now Mom's present to you," said Tommy.

Michelle could feel her cheeks heating up.

She hoped this was okay. It wasn't very expensive.

Troy threw her a look and then opened the small parcel carefully. Inside was a pair of socks. A pair of socks with ballroom dancers on them.

Michelle found herself rushing into speech. "You said you were the team's best dancer, so I thought…" Her voice faded away.

Troy laughed. "If I wear these and any of my teammates see them, I'll be mocked mercilessly. But the next time I go out dancing, I'm wearing these anyway. What do you think, kids? Will I dance better in these?"

The kids nodded politely, but they obviously believed socks were pretty lame. They *were* lame, Michelle agreed. But what do you get a hockey superstar who has everything he could want when you have no money?

Michelle busied herself getting the kids to pick up all the paper and tidy up their stash. Troy went to the kitchen to make the waffles, assuring everyone that he was good at cooking breakfast. When Michelle came over to get more coffee and offer assistance, Troy spoke in a low voice.

"The socks are great, really."

Michelle glanced up at him. He really was

tall, with a broad chest that looked more than capable of handling any problem a woman might have—and which Michelle should spend less time dwelling on. "But compared with what you spent—"

Troy grabbed her hand. "I've got more money than I need and nothing much to spend it on. I know you wanted to make this Christmas special for the kids. I do, too. I'm enjoying being a part of your day. I never had this kind of Christmas. Let me have some fun."

His eyes were warm, and his expression sincere. Yes, he'd manipulated the situation, but he was right—the money meant little to him, and he was helping to make the day special for the kids.

"Plus, this should get me out of doing dishes, shouldn't it?" His eyes sparkled as he broke the serious mood.

Michelle took back her hand reluctantly. It had felt better than it should have. This is temporary, she reminded herself.

"Okay. If you're sure you can handle waffles, I'll go get ready so I can prep the turkey for the oven."

She escaped to her room. She wasn't sure if she was doing the right thing by allowing Troy to become a bigger part of their lives, but she didn't have that many options. She'd invited Troy today, thinking she was paying him back for all he'd managed to do for them. Instead, it was harder and harder to picture their lives without him. That made her edgy, but she didn't have time for introspection; she had a turkey to cook.

TROY WATCHED MICHELLE GO. He was glad she'd left. He wasn't sure what he'd been doing.

He'd never met anyone so hard to help. He wasn't doing anything big for her or the kids.

But something had changed. He wasn't thinking about how this would reflect on him and his standing with the team. He was thinking about a brave woman with tired eyes doing her best for her kids, and he wanted to step in and ease that burden. No, not exactly. Not ease it, but share it.

This was new terrain for him. He wasn't sure if this path he was on was going anywhere, and he wasn't sure how to ensure he didn't step off and plunge down a cliff. Plunge off and take the whole family with him.

He'd always avoided dating mothers since they came with responsibilities. Parents couldn't be spontaneous, or do anything crazy.

Troy liked being free to do what he liked when he liked, and moms had never fit that profile.

But there was another thing about moms. Moms by definition had kids. And kids were easy to hurt. They didn't have emotional protections like adults, and he knew how much being abandoned could affect them. He might not be a saint, but he never wanted to be the kind of bastard who broke a kid's heart.

So what was going on here?

The kids distracted him from his thoughts. After the excitement of opening presents, they were hungry for waffles. He forbade them from getting into the candy, and started warming the griddle. He gave them the task of setting the table and asked them to find the butter and syrup.

By the time Michelle reemerged with her hair braided back and fully dressed, he'd been able to push aside that moment in the kitchen. After all, he and Michelle weren't dating. They were just friends.

But she'd looked good with disheveled hair and wide eyes, a ratty robe and unmade-up face. That was disturbing. It was one thing to appreciate her when she was wearing a sexy dress. It was another to be moved by someone who wasn't even trying.

THE TWO BLAZE players Troy had invited to Christmas dinner were new to the team, and had come from Finland and Switzerland. They were not the two who'd gotten into trouble in LA—as Troy had suspected, those guys had been quickly traded.

Troy figured team management should be pretty happy with him taking these two somewhere as wholesome as the Robertson family Christmas. Maybe this would help him finally overcome that misstep in LA. Nils and Johan were still finding their feet in Toronto and were grateful for a home to spend the holiday in. Their English was impeccable, if a little formal, but Michelle made them welcome and they soon eased up on their somewhat stultifying politeness.

While Michelle stuffed the turkey, Troy and Tommy worked together to set up Troy's new gaming system. He'd added some extra controllers and games to the package before he had the store wrap it up. When Michelle insisted she was fine in the kitchen on her own, the three hockey players and the kids—though honestly, all five of them were being kids at the moment—took turns playing the games. Michelle kept an eye on them as she worked.

The two rookies had younger siblings and

were able to easily make friends with Michelle's kids. Angie, in fact, was hit with her first serious crush on Nils. Michelle found it funny, and also painful to watch as Angie tried to deal with these new feelings. Michelle couldn't embarrass her by letting on that she'd noticed, but she had a lot to teach Angie about how to deal with the opposite sex in a way that was neither platonic nor adversarial.

Troy also noticed. Michelle caught him frowning at poor Nils. Nils was uncomfortable with Angie's attentions, but Troy only noticed that Angie was looking at Nils with puppy eyes. Angie's crush on Nils, however, did not convince her to let him win the video games.

"Nils," Angie said, lingering over his name. "Do you want me to show you how to get extra strength for that?"

Angie sat down close to him, reaching for his controller. Nils leaned back. He looked up and saw Troy glaring at him and tried to inch farther away, totally missing Angie's tutorial.

"See, when you have that, you can go back to the forest and—wait, let me get you past this boss. He's pretty tough. Watch me so you can do it yourself another time. You're doing really well for your first try."

Michelle hoped Nils had a good amount of confidence because Angie's reassurances would have a debilitating effect on anyone with a crisis of insecurity. She was laying it on way too thick.

So was Troy. "Lower your hackles," Michelle hissed to Troy when he passed by her.

"Do you see the way she's looking at him?" he answered, a glare in his eyes.

Michelle figured the other man had triggered some kind of protective instinct Troy had for Angie. That was nice, but it wasn't his place.

"Do you see the way *he's* looking at *her*?" Michelle countered. "She's been giving him so much advice on how to improve his game that he can't get far enough away from her." She nodded over to the living room where Nils was almost climbing the arm of the couch to keep some distance between him and her besotted daughter.

Troy set his jaw. "Still, I should say something to him."

Michelle shook her head at him. "Just ignore it—you don't want to embarrass Angie. These crushes are as short-lived as they are intense."

"As long as he isn't getting any ideas."

Michelle rolled her eyes. "Nils is no more interested in her than he is in me."

Troy's head snapped around. "Is he—"

Michelle laughed. "No. I'm, well, not old enough to be his mother, but an aunt, maybe. He's not thinking of me that way, I promise."

"Don't be so sure," Troy muttered.

But Troy did rein himself in after that, and they had a great meal gathered around Mrs. Epps's table. Michelle was showered with compliments over her cooking, and she basked in their approval.

The Canadians asked Nils and Johan about Christmas in their countries, which they were happy to share. The three hockey players were good sports about wearing the cheap paper crowns that came in the Christmas crackers, and a lively trade exchange was set up for the silly little toys that came with them. Apparently, if you were born with that competitive gene, it applied to everything.

The three men told Michelle that they would clean up, after all her hard work. She protested, but was overruled. Angie advised them on where to put things once they were cleaned and dried, and Tommy gave Michelle her first opportunity to try the new video games.

Tommy leaned over and whispered, "Does Angie like Nils?"

Michelle glanced over at her daughter. Angie was complimenting Nils on how well he was drying a platter. Troy was keeping an eye on them while scrubbing the roasting pan. She bit back a grin.

"I think so, but we shouldn't say anything."

Tommy nodded. "She calls me a dork, but at least I'm not that stupid. I'm not going to get married. I'm going to stay with you."

Michelle hugged him. "You're welcome to live with me as long as you want, but you might change your mind."

Tommy shook his head. Michelle heard Angie asking Nils if he ever played hockey with girls. She winked at Tommy, and they went back to their game.

THE MEN HAD brought drinks and snacks as their contribution to the day, and with all of that on top of the turkey dinner, everyone was still almost painfully full when the two young players left. Michelle thought Nils might have been a little more eager to go because of Angie's unremitting attention. She'd talk to Angie later, in private, and with a lot of care. She sighed. It was beginning.

Michelle was tired of the video games, and since Angie had started to ask Troy about Nils, and Michelle suspected that would not go well, she suggested a movie.

"What's your favorite movie, Troy?" Angie asked.

"*Slapshot*, definitely."

Angie turned to Michelle, a hopeful gleam in her eye.

"No way," Michelle said firmly. "When you're older."

Troy just grinned.

"Tommy," Michelle said. "You pick."

"*Finding Nemo*!"

"What? No! That's for babies," Angie complained.

"I haven't seen that one," said Troy. "I'd like to see it—unless *I'm* a baby?"

Michelle could understand that Tommy related to the movie, where a father tried so hard to find his kid, but again, she wasn't going to say anything in front of Angie and Troy.

"I like Dory," Troy said when the credits started to scroll at the end.

"There's a movie about Dory now, too," Tommy told him.

"Okay, then, next time we watch *Finding Dory*," Troy responded.

They all agreed and it hit Michelle. They were making plans with Troy, like it was perfectly normal. There was no reservation or qualifications, just an assumption that there would be a next time. It felt good, and that worried her.

She convinced the kids to go to bed, but as Michelle went to tuck her daughter in, Angie had an intent look on her face.

"Mom, do you think Nils has a girlfriend?"

Michelle sat down on the bed. "I don't know. He's a professional hockey player, and Toronto is a big hockey city, so there are probably a lot of women who would like to go out with him." She tried not to emphasize the word *women* too pointedly.

Angie frowned. "Is ten years a big difference for two people to be in love?"

Michelle chose her words carefully. "It depends on the ten years. Think about how different you are from a two-year-old."

Angie wrinkled her nose. "But when you get older..."

"When you get older, it becomes less of a problem. But that's when both people are grown up and know what they want."

"When do you get that old?"

Michelle hugged her tightly. "Sweetie, I

don't even know if *I'm* old enough yet. But I do know a lot more now than I did ten years ago. I'm at least certain of what I don't want, so I'm getting closer."

"Nils doesn't like me, does he?" Angie asked frankly.

Michelle smiled. Her daughter was direct. How that would work in her romantic life, Michelle couldn't predict, but at least her daughter would never play coy.

"I don't think he likes you as a girlfriend. When you're twenty-two, as he is, twelve seems almost as young as two seems to you," she answered, feeling her daughter's pain.

"Maybe when I'm sixteen," Angie said, settling down on her pillow. "That's soon."

Michelle swallowed. Four years from now. Angie would be old enough to drive, and date. She hoped she wasn't looking to date twenty-two-year-olds then.

TROY NOTICED MICHELLE had a stunned expression on her face when she came down the hallway from Angie's room. Troy had stayed to tidy things up a bit. He poured her a glass of wine.

"Thanks," she said and took a large swallow.

"What did Angie do to you?" he asked with a grin.

"She's hoping that when she's sixteen and dating that she won't look like a kid to twenty-two-year-olds. That's in less than four years."

Troy took her wineglass and knocked back a mouthful.

"I'll get you more. That's enough to knock anyone for a loop."

Michelle curled up on her favorite spot on the couch, and Troy leaned back on the other end. He turned sideways so he could watch her. She was staring across the room, but seeing something else entirely. She looked a little tired, but at ease, not tense.

"So, did it work?" he asked.

It took a moment for his words to reach her.

"What?" she asked, puzzled.

"Did the kids have a good Christmas?"

Michelle's shoulders relaxed, and her mouth stretched in a warm smile. "I think so. We Skyped with our extended families last night, and then talked about Mitch. We couldn't forget him, so I decided we'd just face it head-on, deal with it and leave Christmas Day for fun."

Troy wondered about this man, Mitch. Michelle didn't speak about him often, but what kind of guy would leave this family behind?

The man had served overseas, so full points for that, but he'd left Michelle with a big burden.

Troy wanted to believe Mitch must have had some kind of weakness to snap like that, but he was pretty sure Michelle wouldn't care to hear him say that. And in a moment of rare humility, he realized he didn't know anything about PTSD and what happened to guys in service. Would he, Troy, ever take such a drastic step?

He flashed back to the cancer ward. His stomach knotted. He still woke up at night sometimes, sure he could feel the cancer creeping into his body again. If that happened, if the doctors said it was terminal and he would have to endure excruciating pain, would he want to end things? He could understand that choice. But what if he had a family, people he loved who were going through it with him? He just didn't know.

He realized Michelle was staring at him.

"Sorry, mind was wandering. What did I miss?"

She smiled. "I just said thanks for coming, and bringing Nils and Johan. It really helped. We had a good Christmas, but a different kind of celebration than we'd had before. It was mostly clear of bad memories, and that's exactly what I'd hoped for."

Troy was pleased to hear that, but he shrugged. "The guys and I should be thanking you. This was nicer than eating at a hotel. Sometimes I forget that Christmas is not just another day."

Her expression turned stern. "You spent way too much on those gifts."

Troy rolled his eyes. "You may have noticed I got some value out of that. We were playing on Tommy's system all day. Honestly, the one you had is complete junk."

Michelle raised her brows. "And perhaps you'll wear Angie's skates sometime? Or do something on that laptop?"

Troy noticed she hadn't said *her* laptop. She hadn't taken ownership of it yet.

"That was actually for the kids' benefit. From what they've told me, you've come very close to saying bad words when your old one wouldn't work right."

Michelle laughed. "Troy Green, defender against the corruption of minors."

"Yeah, I think I'll get a shirt made." Troy liked to hear her laughing. He liked being the one who made her laugh.

"So what are you guys doing over the

break?" he asked, some ideas already forming in his head.

"Tomorrow we're going to the O'Reillys'. They apparently have a big road hockey game and get together every year on Boxing Day. Angie's keen to go, and Tommy likes the O'Reillys, too."

Troy felt a pang. He hadn't been invited. Well, Michelle couldn't invite him to someone else's event, but she hadn't mentioned it. He was on his own. He realized he'd been counting on the Robertsons being around to keep him busy.

He obviously needed to get back to his normal life. He didn't even know how long the family would be here, next door. Plus, they were only friends, right? Mom and kids, not the situation he wanted in a dating scenario.

"I was going to go to the aquarium one of these days. You want to come?" he heard himself asking instead. Apparently, the message from his brain hadn't reached his mouth.

Michelle's face brightened. "That would be fun. The kids would love it. But this time, we'll make you dinner afterward."

Troy sighed. She was still bothered by the money thing. He wished she didn't throw that up all the time. Whatever had made her so defensive about accepting help probably went back to the situation with her husband. But it wasn't up to him to push her limits on that, was it? Maybe it was.

"It's a date," he said lightly. "How long till Mrs. Epps comes back?" he continued, following his own train of thought.

"She's supposed to come home at the end of June, after the kids are done with school. I suspect she's deliberately staying away so that we can stay settled till then. Are you eager to have the penthouse floor a kid-free zone again?"

Troy just shook his head. June. Hockey season would be over by then, Troy thought. He normally took off in the summer, unless the team went far in the playoffs. It was his vacation time. Of course, he didn't really have to leave…

"Where are you going after that?" he asked.

"Wherever I can get a job. I should be finished school by April, so I'll start looking as soon as I get through my exams."

"Do you plan to stay in Toronto?" Troy asked. He was mentally going through his list of contacts. Surely he knew someone who'd hire a bookkeeper. His sponsors, the team…

"I doubt we can afford the city."

That halted his thoughts. "So home to Winnipeg?" he asked, his mood dropping.

Michelle shook her head. "The fresh start has been good for us. We won't move back now. Maybe somewhere on the outskirts of Toronto, or one of the small towns nearby. Not too far away."

A small town? That sounded pretty remote.

"Maybe you'll find a job here that pays enough," he suggested.

Michelle looked at him from under her eyebrows. "Not likely. I'm not really a bookkeeping protégée. I'm just keeping my head above water with this stuff."

Troy examined her expression. "Don't you enjoy it?"

She shrugged. "It's not that exciting, but it's stable work, if I can get through the course."

"Isn't there anything else you'd like to do?" he asked.

"I barely finished high school. After my time in the army, I only know how to run recruits through their drills. I don't really have any marketable skills."

"Is there something you can do in that field? You don't want to be stuck doing something you hate."

Michelle looked at him levelly. "Karen said

the same thing. But I have kids, and I'm responsible for them. So it doesn't matter if I'm bored, or struggle a bit. I'll do what I need to do to take care of them."

Troy again wondered how her husband could have left her with this burden to carry alone. At least that was one thing he wouldn't mess up. The cancer treatments had made him sterile, so he wouldn't have kids to leave behind if something happened to him.

"It just seems wrong that you have to be miserable to take care of your kids," he said stubbornly.

Michelle shrugged. "Well, that's my problem. Not one you'll ever have to deal with."

He stiffened at the echo of his own thoughts. "How did you know that? I haven't told anyone."

Michelle looked confused. Her mouth parted.

"If it got out, it could have a big impact on my game—" Troy continued.

"I'm sorry, I just assumed…" she said, puzzled.

"Assumed? Why?" Troy was shaken. Was his secret not so secret after all?

"Look at what you spent on presents. You insist on paying for everything, you've got those cars, you're a professional athlete... I'm sorry. If you've got financial issues—"

Troy shook his head, relieved. "No, I'm fine for money. One good thing my dad did was make sure I was careful with my finances. I thought you were talking about something else. Never mind."

Michelle studied him, and he couldn't blame her. He'd flown off the handle there. And now she would be trying to figure out what he'd been talking about... He'd normally quickly pivot to a harmless topic, but he knew Michelle's secret. Maybe she'd feel things were more equal between them if she knew his.

"Okay, here it is. I can't have kids." Troy couldn't believe he'd actually said it out loud. He waited for her reaction anxiously.

She was quiet. Then, "Because of the cancer?"

He nodded.

"Wow." Michelle paused for a moment. "That's quite a thing."

Troy nodded again.

"I guess I can understand why you'd want to keep that quiet."

Troy tightened his lips. "I play a pretty physical game. I can't let anyone think I have a weakness. But that's not all of it. Have you heard of chirping?"

Michelle blinked. "Chirping?"

"Yeah. It's basically trash-talking. A lot of that happens on the ice. If this was out there, I can just imagine what the other players would come up with. I have a temper occasionally and those chirpers would get to me."

Michelle nodded, considering what he'd said. "What about the non-hockey consequences? Have you coped with that?"

Troy quirked up his lip. "You mean no little Troys in my future? I haven't really worried about that yet."

"Do you want to have kids?" Michelle asked.

Troy shrugged. "Someday, I guess. I always figured that's how everyone does it, right? Find someone, settle down, have the family. I hadn't really thought much about it. I was having a pretty good time the way things were."

"And now?"

"Now that I don't have a choice? I get mad about it sometimes. My dad would have—" Troy broke off.

"He'd have been disappointed?"

"I'd have been a failure in his eyes," Troy said flatly.

"Not to be too personal, but your dad sounds like a moron," Michelle said drily.

Troy laughed. "Yeah, that describes him pretty well."

"There are other options," she said. "Adoption, sperm donors…"

Troy cut her off. "I know. The doctors were very nice and understanding when they gave me the news. They made sure I understood all the options available. I wasn't ready to deal with it then, and I still don't know if I'm cut out to be a father, or if I want to be one. Guess it depends on my partner. But that could be a deal breaker for some women, right? When do you tell someone you're seeing that having kids isn't an option? At least, not the usual way."

Michelle gnawed on her lip. She was thinking seriously about this. "You're right. There are things you don't want to share until you really know someone and trust them. But you don't want to be in a relationship under false pretenses, either. I'm not sure what the answer is to that."

Troy tilted his head. "Well, what about you? When would you want to find out that bit of information?"

"It's different for me. I'm not twenty-three,

I'm thirty-three. I've got two kids, and I don't plan to have any more."

Troy remembered she'd said something about that before, but he was still surprised. Michelle was such a good mom. "Are you sure about that?"

She nodded. "But I also don't plan to get married again, so it's not an issue for me anyway. Have you ever gotten to the stage of talking about kids with someone?"

Troy snorted. "Are you kidding?"

Michelle creased her brow. "Well, why not?"

"I told you, I was just having fun."

"Ah. So having fun means never getting serious." Her tone was dry.

There was an implied insult there, but Troy couldn't disagree. It wasn't very mature. "I thought so. Might be just as well. I don't know that I'm the responsible type."

"You mean you aren't a responsible adult after all?" Michelle teased.

"When Angie came to my door that night, I really wondered what the hell she was talking about. I'm sure she's the first person to call me responsible."

"Maybe you're selling yourself short. You've done a good job with the kids so far. And did I thank you for putting me to bed

that night? I don't normally let myself get…
like that, because I do have to be responsible."

Troy smiled at the memory. "I'm glad you had
a chance to have fun. Everyone should have that."

"You've been great with my kids. So maybe
you should give yourself more credit."

Few people would consider Troy to be too
modest. But it was nice to hear that one person
didn't think he was a complete goof-off.
And someone he liked and respected, at that.

He tried to remember when he'd last talked
so honestly with someone. It had been a while.
A long while. Michelle, after their first unpromising meeting, had accepted him as he
presented himself, without coloring it with
his history, a lot of which was nothing to brag
about. The person he was now truly was a
more responsible person. Maybe last year had
changed him a bit; maybe it had just been time
to grow up. He liked the person he was now.

It was a relief, as well, to share his secret.
Someone else knew and didn't seem fazed
by it. She didn't think less of him. He looked
over at Michelle and found her holding back
a yawn. Instead of finding his secret noteworthy, it was apparently boring her.

Troy stood. "If you've got places to go tomorrow, I should let you get to bed. Thanks again. I really enjoyed the day."

Michelle stood, as well. "It was a good day. Thanks. And merry Christmas."

She reached up and kissed him on the cheek. He stilled. It was a simple gesture. She probably came from a family that did that a lot. But there hadn't been a lot of affection in his family.

She drew away and hesitated. He didn't want to make things awkward, but he wasn't sure what to do. A part of him wanted to reach a hand to the back of her neck and pull her in for a proper kiss. That wasn't how this script was supposed to go, though. They weren't dating, and with Michelle, he might just end up on the floor inspecting the carpet again.

"Thanks," he repeated instead, and headed for the door.

Back in his apartment, he stood in the dark. It had just been a quick kiss on the cheek. It was Christmas, they'd spent the day together, they'd been talking intimately—it had just been a polite gesture. But he hadn't reacted politely. He'd better watch that.

MICHELLE CLOSED THE door behind her. What had come over her? She wasn't normally a kissing person. It had just been a polite brush on the cheek, but Troy had stiffened. Had she been too forward?

She carefully turned off the Christmas lights, leaving the room in darkness. It was the intimacy of that conversation, sitting in the dim light of the decorations, after what had been a pretty emotional twenty-four hours for her.

She stood, looking out over the city, the lights bright without any on behind her.

How did she feel about Troy? She hadn't had much time for introspection since they'd moved next door to him. Even her dreams had been about bookkeeping. But she was on a break now, and with Christmas taken care of, there was no longer any pressure on her for a while. Maybe she needed to take a good look at what was going on.

Lately, Troy had become her best friend in the city. She valued that. He knew what had happened with Mitch, but that no longer seemed to be his motivation for hanging out with them. And he'd just shared something private. It indicated he trusted her. She was touched by that.

But she was also feeling some things that weren't really friendly. She couldn't deny that he was an attractive man. One of the first times she'd seen him he'd been wearing nothing but shorts, and she'd have had to be dead not to have admired him. He had a confidence she envied, and was showing a consideration for her and the kids that she couldn't help but appreciate.

So maybe she did have a bit of a crush on him. It had probably been inevitable. She'd been on her own for a long time, basically since Mitch had been deployed overseas.

She'd expected things to be the same between her and Mitch once he returned, but the man who'd come home hadn't been a partner. He'd been someone who needed help—another responsibility. So yes, she'd been on her own for a long time.

She was in a new city, the kids were gaining independence and the good-looking hockey player across the hall was spending time with them. She could sympathize with Angie and her crush on Nils. But she wasn't twelve. She had nothing to offer Troy, even if he had any romantic interest in her. She couldn't let this crush get out of hand.

CHAPTER EIGHT

BOXING DAY WAS a full and fun day. A day with the O'Reillys was not a day for introspection and gloom. After wearing themselves out playing road hockey, the teams came in and helped themselves to the mountains of food available. Michelle enjoyed being part of the group.

Then the hockey aficionados gathered around the TV to watch the World Junior hockey championships, cheering on Canada. Angie was in the thick of that, while Tommy went off with Bradley to play video games. Michelle helped clean up, despite being "company." She finally dragged the kids away after dinner, everyone full of food and thanks.

It wasn't hard to get the kids to bed. They'd been up early the past couple of days, wound up with excitement, and it was catching up with them. Michelle checked up on them after only a few minutes and smiled when she saw them sound asleep. It had been that way since they were born. They were completely lovable when they were asleep. For a while, there was nothing to worry about.

She didn't want to watch TV, so she turned the music on low, dimmed the lights and opened the curtains to watch the city. It was calming. She rarely had moments to do nothing.

When she heard the quiet knock, she knew who it must be. She reminded herself that she needed to be sensible around Troy. As long as they kept things at the friend level everything would be fine...but when she saw him, she couldn't hold back a smile.

Troy smiled back at her. "I hoped you might still be up."

She opened the door to invite him in. "Drink?"

When he nodded, she went to the kitchen to get it for him. When she joined him, she saw he'd gone to the windows.

"I do this, too, sometimes. It's hard to imagine how many other people are out there, all doing their own things, each little window another world."

Michelle stood beside him and passed him the glass.

"Did you have a good day?" he asked her.

"The kids are down and out. That tells you all you need to know."

Troy turned and looked at her. "What about you?"

Michelle took a moment. "Yes, it was good. They're a nice group of people."

"Do they really all have red hair? Reimer swears it."

Michelle laughed. "Well, the parents' hair is getting kind of gray, but the kids all do, and some of the grandkids."

"Must be quite the family picture."

"I don't know if they could get everyone to stand still long enough to take a picture. They're all hockey mad, too. How was your day?"

TROY HAD HAD a perfectly acceptable day. He'd gone out with some friends, had a nice meal, watched the World Juniors at a bar. But he'd been happy to head home. He wanted to set up a date for the aquarium visit with Michelle and the kids. So when she asked about his day, it took him a moment to remember what he'd done. He'd done nothing memorable.

"Fine."

She looked up at him, a sparkle in her eyes.

"You watched hockey, didn't you?"

He laughed. "Did you have to watch, too?"

"No, there was an option to clean up instead, and I took that."

Troy raised his brows. "You considered that a better option? You really need your horizons opened."

"Hockey is more fun live. I get bored watching it on TV. Angie tells me that I just don't understand the game."

"Angie is right. You need some lessons."

He drank in the sight of her. She was relaxed and had her hair down. He liked that. When her hair was tied back, Michelle was in Responsible Mom mode, worried about her family, doing the right thing. Michelle with her hair down was the woman who'd left her cares behind for a while. That Michelle was the woman who'd danced with him. And he realized the lessons he'd like to share with Michelle had nothing to do with hockey.

Something thrummed in the air between them. Did she feel it? Or was he getting buzzed on the beer she'd given him?

The song changed to the one they'd danced to that night.

"I think it's our song," said Troy, extending a hand to Michelle.

Michelle flushed. "I may have some memory of dancing with you, but that whole night is a bit fuzzy." Still, she set her glass down and gave him her hand.

He pulled her into the small square of open space. She followed lightly, easily.

Troy was surprised all over again by how well they danced together. Michelle seemed to understand instinctively where he wanted her to be. She felt the music, just the way he did. He thought he could move around the floor with her in his arms for a long time and not ask for anything more.

"You really are a good dancer, Troy," she said.

"It's my claim to fame, remember?" he responded. The song changed to a ballad, and he tucked her against him. She molded herself to him, and this time she was sober. She still fit perfectly.

"So, did you come by just for some dancing?" she asked abruptly, breaking the silence.

"I would have if you'd asked. But truthfully, I wanted to set a date to go to the aquarium. I wasn't sure how busy you would be over the break."

Michelle shook her head. "We're not the busy ones. You have to practice and play, don't you?"

"Practice starts up again tomorrow. But I could go any afternoon or evening we're not playing."

"We don't have anything planned, so you tell us when." She was talking to his chest, not looking up at him.

"Tomorrow?"

"It's a date."

The words seemed to linger in the air.

They both let the conversation peter out, and as another slow song played, they moved together to the music. Troy could smell her shampoo and was tempted to feel a strand of her hair. He wondered how silky it would be. Would she be okay with him touching her? Would she flip him to the floor again? Had that kiss last night been a sign that she was thinking of him as more than a neighbor? He was about to tighten his grip, wanting to move her even closer, when he felt her pull away.

Angie was in the hallway.

"Hi, Troy. Mom, did I leave my hat at the O'Reillys'? I couldn't find it in my backpack."

Michelle pulled all the way out of his arms. She walked over to the doorway, where some coats and her purse were hanging on a coat rack. "It's in my bag—you almost did leave it behind, but Bridget saw it and gave it to me, since you were already outside." She reached into the bag and pulled the hat out.

"Oh, thanks," Angie said, taking her hat.

She hugged her mother. "Love ya. G'night, Troy."

She returned down the hall to her room, but the mood was broken. Michelle switched off the music and asked Troy if he wanted to watch TV. He said no, and left for his place. Apparently, he had been the only one feeling anything out of the ordinary.

THE NEXT DAY when Troy knocked on the door, everyone was ready to go. The kids had been so excited about their trip to the aquarium it had been easy to convince them to get dressed. Michelle herself had felt a little flutter of excitement. She worried about that flutter.

Michelle blinked when she saw how Troy was dressed. He normally wore expensive clothes that fit him well. Today he was in sweats, loose and well worn. He hadn't shaved, and had sunglasses pushed up on his head.

The kids pulled on their coats and raced into the hallway. Michelle slid on her jacket more slowly and raised her brows at Troy, her gaze moving over his gray sweats.

He grinned and shrugged. "I asked if we could do a private tour, but that only happens if you book the whole place. I didn't give them enough notice for that, so I was hoping to attract a little less attention. There might be some hockey fans there."

"If I call you Todd for the day, will that help?" Michelle teased.

"Anything but Todd," he answered. "Todd was the name of the worst guy I ever roomed with."

At the aquarium, Michelle had to restrain herself from arguing as Troy paid admission. He had his hood up, sunglasses on, as they entered. But he needn't have bothered. The first exhibits were in low, dark lighting.

There were displays on the wall meant for kids, but hers left them alone, considering them too immature for their attention. Not Troy, though. He moved everything that could move, and stuck his hand in the display to find out how cold the water was in the Arctic. Soon she and the kids were participating, as well.

The lighting brightened as they walked onto the slow-moving track that took them through Danger Lagoon, but Troy went unrecognized.

The place was packed with tourists, many from overseas, and apparently not many hockey fans. The tourists were far more interested in spotting a sea turtle and oohing and aahing at the proximity of the sharks than in recognizing a hockey player. Michelle teased

Troy by calling him Todd, but even when the kids yelled out "Troy" no one turned.

The tour ended in the gift shop and she managed to restrain Troy from buying them too much.

But as she watched him corral the kids out the exit with an easy confidence, she wondered if she'd dodged the true danger.

"I HOPE YOU like tacos," Michelle said to Troy when they returned to the condo for dinner. "It's what the kids decided we should make for you."

"I love tacos," Troy said. He would love pretty well anything they wanted to put in front of him at this point. He was starving. "What kind are we having?"

"We don't do fancy. Just what the box says."

They did have a box kit. And not the name brand, he noticed. Michelle cooked up the ground beef and seasoned it. Tommy grated the cheese, and Angie carefully chopped lettuce and tomatoes and onion.

"Can I help?"

"You're a guest. Guests don't help make the meal," Michelle insisted.

He sat on a stool on the island, drinking a beer he'd brought from his own place.

"All right. I like fingers in my tomatoes anyway," he teased Angie.

She sniffed.

Tommy set out the sides as he laid the table. Then they all sat down to enjoy.

If he'd ordered the tacos in, he would have eaten twice the amount. He was an adult and needed a lot of fuel. But he knew money was tight, and was careful to match the others as far as taco consumption went.

The meal might have lacked in quantity, but it made up for it in laughter. He bragged that he was the only one of them who could eat a taco without breaking the shell. The kids accepted the challenge. He let Tommy win.

A few months ago Troy would have shuddered at the suggestion that he share a meal with a mom and a couple of kids. He would have assumed the meal would be incredibly boring.

But it wasn't. It was fun. Fun because they knew each other now and had some inside jokes. It was a closed circle, and Troy was inside it for once.

As Michelle stood to arrange dessert, Tommy bombarded Troy with questions.

"What would we have done if one of the sharks from the aquarium attacked us?"

Troy frowned. "The sharks were all safe in

their tanks. If one got out, it wouldn't survive out of water, so I don't think you have anything to worry about."

"Okay, but what if you were swimming and a shark attacked?"

Troy scratched his cheek. "There aren't any sharks around here, Tom. Lake Ontario is fresh water. Nothing to attack you there."

"But if you were swimming in the ocean?" Tommy persisted.

Michelle broke in from the kitchen. "We're not going to be swimming in the ocean anytime soon."

"You can look it up on the internet," Angie said, bored.

Troy wondered why Tommy was worried about shark attacks. Was it from something in *Finding Nemo*? Did he normally worry about things like this? Michelle and Angie didn't seem to find his questions odd, but Troy wondered.

Michelle brought out dessert—ice cream sundaes with chocolate sauce and peanuts. Troy made the biggest, and managed to eat it the quickest, claiming the title of sundae champ. Angie ran for her Christmas cracker crown and put it on Troy's head to celebrate his win.

Angie had planned the evening's entertainment. Someone had sent her the Blaze championship DVD, and she wanted to watch it with Troy. She pulled him over to the couch and curled up beside him. Tommy sat on his other side.

Michelle grinned at him. "You're the guest of honor."

Sitting on the couch, sandwiched by the two kids, felt good. And he hadn't watched this recording for a long time. Not since he'd gotten sick.

That playoff series had been incredible. The year prior to the Cup run, the Blaze had been swept in the first round. That year the Blaze had scraped their way into contention when Mike Reimer, then a new goalie for the team, had regained his championship form and been the star.

Troy and the other team members had played well, but Mike had carried them to the Cup, and they all acknowledged it.

Now Troy hoped the family wasn't going to be disappointed that they weren't sitting with the star of the series. He had fans, and a few detractors, but these were kids, and friends. Their opinion meant something to him. Angie, of course, would be blunt.

Angie was focused on the skaters, though, not the goalie. It didn't matter to her how good he was. She was interested in goal scoring, not pucks being stopped. She peppered Troy with questions. In the first game of the first series he had a breakaway and scored. How had he felt? How had he decided where to shoot and when?

Troy hadn't thought Tommy had a big interest in hockey, but he was impressed by a fight Troy had been in.

"Do you fight a lot?" he asked Troy seriously.

Troy shot a look at Michelle. Should he downplay this? Michelle was listening but not freaking out. He guessed a soldier wouldn't be upset much by a hockey fight.

"I wouldn't say I fight a lot. But occasionally. We get pretty excited out there, and we can lose our tempers. And sometimes you have to stand up for your teammates."

Tommy nodded seriously. The kid was almost always serious. He'd lightened up a bit at the aquarium and over dinner, but he was back to his usual self now. "Are you a good fighter?" he continued, gazing at Troy intently.

"I can hold my own. I've got a pretty good

score at hockey fights.com," Troy said. He didn't want to brag, but...

"You're big, too," Tommy said.

Troy shrugged. "Pretty big, I guess. I'm not the tallest on the team, or the heaviest, but I'm not the smallest, either."

Angie was tired of talking about fights. She was aware it would not be one of her strengths when she was playing.

"Can we keep going with the DVD? I want to see the Cup." She said the word reverently.

Watching the game, Troy was swept back into the excitement of that spring. It had been the highlight of his hockey career. Each man on that team had played better than they had in their lives. They hadn't been the best players individually, but together they'd been better than the sum of their parts. It had also been before he'd been diagnosed with cancer, and Troy had still felt invincible.

They all cheered when Mike made the last save. The DVD showed a redhead racing onto the ice and knocking the goalie over.

"Is that Bridget?" Angie asked.

Troy nodded. "She was our good luck charm during those playoffs." He remembered how irritating he had found her initially, but by the end she'd been one of the team.

The DVD had taken a while to watch, since Angie had kept pausing it to ask Troy questions. Now that it was done, Michelle sent Tommy off to bed while Angie talked more hockey with him.

"Is there anything that feels better than winning the Cup?" she asked.

Troy considered for a moment. When he had taken his turn to hoist the surprisingly heavy hunk of silver and skate it around the arena, he'd thought that had been the best it could get.

But then came the cancer diagnosis.

It had not been the first time Troy had struggled in his life. Some guys might make it to the top in a pretty easy ride, but Troy came from a small town, with a difficult father, and not much money. He'd been blessed with a lot of talent, but he'd had to work hard.

But the fight against cancer was something totally different. He'd felt helpless for the first time since his mother left, and none of his money or talent could force the outcome he wanted.

If he was honest, the day he'd been told the cancer was gone had been incredible, in a completely different way.

But that victory had been humbling and private, and something he hoped never to repeat again. The Cup he intended to win again if he could.

He wasn't going to tell all that to a twelve-year-old, though, so he simply said that not much could top hoisting the Cup over your head.

Angie gave him a skeptical look. "Not much? What could be better?"

Troy racked his brain for something to tell her that didn't involve cancer. "Some guys say getting married or when their kids were born are better."

"Would you say that?" Angie asked, forehead wrinkled as she pictured her own future.

Troy was spared answering by Michelle.

"Angie, that's getting pretty personal. It's also getting late. Off you go."

Angie sighed but gathered up the DVD and her Blaze hat and jersey that she'd brought out for the viewing.

"Sorry, Troy," she said with a sidelong glance at her mother. "But thank you. I liked hearing about the Cup from you."

She spoke with the confidence of youth, sure that one day this was coming to her. Troy knew that his confidence had never been so unshakable since his cancer. He hoped for her sake that Angie could keep that conviction for a good long time.

Michelle offered him some wine, but he shook his head. She sat back down in the big chair with a glass, leaving him alone on the couch.

Troy had thought they'd shared a moment last night, but Michelle had given him no indications that she felt the same today. She'd kept her distance tonight. He had a big game tomorrow, so the smart thing would be to go now. Plus, he was hungry.

So he rose to his feet. Michelle had been staring into space, and she turned to look at him. He wasn't sure what she'd been thinking about, but her posture showed that the burden was back on her shoulders. He really should leave.

"Big game tomorrow, so I'd better get going. Thanks for the tacos." He smiled at her, wishing he could bring back the carefree Michelle.

Michelle followed him to the door. "Thanks for the trip to the aquarium."

"It was fun. I'd heard about it, but it's not a place you want to go alone."

She opened the door. She still carried that weight, and he had to do something to help.

"Don't worry, it's going to work out," he said.

She glanced up at him, startled. He leaned down and brushed his lips against her cheek.

"Good night," he said, and left. He could feel her gaze on him as he went down the hall and entered his condo. His clean, quiet, empty place.

MICHELLE SLOWLY CLOSED the door. Why had he kissed her?

She supposed she must have looked worried. Her mind had been on their impending return to a hectic schedule. And she was about to start one of the hardest courses: tax. Poor Troy—she must have been poor company. No wonder he'd felt sorry for her. Sorry enough to kiss her.

Last night she'd felt some kind of undercurrent running between them. Fortunately, Angie had broken things up before Michelle had done something stupid. She had tried hard to keep her distance from him today.

Michelle sighed. This was getting to be too much like dating, and they needed to stop.

She wasn't interested in getting involved with anyone. She wanted to raise her kids before getting into another relationship. She certainly shouldn't get ideas about Troy. He was being very kind, and yes, he'd said it was helping his image with the team, but she knew he was biased because he knew their family history.

She also wondered if, without realizing it, he had been affected by his diagnosis of sterility. He apparently hadn't thought much about having kids. But then she'd arrived with two of them in tow. He could be trying them on for size, finding out if he wanted his own kids someday. She didn't believe he was doing it as a cold-blooded experiment, but how could that not be a factor, if only subconsciously?

She was more than grateful for his help. But she had to remember it was temporary. She couldn't burden him with any further expectations, or open herself to disappointment.

AT THE END of their break, the day before New Year's Eve, Angie rushed in from a trip to the corner store for milk. "Troy asked if we wanted to go to a game tomorrow! I said yes. That's okay, right? We didn't have anything else going on, did we?"

Michelle looked up from the stove. She was making some meals to put in the freezer for the busy weeks ahead.

They hadn't heard anything from Troy for a few days, but Angie had said the team had away games. Not that Troy owed them anything. Still, she'd been relieved when Angie had mentioned the team's road trip. Michelle had been mortified to think that Troy might have been avoiding them—or her.

Tomorrow was New Year's Eve. In the past, Michelle and Mitch had gotten a babysitter so they could go out to dance in the New Year. At least, before he'd been deployed. Last year Michelle had been sent out to a party by her concerned family and friends, and cried through most of it. This year the kids wanted to stay up till midnight. Michelle had agreed they could stay up to watch the ball drop in Times Square, and then go immediately to bed. It was something new for them, she figured. A new tradition to help them in their new life.

Adding in a hockey game shouldn't be a problem. She'd wish Troy a happy New Year after the game, and that would be that.

ANGIE WANTED TO get to the game early again, and since Tommy had no objections, they were at the rink in plenty of time to find their seats and watch the warm-ups.

Angie and Tommy ran down to the glass

to see everything as closely as possible. Troy spotted the kids and skated over to them. He smiled at them, then looked up to where Michelle was waiting in their seats and waved. She waved back with a smile. Then she heard Angie scream, "Nils!" when she noticed him on the ice. The young winger gave a start and almost fell.

The kids returned to their seats for the game, and Angie diligently explained the plays to her mother. Michelle now knew more than her daughter thought, but was willing to let her demonstrate her expertise. Angie tended to watch Nils closely whenever he was on the ice. Michelle watched Troy.

Hockey was a physical game. Troy used his size and force to control the play. Honestly, if she was out there with the puck and he came after her, she'd be gone so fast there'd be a roadrunner-shaped hole in the boards. She didn't think he needed to worry about any perceptions of being weak.

The Robertsons had a cause for panic when a particularly hard check dropped Troy to the ice for a few moments, but he got up, skated to the bench and played his next shift. No, cancer hadn't taken away his toughness.

The game had taken place earlier in the day

than usual, since it was New Year's Eve. Troy had asked them to meet him at a nearby restaurant. It hadn't exactly been part of her plan, but she'd agreed.

Michelle and the kids got a table and had some drinks while they waited for Troy. When he showed up, Michelle noticed Angie looking behind him, hoping he'd brought Nils. He hadn't.

Toronto had won, so they congratulated Troy. His hair was damp from a shower, and he was still wound up from the game.

Tommy asked Troy if he'd been hurt after the check that had dropped him to the ice.

"Nothing but bruises," Troy reassured them. "I took an extra moment there to get a bit of rest, and to see if I could get a penalty for that guy." He shrugged. "Didn't happen, but that's the breaks."

Angie frowned. "Is that cheating?" she asked censoriously.

"Kiddo, it's my job to help the team win. As long as I don't break the rules, I'll do it."

Angie frowned. She was young enough to believe everything was black or white.

"So how are the Robertsons celebrating New Year's Eve?" Troy asked, diverting her.

"We're staying up till midnight!" Tommy

said, voice rising at the end of the sentence as if he still didn't believe it would happen.

"Really?" Troy responded, sounding impressed.

"We're going to watch the ball drop in Times Square. On TV," Angie stated as if these details would make it more believable.

"What are you doing, Troy?" asked Tommy.

Troy assumed the expression of a freshly kicked puppy. "I don't have any plans. Guess I'll be all alone…"

Michelle was skeptical. "Really?" she echoed.

But Angie had fallen for it. "Troy can watch a movie with us, right, Mom?" she asked eagerly. "We have lots of snacks."

Michelle found three sets of eyes on her. She focused on Troy.

"I can bring snacks, too," Troy promised.

"It's not going to be very exciting," Michelle warned.

"But if we get to watch the ball drop…" he responded.

Michelle rolled her eyes. "You're welcome to come if you want to. Did you want to bring anyone else along?"

Angie looked eager, but Troy dashed her hopes—and Michelle's—when he said it was just him.

THE KIDS WERE having a hard time staying awake, especially Tommy.

"Can we do something that isn't sitting?" he asked, swallowing a yawn.

"Let's dance!" Angie suggested.

Michelle had danced with the kids since they were small. It tended to be more bouncing around than a recognizable dance routine, but they'd always had fun. When Mitch had come home from his tour, he didn't want to dance, so Michelle had just let the kids have fun. She wasn't sure about dancing with Troy there, but Angie had already run to turn on the music.

After jumping around to a couple of fast songs, a slower one came on.

Troy bowed in front of Angie and held out his hand. "May I have this dance?"

Angie flushed in confusion, then, after a glance at her mother, nodded. Troy took her hand and placing their hands in position, moved in a slow circle with her.

Tommy tugged on Michelle's hand. "May I have this dance?" he parroted.

Michelle nodded and stood up with a smile.

Tommy glanced over at Troy and did his best to mimic his behavior. Michelle gently nudged him in the right direction when needed. Troy teased Angie, telling her that he was supposed to lead, and then stood her on his feet to learn the steps.

Tommy looked up at Michelle, his brow furrowed. "How do I lead, Mom?"

Michelle whispered back, "Since you're still learning, do you want to stand on my feet and see how the steps go?"

"The man is supposed to lead, though, isn't he?"

"Normally, but we're just practicing, so it's okay."

This would have been a fun thing to record and play back later to embarrass Tommy when he was grown up, but it was serious for her son now, so she held his hands and they moved carefully to the music. Tommy was concentrating intently, and Michelle kept her face straight.

When the music picked up again, they returned to a group dance, involving a lot of hopping, twisting and flailing. Michelle hoped they weren't disturbing the neighbors below. She watched Tommy trying to duplicate Troy's moves. When it came to dancing, he could hardly pick a better model.

The music slowed again, but this time Angie pushed Troy toward Michelle.

"You guys know how to do it. Show us."

Troy held out his hand, and she placed hers in it self-consciously. The kids sat on the couch to watch. Dancing with a sibling would be lame.

Troy wrapped his arm around her back and drew her close. "Am I going to have to fight *you* for the lead?"

Michelle shook her head. She found it uncomfortable to meet his gaze, so she focused on his chest in front of her. It was a good chest. Strong and broad. Troy was back in his normal well-tailored clothing tonight, and his shirt fit him impeccably. She felt dowdy beside him.

Despite the kids watching, they still moved together well. She was strangely aware of him, and responded to every move he made, following his lead effortlessly. He was a confusing man. On the ice, he was fast and aggressive, yet here he was teaching her daughter to dance, and now leading her with the lightest of touches, graceful and sure. She began to relax.

"That's better," he murmured into her ear.

She glanced up. He was watching her intently. Her breath caught in her chest.

The song ended. He held the position for

a few more seconds, then released her to applause from the kids.

"Does dancing help you in hockey?" asked Angie, focused as ever.

"Hey, it's almost midnight!" said Tommy, relieved that he was going to make it.

Angie switched the music off, and then the TV on. They were five minutes from the ball drop.

"What do we do when the ball drops?" asked Tommy.

"We should toast," said Michelle. Everyone reached for their glasses. Angie's was empty, so she quickly ran for more soda.

"And you kiss someone," said Troy, with a glinting smile.

"I'm not kissing Angie," Tommy said, disgusted with the idea of kissing girls in general.

"Quiet! It's happening!" Angie shouted.

Tommy snuggled in next to Michelle. He wasn't taking any chances on having to kiss his sister.

When the countdown ended and the ball dropped, Michelle turned and kissed Tommy on the cheek. Her son was getting too old for the childish kisses Michelle had loved.

Angie gave Troy a kiss on the cheek and started cheering. Michelle stood to join her and felt Troy behind her. She turned to him and saw a strange expression on his face. "Happy New Year!" he said, and with a gentle touch on her chin, leaned down and kissed her. This time he kissed her on her parted lips.

Michelle hadn't been kissed by a man for a long time. Thankfully, her body remembered how it worked, and Troy certainly was skilled in what he was doing. His lips were firm, gently asking for a response she'd almost forgotten she knew to give. She heard Angie blowing a noisemaker, and pulled back. What was she thinking?

TROY TOOK A moment to gather his wits. He'd wanted to kiss Michelle for days now. New Year's Eve had been the perfect opportunity, so he'd taken it.

But the kiss had jolted him.

He was attracted to her, and he thought she was attracted to him, as well. He'd expected the kiss to be an indicator: Was there enough chemistry between them to go to the next level?

There had been chemistry, and a lot more. Enough that it took him a bit of time to come back to earth.

Michelle looked a little shell-shocked herself. She spun around to the kids, telling them it was bedtime. Angie had a gleam in her eyes, but agreed readily. Tommy was splitting his jaw with yawns.

They each gave Troy a hug, wishing him happy New Year again. Troy said he needed to get his beauty sleep, too, and took himself off. Michelle didn't look him in the eye as she said her own happy New Year.

Troy let himself into his condo. He didn't turn on the lights, but walked over to the window. Below, the city was alive with parties, people spilling into the streets to greet the New Year. He paid only cursory attention to them.

He couldn't stop replaying their kiss.

He'd wanted to stay in her place, wait for her to come back after putting the kids down and pick up right where they left off.

But as his blood cooled, his brain began to work. The chances of mother-of-the-year Michelle Robertson indulging in a makeout session in her living room were slim to none. And as he remembered, one of the kids could come in at any time.

What did he want from Michelle anyway? He remembered all his own arguments against dating mothers. They had responsibilities, and that wasn't something he wanted to take on. And just as important, they had kids, and kids shouldn't be hurt.

Right now, though, the idea of responsibility wasn't scaring him. It wasn't a vague thing anymore; these were two kids he was attached to. Being responsible for them sounded okay. Better than okay. Being part of their family tonight, and the taco night...he'd truly enjoyed that.

And he'd move heaven and earth to make sure those two weren't hurt.

Did he really want a relationship with Michelle? With the kids? He probed around in his head, but the fear, the reluctance—it wasn't there. Instead, there was a growing feeling of certainty. This was what he wanted.

He started to move, to go talk to Michelle, but he'd spent a while working this out and she was probably asleep. He'd talk to her tomorrow.

He sat down in his favorite chair. He looked around his place.

It was a single guy's pad, no doubt. That was what he was. He'd never had a relationship longer than a few months. He remembered the comments old girlfriends had made—that he was a kid himself. He frowned. Would Michelle believe he was in this for the long haul? Could he convince her? Convince her he was ready to commit to her and the kids, and anything else that came up?

He remembered her saying she didn't plan to get married again, didn't want to have more kids. So maybe the issue of kids wouldn't be a problem for them, but she had some hangups from her first marriage.

He'd just have to show her. Show her that he was reliable, that she could count on him, that he was around for the long haul. He tried to convince himself that kissing her senseless might help with that, but he realized that kissing her at every opportunity might only reinforce his player image.

Okay, he was ready to start Operation Michelle. He'd show her he could be just as responsible as she was. That family wasn't going to know what had hit them.

And when he had that accomplished, operation Kiss Michelle Senseless was going to be next.

CHAPTER NINE

"KIDS! COME ON! We have to leave now!" Michelle yelled.

It was the first morning back at school after the Christmas break, and they were all dragging their feet. No doubt staying up on New Year's—just two nights ago—didn't help. Michelle told herself not to dwell on New Year's.

Especially not to dwell on that kiss. She'd probably overreacted. After all, how long had it been since she'd been kissed? Since before Mitch deployed? So, yeah, she was probably a little kiss-starved. She hoped, really, that Troy hadn't meant anything by it. She'd tried the happily-ever-after, and it hadn't worked. Now she relied on herself only. If Troy thought there might be a future for them, she'd have to correct him.

She shook her head. Time to stop obsessing about this. "Kids! Come *now* or bedtime is moving up an hour!" Michelle yelled.

They came running out of their rooms, and

Michelle sighed. The three of them would be fine on their own…if they could ever get out of the condo on time.

They ran into Troy later that day as they were coming home. Michelle felt awkward, but Troy was his usual self.

"Can I drop in later?"

Michelle nodded, suddenly incapable of speech. Usually he just stopped by; he didn't make an announcement about it. She remembered her promise to herself to clear the air between them.

After the kids went to bed, Michelle tried to study but the words on the page made no sense. Michelle kept finding herself staring at the same sentence without taking it in. She was relieved when she heard the ping of the elevator. She slammed the book closed. Hopefully tomorrow the words would be clearer. She was at the door when Troy knocked. She braced herself.

His hair was damp from the shower but his movements were a little jerky, his eyes a little brighter. She'd noticed he was like that after games—like a spring unwinding.

"Is everything okay?" Troy asked.

Michelle relaxed a bit. "One of those days." She shrugged. "Did you want to come in?"

He followed her through the door. She sat back at the breakfast bar, rather than the couch. Things had been getting too familiar between them, so some space would be good.

"Oh, condolences on the game," she offered.

Troy smiled. "You watched the game."

Michelle shook her head. "Not really. I let Angie watch while she did her homework. I know, I'm a bad mother, but it was her first day back at school. She showed me her work—it looked okay."

Troy shrugged. "Can't win all the games, unfortunately. Reimer should be back next game and that will help. Are you okay? You seemed a little tense. School? Kids?"

"Yes, and yes. Plus, I have a headache. It was just a difficult transition back to the usual routine after the break." With an abrupt tug, she pulled her hair tie out. Her hair fell free over her back and shoulders, and she rubbed her temples. "That helps. Should have done it sooner."

Troy was eyeing her hair. "Did you have to cut it for the army?"

Michelle shook her head. "You can go short or long, but it has to be tied back out of the way. I was vain, and thought I'd look weird with short hair, so I kept it long. And then Mitch loved it long." She paused. Troy didn't say anything.

"When he was deployed, I kept it long for when he came home. And when he came back, it was one thing he still liked." She held a strand in front of her, checking for split ends. "Maybe I should cut it now."

"No," Troy interrupted.

Michelle raised her brows.

"It looks good. You should think it over before you cut it off. It must have taken a long time to grow it out."

Michelle sighed. "It did. And I'll soon be too old for hair this long. Might as well keep it for now."

Troy folded his arms across the breakfast bar. "So what were the kids doing to cause problems?" he asked.

Michelle recounted the late morning start, and a few other examples. Somehow, now, telling them to Troy, they were less irritating and more amusing anecdotes.

He countered with some of the things his teammates had done. They both relaxed. Michelle offered drinks. Then she remembered that this wasn't an idle visit. Troy had asked to come by.

Her shoulders tightened as she asked, "Is there anything wrong? You wanted to talk?"

Troy leaned forward on his forearms. "I have some time Sunday afternoon. Wondered if you and the kids wanted to do something."

Michelle felt herself smiling. "That would be nice."

"Okay, after practice I'll stop by. Any place you want to go?"

Michelle looked at him speculatively. "We've never been up the CN Tower…"

Troy laughed. "The ultimate tourist trap. Okay, sure, if you want to go."

"Do you mind? We've talked about going, but if you would rather do something else, we can go on our own."

Troy cocked his head. "I don't think I've been there since I first came to the city. That was years ago. So that's good. The Tower it is. You know, they have that Edge Walk thing."

"Edge Walk?" Michelle's brow furrowed.

"Some of the guys talked about it. You walk around the outside of the tower, about 1,200 feet above ground." Troy's eyes sparkled at the thought.

"Outside? In January?" Michelle asked in disbelief.

Troy pulled out his phone. He tapped and

swiped. "Oops, guess not in January. Maybe this summer we could do it. No, the kids are too young."

Michelle had peeked over the counter to see the information on his phone. She sighed.

Troy looked at her, a glint in his eye. "Would *you* do it?"

"It's safe, right?"

"No one has died from it that I've heard of."

Michelle bit her lip. "I don't know if that's a kind of risk I should take. The kids need a parent."

Troy leaned back, examining her speculatively. "It's the kid issue that you worry about? You're not afraid of heights?"

Michelle sat up straight. "I'm army. No fear. What about you?"

Troy grinned at her. "I'm hockey. No fear. Now, is that a dare, army woman? When the Edge Walk opens up, we are going walking. But this Sunday we'll stay inside."

"Thanks," Michelle said. She had relaxed enough to be disappointed when Troy said he needed to leave.

She shut the door behind him. This was something she truly missed. Another adult, a friend if nothing else, to share things with. It didn't mean the kids would be any faster tomorrow morning, but it had helped Michelle release some of her tension.

And he'd made no romantic overtures, so there was no need to worry about what had happened on New Year's Eve. The whatever-it-was had all been on her side. That was a relief. Anything more, and she couldn't have let this go on.

She really should have let her hair down sooner. The headache was forgotten, and she felt good. She had to remember to do that.

JANUARY WAS NOT a great month in Canada. The weather was cold, the days short and there weren't many things to look forward to. But somehow, they found some way to brighten each week up…usually because of Troy.

They booked some activity with Troy almost every week, and he had taken to stopping by in the evenings. Michelle thought he probably enjoyed an adult to unwind with just like she did. When he wasn't gone for away games, he'd often come over and they'd just talk. They'd discuss movies, TV shows, what had happened in their day… Michelle told him about some of the crazy things she'd done when she'd first signed up for the army, and Troy had stories about playing—on and off the ice. Troy had become her best friend in the city. Angie was his fan, and even Tommy seemed to come out of his shell when Troy was with them.

Sometimes Michelle thought his eyes were warm when he listened to her, but that had to be her imagination. There was no kissing, no more dancing... Troy seemed content with them all being friends. Her attraction to him still hit her by surprise occasionally when she wasn't expecting it, but she couldn't think of a good way to tell Troy to be less nice to them. She'd tried it once in the fall and it had made things uncomfortable. She couldn't imagine telling him that she liked him a little too much so he should keep away. His eyes would get that glint...

And somehow, as much as she tried not to rely on anyone else, Troy was always there. He took Angie to games and sometimes took Tommy to Tae Kwon Do classes. It gave Michelle extra hours to study, and she desperately needed them. The tax course was proving her downfall. She'd failed the first test, and was really worried about the next one. She couldn't bother Karen—this was the busiest season of the year for accountants. She tried to follow what Boni told her, but she just couldn't wrap her mind around the concepts.

So Michelle fretted about tax, but everything else was going smoothly...too smoothly.

Michelle got a metaphorical smack to the head from the kids. One evening they'd gone off to do their own thing in their rooms while she finished a difficult assignment. When she realized how late it was, she went to check if the kids had gotten their pajamas on as asked. She overheard a conversation between them that she should have anticipated. But she'd been blind, accepting things at face value.

"Don't worry. Mom and Troy can get married and then we can stay here. We won't have to move and we won't have to worry about money." That was Angie.

"Are you sure?" Tommy was not the optimist Angie was.

"He comes by here all the time after we're in bed. I'm pretty sure he likes her. And we all like him."

Michelle froze. Should she correct them?

No, she thought. Actions were better than words. She tiptoed back to the kitchen and made a big deal of putting some things away noisily. When she came down the hallway again, the kids were in pj's, and their conversation was over.

Michelle went through the normal evening rituals with them as if she'd never overheard the conversation, but she knew this wasn't something she could just let go.

She'd never wanted her kids to get attached to someone who wasn't sticking around. That was why she'd promised herself she'd never introduce them to someone she was dating until it was very serious.

But she and Troy weren't dating, so she'd assumed she and the kids were safe. She'd assumed wrong.

She decided to talk to Troy first—she didn't want anything the kids might say to come at him out of left field. Once she had that settled, she would talk to her kids. Explain that they got things confused.

That settled, she studied, or tried to, but she was keeping an ear cocked for the sound of Troy coming back from the game. She finally heard the ping of the elevator doors opening, and ran to the door.

His hair was damp and he looked tired, but happy. The team must have won. He smiled when he saw her in the doorway.

"Can I talk to you?" Michelle asked.

Troy nodded and came toward her, but she slipped through the door opening.

"Your place? I don't want the kids to hear."

An eyebrow shot up, but he continued to his door and opened it.

"Can I offer you something?" he said, switching on lights as he made his way to the kitchen.

Michelle shook her head, nerves building in her stomach.

Troy threw himself down on the couch. She wanted to ease his fatigue—get him a drink, put his feet up and help him relax. Michelle took a breath. It wasn't just the kids who were getting ideas. She might as well be honest with herself. This crush was getting out of hand.

"Do you want to sit?" he asked.

She shook her head. She swallowed and began.

"I overheard the kids talking." She paused, trying to find the right words.

"Were they planning a heist or something?" he asked, the corner of his mouth curling up. She caught herself watching the movement of his lips and stiffened her resolve. She needed to remember why she was here.

"They've made some assumptions. I promise, I've explained things to them, but, well, they're kids…"

He looked at her levelly. "Spit it out. How bad can it be?"

"They're talking about us getting married," Michelle said in a rush.

She wasn't sure exactly how she thought he'd react, but laughter was not what she'd have bet on.

"Angie probably figured it would help her move up in hockey. You can't tell me this wasn't her idea," he joked.

Troy didn't seem upset. She had worried he might be shocked, might try to minimize how close they'd become. At least look panicked. But instead, he wasn't even taking it seriously.

Well, obviously. She was not of any interest to him that way. The thought hurt, and that made her angry.

"It might seem funny to you, but they weren't joking," she said tightly.

Troy sobered quickly. "I'm sorry. I didn't mean it like that. Your daughter is very goal driven, and I'm a little surprised she didn't come to me and propose herself."

Michelle blanched. She hadn't realized things could have been even more embarrassing.

She said, "We obviously need to straighten them out. And actions speak louder than words, so I thought we should agree to start spending less time together. A lot less." She relaxed once she'd gotten that out.

Troy's brow creased. "The purpose of that being…?"

Michelle tightened her lips. Was he being obtuse?

"So that the kids realize that we're not dating, we're not planning a future together and so they don't get more attached to you." And so their mother doesn't get more attached, either, Michelle added silently.

Troy leaned back. "What if I don't want to do that?"

Michelle's stomach knotted as she stared at him. She'd assumed he'd want to put as much distance as he could between them once she brought up the *M* word.

"Why not?" she asked nervously.

"Maybe I enjoy spending time with you. Maybe I want to start thinking of a future. Maybe I want the kids to be attached to me. Maybe I'm attached to them."

Michelle blinked. The knot tightened.

Troy leaned forward. "Maybe we should start officially dating."

Michelle's knees buckled and she dropped abruptly into the seat behind her. She stared blindly at Troy, trying to process this.

Start dating? Her stomach fluttered.

But those flutters were familiar. She remembered when she and Mitch had first started going out. The flutters. Then the kids, the flutters changing... Then Mitch had gone overseas. She'd felt flutters again when he finally returned. But he'd been a different Mitch. Her life had been full of flutters after that, but not good ones. She'd been on her own, truly, with two kids and a badly damaged soldier to take care of. She shuddered.

She couldn't do that again. She glanced up at Troy. He looked strong, healthy and eminently sane. So had Mitch before he left. There was no telling what could happen to a person. Troy played a fast and physical sport. And he'd had cancer. Her head filled with pictures of emaciated people with bald heads, reaching arms out for help to deal with the nausea and weakness after chemo...another person to take care of. Another responsibility. Another funeral...

She shook her head. "No." She shook her head again, unable to stop the motion, trying to hold down the panic.

Troy looked baffled.

"Why not? I know I have a a reputation for being irresponsible, but I've changed. I can change more. Between going through cancer treatments last year, and spending time with you guys these past months—I'm not that same guy." His voice was smooth, persuasive.

Cancer treatments. Michelle shook her head again. No, she'd done enough.

"Michelle, look at me," Troy said. His tone was serious.

Michelle met his gaze, but she didn't see the man in front of her. She pictured him in a hospital gown, tubes in his arms, shadows under his eyes, reaching for her help. No.

"Michelle. I care for you—and the kids. I was hoping we'd just naturally explore this thing between us. And I know, after that kiss, there's something there. I've been trying to prove to you that I was responsible enough. And I'm ready to make a commitment to you now. I'm completely serious."

Michelle didn't want any more commitments. Most of the time she felt like she was barely keeping her head above water with the ones she had.

"Michelle, what's the problem? I can prove it to you. Whatever you need."

Michelle fought back the panic and focused on the present. She had no obligations to Troy beyond gratitude for what he'd done. But he'd had a reason for it. They were helping his reputation with the team. She hadn't promised him anything. She didn't have to take him on, too.

"Troy, I said no."

"But why? I'm a good guy, really."

"Troy, this isn't about you. I told you, I'm not getting married again."

"I was thinking we'd start by dating exclusively, see how things go…"

"I'm not getting married again, and I'm not getting involved again. I told you," she repeated more forcefully.

"But you know I can't have kids. I won't be trying to tie you down further. When the kids are out on their own, I'll be done with hockey, and we can do anything you want."

"What I want is to be on my own," she said.

Troy studied her for a moment.

"Is it Mitch? You're still in love with him?"

Michelle wanted to take the easy out, but she hadn't been raised to be a coward. She looked at Troy directly. "I've mourned Mitch. I mourned him when a man returned from over there with his body, but not Mitch inside. I mourned that body, too, when it died. I'm not going through that again."

Troy spoke gently. "Michelle, I have no idea what that was like but—"

Michelle shot out of the chair. "Then let me tell you what that was like." Her chest was heaving as she remembered. "We started out like a fairy tale, Mitch and I. He was tall and strong and people would follow him anywhere. I would follow him anywhere. And we had our kids, and were serving our country together and everything was great. We didn't have a lot of money, but we were happy, and it was enough. Then he went on tour overseas. I stayed here with the kids. I'd asked my superiors to keep me posted at home, for the kids' sakes, but Angie and Tommy still had their go-bags packed in case anything happened and I had to be deployed somewhere fast.

"But nothing happened to me, and Mitch survived. He was coming home and we were so happy, thinking it would be just like it was before."

She began to pace, arms crossed, holding herself together.

"But the man who returned wasn't Mitch. This Mitch had been wounded, badly wounded. You just couldn't see where he'd been mutilated.

"He had...episodes. So he couldn't stay in service. But I had two young kids and a damaged man to support, so I kept working. And I was okay with that. It was my family, and I would do anything for my family.

"But things were bad. At first, people wondered if he was abusing me because of the bruises. He'd wake up in nightmares, thrashing and kicking. I started sleeping on the couch.

"Then there were the mood changes. This nasty, dark anger. I could take it, but when he lashed out at the kids... I had to be the buffer between them.

"I couldn't relax. There were moments when the old Mitch was near the surface, but suddenly, a switch would flip, and the new Mitch was there. We tiptoed around him, never sure what would set him off. We couldn't have people over, because we never knew which Mitch our guests would meet. We couldn't go out for the same reason. And we couldn't tell anyone, because his reputation was all he had left. He'd given so much for his country, how could we take away the last thing he had to be proud of?" Michelle was almost in tears.

"It was like I had another child, but not one I could discipline, or get help for. I tried. I really tried. He refused to see someone, and I said if he wanted to talk, I'd listen. But he didn't want to revisit whatever he'd been through.

"Anything he wanted to do, we'd do, trying to find some way to make him happy. But nothing ever worked. He was in too much pain. I was his keeper and his guardian, but not a partner anymore. I was alone to take care of all of us.

"And then he killed himself. He was considerate enough to do it where the kids and I wouldn't find him. He took a gun, left a note and went out and shot his head off." Michelle wasn't crying anymore. She was numb.

"I was so sad when he died, but there was a part of me that felt this incredible relief. We could relax. We weren't on watch all the time anymore. Not just me, the kids, too. And that was awful, to feel relief when he'd been in so much pain inside that he'd killed himself. So then I was weighed down by guilt and sadness, so much sadness.

"And his parents just kept trying to understand how I couldn't have prevented his death. They kept asking for details of what had been going on in our lives. Mitch didn't want his dad to know he'd been sick, so we worked really hard to keep up the facade. So they believed it must have been my fault. Somehow, I was supposed to watch him every minute as well as work and run the house and take care of the kids.

"The story was all over the base, all over the city. Everyone wanted to know what it was like. And I couldn't tell them. I couldn't betray Mitch, my Mitch, who'd gone over there to serve his country the way he was supposed to. And I couldn't stand to have people looking at us with pity and condescension. I just wanted to blend in with the crowd again.

"So now we have a new start. *I* have a new start. And I will *not* go back to that. I can't. I just could not handle it again. I don't have the strength."

Michelle sat down. She was trembling. She'd never revealed to anyone the details of their life with Mitch after he'd come home. It would have been a betrayal to Mitch. But she'd had to explain to Troy, and once she got started, it had all just spilled out, like a dam bursting.

Troy sat down beside her. He spoke softly.

"You shouldn't have had to go through that. You shouldn't have had to do it alone. But I'm not Mitch. I'm not in the army. I'm not going overseas. It won't be the same."

Michelle looked at him, eyes blazing. "And you can promise you won't get injured? You don't take risks every time you go out on that ice?"

Troy stiffened. "You want me to give up hockey?"

She shook her head. "I don't want you to give up anything. Except us."

He gazed at her from under lowered brows. "What if I did give up hockey? Would that remove enough risk?"

She stared at him. The walls started closing in; she couldn't breathe in enough air. He didn't understand. It wasn't just Mitch who'd been hurt.

"Can you promise your cancer won't come back?" she asked.

Troy drew away. He sucked in his breath.

"No," he admitted.

Michelle stood. "I'll tell the kids you won't be coming around anymore. We'll stay out of your way. We're not here for much longer anyway."

She walked quietly to the door. Once outside, she almost ran back to her place, shut and locked her door, as if it could keep out the memories, the fear. Then she leaned against it, exhausted and trembling. She slid to the floor, hands on her face. She sat there for a long time.

TROY HARDLY HEARD her leave.

He could feel it again. He knew it was just his imagination, but somehow he sensed the cells in his body multiplying, preparing an army to fight against him. He couldn't control his own body.

He'd been cancer free for a year, but you had to wait five to say you'd beaten it. Really, though, you never knew. There were all kinds of cancer. And if it came back again, he might not win this time.

The last round had almost taken his career. It had taken his virility. He'd fought hard, harder than he'd ever fought anything in his life to come back and be the same hockey player he'd been. That way, he could convince himself it hadn't happened, that he was still invincible. But he wasn't. And Michelle knew it. And because of that, he wasn't worth being with. He wasn't good enough for her.

He'd been serious when he'd promised her he was ready to commit. He'd been proving it, not just to Michelle, but to himself. He, Troy Green, who avoided responsibility, loved them and wanted nothing more than to take care of them. Even without any physical contact, he realized he loved Michelle. He loved just talking to her after a game. Watching her face, making her laugh, lightening her burden, just a bit. Spending time with the family. And those moments they'd shared...

But he wasn't good enough. He was defective. He had cancer.

He swallowed a sob. And he started to get angry.

They could have been good together. But she wouldn't take a chance. Not with him.

Fine. He still had a great life. He just had to avoid them for a while. Mrs. Epps would be back in June. He could have fun again. If the team's management didn't like it, too bad. He was a good player, and that was going to have to be enough for them. This whole behaving thing was crap.

MICHELLE HAD COME home to study before her test this afternoon. She'd needed every minute of the hour she had. Lately, she'd found it hard to concentrate.

She rooted around in her purse for her keys as the elevator doors opened.

Michelle was used to coming home to an empty hallway now. With only the two condos, there wasn't a lot of traffic. Since that last conversation with Troy, he'd avoided them, just like she'd avoided him. Today, though, the hallway wasn't empty. There was a woman leaving Troy's home.

Pain ripped through her. No. She should be glad Troy had moved on, wouldn't be bothering them anymore.

"Can you hold that?" the woman called, and then turned and kissed Troy on the cheek. She hurried down the hallway to the elevator.

For what Michelle had heard called the "walk of shame," the other woman was doing pretty well. Her hair and makeup were immaculate, as were her clothes. She appeared ready to walk into an office and handle multimillion-dollar deals with one hand tied behind her back. Michelle was all too aware that she was the one who looked like the rumpled, unprepared schlep who was slinking home. It hadn't seemed important to primp before a school run. Who did she have to impress, after all?

The woman nodded to Michelle as she slipped past her into the elevator and pushed the button. Michelle was relieved that the kids weren't with her. She didn't want to have to explain this kind of thing to them. She shot a glance at Troy, who had apparently needed to watch his paramour get safely onto the elevator. The doors slid closed.

He didn't look embarrassed. Instead, she averted her gaze as if she was the one who'd done something wrong. She wanted to get safely inside before she had to look at him again.

"What is your problem?" he bristled from his doorway.

Michelle stood at her door, fumbling for her keys in her bag.

"I'd just rather not have something like that going on in front of the kids."

Troy stalked toward her. "Something like what?" he asked, spitting out each word.

"You're obviously an adult, and can do what you want. But I don't want to have to explain what a walk of shame is to them. It's not behavior I want Tommy to copy, and I'd like

Angie to strive for more." She sounded priggish to her own ears.

Troy slammed an arm across the doorway, just as she found her keys. She looked up and saw anger, real, hot anger in his eyes. This wasn't the easygoing neighbor she was used to interacting with. This was the man who knocked opponents down with the force of his body, won fistfights with other players. This man could be dangerous.

"You're right. I'm an adult, and I don't have to answer to you for anything I do. It's not my job to be a role model for your kids—I'm not good enough for your family, remember?"

He leaned in. "But just so you don't show that lemon-sucking expression to any one again, that was Kristie. She's engaged to a friend of mine. They were at my place last night, and decided they'd drunk too much to drive and took a cab home. Kristie forgot her phone, so she came back for it. That wasn't a walk of shame, which is a damned sexist way to refer to it. And even if it was, you can just figure out a way to deal with it. Not. My. Problem."

With that he turned and strode to his door, slamming it closed behind him.

Michelle stood there, keys dangling from her fingers, mouth open.

She gave herself a mental slap and let herself into the condo. She put the keys down and found her hands were shaking.

She'd never seen Troy so angry. It was upsetting. It was more upsetting that he was angry with her.

She sat at the countertop, studying forgotten.

He'd been angry, and when she thought about it, he was right. She'd judged them both without knowing the facts. When she'd seen that beautiful, well-groomed woman, clearly on good terms with Troy, she'd been...she'd been jealous. Bright, livid, green with envy.

For a while he'd devoted himself to her and her kids, and she'd enjoyed that. It had been nice to talk to another adult, to know someone was looking out for her, even though she'd tried so hard not to depend on it. Today she'd been jealous that someone else was getting that attention.

And if she was honest, she'd been jealous that there was someone who could kiss Troy with such freedom. Someone who didn't dig through a history of shadows and encumbrances before being able to reach out to someone else.

Troy had been right to challenge her on her quick judgment. She had no right to burden him with her expectations when she'd refused to give him any room in her life, or the life of her kids. She felt small, small and ugly. Not just the surface ugly, the inside ugly.

She should apologize to him. She didn't want to have this between them. She stood up to go knock on his door when she sat again. Why would she do that? It didn't matter if he thought poorly of her. It was better if he did. She'd tried to explain to him that she was changed by what she'd been through, and that she was no longer open to a relationship the way people should be. It was better if he just accepted that she was not the person he wanted.

She felt a twinge when she remembered he'd said he wasn't good enough for them. He had it backward. He had been great. She was the one who wasn't good enough.

Michelle sighed. These tough choices, these sacrifices, came about when you cared for someone. She couldn't take on any more. Someday, hopefully, she could think about what she wanted first, but that day was a long way off yet, and she was tapped out.

She wanted to put her head down and not wake up for weeks.

Instead, she grabbed her notes and started reviewing them for her test. She heard footsteps in the hallway and knew Troy was leaving, probably for practice. She realized she'd been looking at the same page for a few minutes and not taking in a thing.

Focus! she told herself. It had been the right decision to put distance between her and Troy. So, just like she'd always done, she needed to knuckle down and get through it. No crying, no whining. She was strong. She was army! She swallowed a lump in her throat.

TROY SLAMMED THE DOOR. How dare Michelle look at him that way, like he'd somehow disappointed her. She'd assumed he was sleeping with Kristie. He might have had a few girlfriends, but he would never put the move on a friend's partner. Okay, yes, Michelle didn't know who Kristie was, but what if she had been someone who'd spent the night? It was none of her business. She'd made that clear. He didn't make the cut. He'd been sick. Cancer survivors need not apply. It was…

It hurt, was what it was. And so he'd over-reacted and yelled at her, his anger blazing through. He probably should apologize, but damned if he would. He'd felt such a lash of fury when he saw her, judging him and finding him wanting again, that he had lost his control. He was sorry if he'd hurt her, but if he went over there now, he might say worse. He thought he'd come to terms with how things had ended, but apparently not. Better just to keep avoiding the family across the hall.

He dropped into a chair. When was Mrs. Epps coming back? Soon? He wasn't sure if he wanted her to return or not. Even though he didn't see much of the Robertsons, he was going to miss running into Angie and Tommy.

He was finding it hard to fill his time now without the family outings. He'd gotten used to spending his free hours with the Robertsons. He'd started to care about them. Now he just didn't have as much fun going to the clubs.

Enough. He rose to his feet. He needed to get to the arena for practice. No more moping around. Michelle had made herself clear. The Robertsons would be gone before long anyway, and he wasn't allowed to be part of their circle. He had to work on what his life was going to be like going forward, without them.

He threw on a jacket and grabbed his keys. But he paused and checked the hallway before he left. He didn't want to run into Michelle.

MIKE REIMER PASSED Troy in the team dressing room after practice.

"Let's get a coffee," Mike suggested.

Troy looked up from the skates he was unlacing.

"Is there a problem?" he asked, knuckles whitening around the laces.

Mike shrugged. "Just wanted to talk."

Troy nodded curtly. Something was up. Mike and Troy didn't hang out together. Mike wasn't the team captain, but that was only because he couldn't be, since he was a goalie. In every unofficial way, Mike led the team.

Troy waited for Mike outside the change room, arms crossed. Other players passed, and Troy gave them each a small nod. No one lingered to talk to him. That was different. People used to enjoy hanging out with him. Troy used to joke with them, but these days he didn't feel like joking. Apparently, they'd noticed.

Mike finally made his way out. "Why don't

we go to my place? I'll drive and you can follow me."

Troy raised his eyebrows, but nodded again. Mike gave him the address and Troy put it into the truck's GPS. He arrived right on Mike's tail.

He swung out of the truck, seeing the sports car that Bridget normally drove in the driveway. "Bridget here?" he asked warily.

"Nah. She's gone to a meet in Europe." Bridget coached one of the top swimming clubs in Canada. Troy might not be her biggest fan, but he had to respect her accomplishments. She knew her stuff.

"So I'm not getting tag-teamed here?" Troy asked.

"No. But I can set that up if you want," Mike said with a slight smile.

Troy looked around as he followed Mike into the house, but he didn't say anything. Mike led the way to the kitchen and started the coffeemaker.

He indicated a stool at the breakfast bar and Troy sat down.

"So what trouble am I in?" Troy wasn't interested in small talk.

Mike leaned against the counter and crossed his arms.

"Did you do something?" Mike asked mildly.

"Just spit it out. You didn't invite me here because you want a new BFF."

Mike nodded. "Okay, then. What's wrong with you?"

"Nothing. We good now?" Troy said, starting to get up.

"You haven't had your coffee yet," Mike reminded him.

Troy sat back down. He waited.

Mike sighed. "Okay, we'll do it the hard way. Is it the cancer again?"

"What is it with people obsessing over my cancer? It's gone. I've got a clean bill of health. I'm fit. I'm playing well. So what's the problem with everyone?" Troy snapped.

Mike looked at him assessingly. Troy stared back.

"So you're feeling good, the doctors are all happy?"

"Do I have to get a banner made up? Put it on the jumbotron? I don't have cancer, not now."

"I know it's not drugs. You're smarter than that. Money? Been gambling?"

"What the hell has that got to do with you? Do I look stupid?"

"I'll take that as a no. Just checking all the options. I guess it's door number three. Michelle?"

Troy winced. Did everyone know his business?

Mike continued. "Something has you in a lousy mood. Everyone has a bad day, but you've been miserable for most of the month. I swear one of the rookies missed a pass at practice just because he thought you were coming after him."

"Then I'm doing my job, so it's none of your damn business."

Mike nodded. "You're right. But it's affecting the changing room, so it's having an impact on the team."

"What are you saying? I need to play nice? Smile more?" Troy drew his lips up in a grimace.

"I've heard it helps to talk to someone," Mike offered.

Troy scowled. "Did you draw the short straw?"

"Something like that. You've been with the team a long time, you're a vital part of it, and if there's anything I can do, I'm offering. Or maybe I could get Bridget to talk to Michelle?" Mike said.

Troy noted sardonically that Mike was pretty tepid on that suggestion. No, he didn't want to get involved in someone else's love life. Smart guy. And involve Bridget? Troy shuddered.

The coffee machine beeped, and Mike got out mugs and milk and sugar. Troy considered for a moment. He'd been in a foul mood for weeks; that was true. He hadn't realized that it was a problem for the team. Hockey was the one thing he had left, so he needed to make sure he didn't mess that up. He certainly didn't want anyone thinking it was a physical problem.

He let out his breath. "Michelle and I are, well, not anything now. She gave me the boot."

Mike nodded. "That would explain it. I'm sorry. I liked her, and I liked the way you were playing while you were spending time with her. Any chance of working it out?"

"You can ask her to take one for the team, but unless I can change history and not get cancer she won't change her mind."

Mike passed him a coffee. Troy caught his puzzled expression.

"Yep, out of all the things that could have been the breaking point, it was having cancer that did it."

"Is it some kind of genetic thing that she's worried about passing on to future kids?" Mike asked.

Troy snorted. "No, she's already decided no more kids."

He took a sip of the coffee. He stared at the countertop. Marble? No, probably granite. He found himself telling Mike the rest.

"She went through some stuff with her husband before he died. Don't spread it around, but he came home after a tour of duty with PTSD, and they had a rough time. She says she won't take the risk of something like that happening—having to take care of anyone else."

"So she's scared?" Mike asked.

"Scared, overburdened, something. Believe me, she was pretty clear that this was not a thing she'd compromise on. I even offered to give up hockey, but I can't change the fact that I had cancer," he said bleakly. The pain of her rejection was still there. Something else to be chalked up to the cancer account.

"Anything I can do?" Mike asked.

Troy shook his head. He'd racked his brains trying to come up with some way around this, but at the end of the day, he just wasn't good enough.

"They'll be moving on at the end of the school year, so I'm just trying to avoid them till then." He remembered the altercation in the hallway. He definitely needed to avoid Michelle.

"Want to move in here for a bit?" Mike offered.

Troy paused with the coffee cup partway to his mouth.

"With you and Bridget?" He hoped he didn't sound as horrified as he felt.

"Sure. Bridget isn't around much for the next few weeks, so it's just me."

"Still, she's not my biggest fan," Troy reminded Mike.

"She's come around a bit. It's my last year playing in the league—I want this team to do as well as they can. Believe me, Bridget understands competing, and she'll be on board for anything that would help."

"You're seriously retiring?" Troy asked, still not quite believing it.

"I'm ready to move on to the next thing," Mike said calmly.

Troy raised his brows.

Mike smiled. "Don't tell anyone, but Bridget's pregnant."

"Wow. Congrats." Mike didn't have any

issues related to becoming a father, Troy thought sourly.

Mike shrugged. "We couldn't raise a family the way we want to with the careers we have, so I'm retiring."

Troy shook his head. "That's quite the sacrifice."

"Not really. I've won the Cup four times, I've had some good years, now I'll get out before I start going downhill. It's Bridget's turn to shine."

Troy examined the other man closely. For a guy as good as Mike to give up hockey was a big deal. But he didn't seem the least bit bothered by it. In fact, based on the look on his face, he was pretty pleased. And how could Troy really call him out on that, when he'd pretty well promised to do the same for Michelle? Sure, that had been when he was upset, and he didn't know if he could really have retired, but…

Troy thought things over. Being away from Michelle was probably a good thing. He would miss seeing the kids, but she probably didn't want him hanging out with them anyway. After all, they might catch cancer from him. It would probably be best for all of them.

"I might just take you up on that offer, at least for a while," he acceded.

Mike smiled. "I'll warn Bridget."

BRIDGET TOOK IT better than Troy expected. He didn't know exactly what Mike told her, but she didn't give him the evil eye when he met her over coffee the morning after she got back from her latest trip.

Bridget stared at his coffee enviously, and made herself some herbal tea.

"So, Green."

Troy looked up at her.

She sat beside him. "I warned you that not telling Michelle about paying for Angie's hockey would blow up on you. I promise, we didn't say a word."

Has it come this far? I'm talking about a relationship with Bridget?

"She still doesn't know about that," he said.

Bridget paused. "Then what did you do?"

Troy snapped at her. "Why do you assume *I* did something?"

Bridget shrugged. "Mike said you were staying here for a while and that you were avoiding Michelle. I connected the dots."

"Well, you missed a few. I didn't do anything."

Bridget squinted at him. "*Are* you avoiding Michelle?"

Troy wanted to tell her to mind her own business, but he was staying in her house.

"Yes," he said tersely. He checked the time. Surely he needed to head to practice soon.

"Did she do something?" Bridget persisted.

"No. Nobody did anything."

Bridget crossed her arms. Her voice was tight. "You're ghosting her. You got tired of her and the kids and you're trying to avoid them till they give up on you."

Troy glared at her through narrowed eyes. "Thanks for the compliment."

Bridget stared at him for a moment. "Okay, sorry. I just don't understand. You were all getting along so well."

When Troy didn't respond, she continued.

"Would you like me to talk to her? We've become friends."

Troy shuddered. "No."

"But—"

"No, Bridget. There's no talking that needs to be done. Michelle was very clear."

"I never thought I'd be saying this, but if you want me to give her a character reference for you... I mean, you've changed, and maybe—"

Troy glanced at her, wanting so desperately for her to stop, wishing she really could say something to Michelle to change her mind.

"Bridget, I appreciate that you want to help, but you can't. No one can. And I'd rather not discuss it."

Bridget looked at him sadly.

"Maybe she'll change her mind?"

Troy sighed.

"And maybe I'll not actually have had cancer at all."

He couldn't talk anymore. He abandoned his coffee and left, not really caring if he was being rude. He'd give Bridget credit for wanting to help, but this was one case where talking sure wasn't going to do it. He'd come to their house to avoid the Robertsons, and if Bridget was going to discuss it constantly, he'd go elsewhere.

She didn't, though. The topic didn't come up again.

CHAPTER TEN

THE POET WHO claimed April was the cruelest month hadn't lived through February in Toronto. Sure, Michelle had been through winters in Winnipeg, also known as Winterpeg. But though it was colder in absolute temperature there, it was a dry cold, and the days were bright. Here, it was gloomy and damp, and the cold got right into your bones. Sometimes Michelle wondered if she'd ever really feel warm again. March rolled in without bringing any change for the better.

School was a struggle. Karen had made some time to help her again, but she wasn't free often, and Michelle was finding it hard to focus on the coursework.

The kids, especially Angie, were upset that Troy wasn't around. Tommy had retreated into his shell, and Angie tended to stomp off to her room a lot. Money was tight, and she had to admit, she missed Troy, too. Those evenings when he'd dropped in, and she'd had a chance to be an adult for while, had helped her more than she realized.

Her school friends wanted her to come out with them again, but money was tight, and she just wasn't in the mood. She couldn't talk about the things that really affected her with them. They weren't having the same problems with classes that she was, and even if they ran into trouble, they could always retake the class next year, or try something else. Michelle didn't have that luxury. And the thing with Troy? No, they didn't have anything like that going on.

She was surprised when she got a text from Troy at the end of the month. She hadn't run into him again in the hallway, and hadn't heard the elevator pinging to signal his return after games. She assumed he'd found someone else with less baggage to spend time with, and told herself it was for the best.

It was a simple text:

Can I take Angie to her next game?

But Michelle stared at the message. Why? Why now, why at all?

The screen didn't answer. One way to find out.

Why? she texted back.

I want to see how she's doing.

Michelle bit her lip.

It didn't sound like he wanted to see *her*, just her daughter. That was *not* disappointment she felt. It was…well, it didn't matter what it was.

Would it upset Angie to see Troy again? Michelle didn't think much could upset Angie more at this point. Maybe if Angie still could visit Troy once or twice she might be less upset with her mother. Angie wasn't selfish, but she was certainly trending toward self-absorbed right now, and being with Troy was something Angie viewed as an asset to her hockey prospects. She'd also grown to like him as a friend.

She sighed. There was no manual to tell you when you were being a good or bad parent. Nothing covered all these situations. You tried, but Michelle knew that she, at least, failed a lot.

Okay, she texted back, hoping she wouldn't regret it.

Time?

Michelle responded, and Troy said he'd meet Angie downstairs. Michelle realized she was right—Troy was avoiding her so much he wasn't even staying in his own condo. Lovely. Michelle was an albatross dispersing misery everywhere she went. She'd just wanted to do the right thing. How had it become such a mess?

ANGIE THREW HER hockey bag into the backseat and jumped up front with Troy. She was grinning widely.

"Hey, Troy! How are you? Thanks for taking me to the game!"

Troy smiled. It was soothing to the ego to have someone be so happy to see him. He and Mike were getting along surprisingly well at his place, but Bridget was still a little reserved. Troy was trying to work on his mood in the locker room, not that his teammates seemed convinced.

"So how is hockey going?" he asked Angie.

The girl launched into a nonstop, game-by-game account of the last few months. A chance to talk over her favorite topic with someone who knew it well was a thrill for her. For all her focus and drive, Troy noticed that Angie talked less about points she'd accumulated, and more about the skills she was working on and how the team was faring. Michelle had done something right. Troy had already called her coach, so he had a good idea of how well Angie was progressing, but he enjoyed hearing her talk. And keeping the focus on hockey kept Angie from broaching any difficult topics.

Unfortunately, the rink wasn't far enough away. Angie turned to him and asked bluntly.

"Is it because of Tommy and me?"

"Is what?" asked Troy, stalling.

"That you're not around anymore. Mom said we'd helped you with the team, but we couldn't take up your time anymore. But we're not morons. Something happened, and Tommy and I wondered if we'd done something."

How was he supposed to respond to that? He could push the blame back on Michelle, but that wouldn't help this kid. She and Tommy needed their mother, and even though he was upset with Michelle, he wouldn't wreck their family dynamics as some kind of revenge.

But he also wasn't going to let the kids believe they'd done something wrong.

"No, it wasn't anything to do with you and Tommy."

"Well, what was it?" she persisted.

He sighed. He wasn't equipped to handle this kind of thing. "You're not going to like me saying this, but it's complicated. It's between your mother and me, and not really something I can explain."

"Is it because of Dad?"

Troy almost swerved into oncoming traffic. "Your dad? How would he have anything to do with it?"

"He was sick before he died. It was hard. But you're not sick, right?"

Troy took a breath. "I was sick. I had cancer."

"I know that. That's not news any more. But it's gone now, right? That's why you can play again."

"The rule is that you have to be cancer free for five years before you can say you've beaten it. It's been a year, and I hope it's gone, but it could come back."

Angie studied him intently as if she could see something in his face that would indicate the chances of his cancer returning. Troy could tell her it wasn't there—he'd looked.

"What if Tommy or I get sick?" she asked.

Oh boy. "Your mom will do everything

she possibly can for you two, you know that, right?"

"But what if she gets sick, too?" Angie said it softly, but she was scared.

Troy swallowed. What do you say to a kid who's lost one parent and is afraid of losing the other?

"Then you call me."

Angie stared up at him, eyes wide.

"You understand, I don't have any legal standing. But you call me, and I'll make sure you two are okay. Somehow."

Angie nodded, taking this as a promise. Troy nodded back, accepting it as the same.

Troy was noticed at the rink, of course, and had to pose for some pictures with the fans he encountered, but at the end of practice he headed down to Coach Albee and asked about Angie. She was doing well, and Troy was proud of her.

He was disappointed that he wouldn't get to be part of her future. He'd keep an eye on her, though. With her determination, she'd make something happen. Troy wanted to be there when she did.

After the game, Troy asked Angie if he could take her for some food. Angie texted her Mom for approval, and then she and Troy stopped for burgers. He'd searched in advance for a kid-friendly place. They talked hockey—how she was playing, how the Blaze was doing, even a question about Nils. Troy bit back a grin as he told her Nils was handling being sent down to the farm team just fine.

When they got near to the condo, Troy noticed a frown settling on her brow. As he pulled up to drop her off, he said, "Don't take this out on your mother."

Troy himself was still reeling from anger to disbelief with Michelle, but he would never take it out on her through the kids. He was angry, but no longer wanted to wound anyone.

Angie's jaw set. "Why not? It's all her fault. You said it wasn't us."

Troy sighed mentally. How to navigate this one?

"Angie, your mom only wants the best for you and Tommy."

"But she's wrong," Angie said with conviction.

"You don't know that," Troy heard himself saying, though he thought Michelle had it wrong himself. "I told you, it's complicated."

Angie glanced at him out of the corner of her eyes. "So it's about sex," she said.

Troy choked. "No— What—? That's none— Where did you—?"

Angie was looking at him curiously. "I'm not a child. I know that's what grown-ups fight about."

"Well it's not in this case." Man, he thought. How old was she? He tried to think of a way to explain.

"Angie, say you wanted to change your hockey stick. You don't believe you're using the right one. Now, if Tommy started to fight with you about that, what would you say?"

Angie rolled her eyes at him. "You're trying to say you're a hockey stick?"

Troy had to smile. "Okay, I'm not good at this. But just like Tommy doesn't know hockey sticks, you don't know what's up with your mom. Just understand there's a lot involved there, but we all want the best for you and Tommy."

Angie sighed. "She's still wrong. You both are. But okay."

NEXT, TROY TOOK Tommy to one of his Tae Kwon Do lessons. It was easier to spend time with Angie than Tommy because he and Angie had more in common, but he had a feeling there was something going on with the boy.

He wasn't sure what it was, and would probably never understand, but Tommy marched to a different drummer and Troy wondered why. The kid was so quiet and intense. Unlike the other kids in his class, he didn't goof off on breaks. He was *on* the whole time.

They had time after the class before Tommy had to be home, so Troy suggested they stop for some hot chocolate. They sat in a booth, and Troy searched for the right words.

"So, Tom, when do you get your black belt?" Troy asked, trying to open him up.

Tommy shrugged. "It takes a while. I'm working on my blue belt now."

"Do you have to register yourself as a lethal weapon if you make it all the way to a black belt?" Troy asked with a smile.

"There are nine levels of black belt," Tommy answered, seriously as usual.

Troy had had no idea.

But before he could ask further about the levels, Tommy said, "I haven't heard that anyone had to register themselves." Tommy's brow creased.

Troy hoped he wouldn't get the kid in trouble if he started asking about registering himself after this.

But that wasn't what Tommy was worried about. He'd been talking to his sister.

"Angie says if anything happens to Mom we can call you. Can we call if we get in trouble or something, too?"

This kids thing was full of land mines. What would Michelle be okay with him saying?

"As long as it's not going to make your mom mad? She's the one in charge."

"Okay," Tommy said. "And you can call on me, too."

"Sure thing, Tiger," Troy responded.

And just like with Angie, Troy felt he'd promised something that meant a lot to this kid. He couldn't imagine what trouble either of them could get into. They weren't delinquents, and he was sure Michelle wouldn't let them become anything close. But if it eased the kids' worries, he was happy to make them all the promises they wanted. And he was determined to keep them.

Tommy relaxed a little after that. When Troy asked about school, Tommy told him about the tornado project he'd done for the science fair earlier that year, and he'd memorized exactly what one should do if a tornado hit. Troy figured if a disaster ever happened, Tommy would be the best prepared person he knew.

MICHELLE APPLAUDED ALONG with the other friends and family. It was the promotion ceremony, and Tommy had earned his blue belt. Michelle hoped this would give him a confidence boost.

Michelle had decided to come to the ceremony rather than attend Angie's final interview with her hockey coach. As had to happen eventually, both events had been scheduled for the same night. Angie, who fought harder and harder against her mother's concern all the time, had insisted she didn't need Michelle at the interview.

"You don't know anything about hockey, Mother. You're just going to sit there and nod. Next year I'm going to do it all on my own anyway, so you might as well go see Tommy get his fancy belt."

Michelle had refrained from snapping at her with difficulty. What Tommy was doing was just as difficult and important. Angie did have a point, though. Michelle was mostly clueless about hockey subtleties.

Unlike Troy, said a little voice. Michelle stared at Angie, almost sure the girl had spoken the words. But no, it was Michelle's own voice she'd heard in her head. She sighed.

But to be honest, Michelle had no concerns

about Angie's hockey skills, and knowing how well she'd done this year, she was sure Angie would be ready to celebrate afterward. So with two bits of good news, Michelle had planned a celebratory dinner. Michelle was taking time away from studying, but as much as she needed that, she also deserved something to break up the funk she'd been in.

Michelle and Tommy walked home—Brittany's mother was dropping Angie off at home. Tommy was in street clothes again, but was carrying his new belt in his hands, a smile on his face. Michelle thought it must be one of the happiest moments Tommy had had here in Toronto. This year Michelle had had to make her courses a priority, and Angie was enough of a force of nature to make sure her interests always received attention, while Tommy was quiet. Next year Tommy would be the top priority. She tried not to overlook him, but she had to do more than that.

The snow was finally almost gone, and there was hope spring would arrive soon. Michelle would be happy once school was done. Not that hunting for a job was going to be a barrel of laughs, but she'd at least feel like she was finally starting to make progress.

She was looking forward to getting their

own place, as well. The condo was spacious and comfortable, but it was too close to Troy's. Not that he was around anymore, it seemed. If he was ever there, it was when they were elsewhere, and he certainly knew their schedules well enough to be able to manage that. Still, just the sight of that other closed door was depressing.

They hadn't heard from him since his outing with Tommy. Michelle wasn't sure what he'd said to the kids, but it had helped. She was surprised: he'd been so angry that day in the hallway that she was sure some of that would spill out when he was with Angie and Tommy. She didn't believe he'd ever do anything to hurt the kids, but...she blinked back tears. Troy seriously underrated himself.

Michelle would have loved to grill the kids on what they had talked to Troy about, but they were old enough now to understand what she was doing. And how would she justify it? If she had questions about Troy, as an adult she should be able to talk to him, not pump her kids for information.

She wished she still was talking to him. She'd panicked that day he'd wanted to start some kind of serious relationship with her. If she could go back now, would she answer the same? She wasn't sure, and she didn't see a chance to find out. Michelle shook her head. She was just tired and stressed. She'd made her decision, and she'd get through this funk somehow.

She unlocked the door of the condo, deliberately trying to ignore the other doorway and only thinking of it more as a result. Inside, their condo was dark and empty.

"Angie?" Angie should have been home already. But only silence greeted her.

Michelle texted Angie to ask where she was and when she would be home. She went down the hallway to check if by any chance Angie had come in, left the lights off and was listening to music in her room with the headphones on. Her room was empty.

She pulled out her phone again. No message from Angie. Michelle texted again.

Where are you? and waited. Nothing.

She turned and saw Tommy watching.

"Brittany's mom should have dropped her off by now. Maybe the team had a party after?" she asked.

Tommy shrugged. "Do we have to wait for her?"

Michelle hit the call button on her phone to connect with Angie. She was starting to get angry. She had thought Angie was getting over her anger about the way Michelle had ended things with Troy. Had something set her off and she was getting back at Michelle by ignoring her text? Had she put her phone down? Had she maybe got bad news from her coach?

The phone went straight to voice mail.

"Angie. This is your mom. Call me right away."

Michelle hung up and waited. Tommy watched.

Michelle sent five more texts and called five more times, with no response.

Anger was replaced by worry. She scrolled through the contacts on her phone and called Brittany's mom.

"Hi, this is Michelle. Did the girls go out somewhere after their interviews?"

"Hi, Michelle. No, I hadn't heard they were going out. Why do you ask?"

"I hadn't heard anything like that, either, but Angie isn't here and isn't answering her phone. What time did you drop her off?"

"I didn't drop her anywhere. She was still at the arena when we left, so I assumed you were picking her up."

Michelle felt worry trickling down her spine.

"I must have misunderstood her. I had a conflict today, so she told me she was getting a lift with someone, and I thought she'd said Brittany. Brittany doesn't know who gave her a ride?"

"Let me ask." There was a pause that seemed to take years. "No, I'm sorry, she doesn't."

"Okay, thanks for asking. I'll just call around. If you hear from her, will you let me know?"

Worry was inching toward panic.

Michelle called some more parents. There was no good news.

Tommy had put down his belt and was reflecting her anxiety back at her. Michelle wanted to reassure him, but she had no idea what to say. She finally dialed the coach's number. A couple of the parents had remembered seeing Angie at the rink, but none of them had given her a ride there or back. Michelle wondered if Angie had received some bad news about hockey, and that had led her to do…something.

Michelle looked up the number of Coach Albee and punched the digits with shaky fingers.

"This is Michelle Robertson."

She listened as the coach told her that Angie was one of the best players he'd coached at this age, and that he hoped she would still be able to play next year. He hadn't wanted to say too much to Angie herself, so he was glad Michelle had called.

Michelle broke in. As much as she was glad things were going well for Angie, she had something more pressing right now.

"You did meet with Angie?"

"Yes, and I said I wanted to talk to you. Isn't that why you called?"

"No, I haven't spoken to her at all. She hasn't come home since the interviews. Do you know how she was getting home?"

"I think she mentioned the subway. I hope that helps."

After concluding the call with the coach, she frantically opened the transit app on her phone, looking for problems on any of the bus or subway lines between the rink and the condo. There was nothing.

She finally dropped the phone in her lap. Tommy came over and sat beside her on the couch.

"Where is she, Mom?"

Michelle shook her head. "I don't know.

The coach thought she was planning to come home on transit. That was two hours ago."

"Did something happen to her?" Tommy asked, his hands fisted.

"Something must have come up, and maybe her phone wasn't charged. But I'm going to have to talk to her when she gets here. I see a grounding in her future."

Michelle hoped that was all that it was. It had to be. But adrenaline was coursing through her body, telling her she needed to go somewhere, do something.

Tommy sat by her while she called the Toronto Transit Commission to see if a young girl had been noticed, been hurt, anything to explain why Angie wasn't here, in the condo, with her mother yelling at her.

Michelle wanted to go search, but had no idea where to begin. The coach had taken it upon himself to walk the route from the rink to the bus stop, but he'd called to say he'd found nothing. Michelle and Tommy walked from the subway stop to the condo several times, to no avail. Michelle had finally picked up some pizza, which was now sitting cooling on the island counter. Neither of them was hungry.

Michelle wanted to search the streets be-

tween the rink and the condo, but she had
Tommy, and there was no reason Angie would
have walked that distance. If she needed help,
she had her phone, so why wasn't she answering?

Michelle had even called some hospitals
in the area, but they had no information for
her. She was about to call the police when she
heard the ping of the elevator door. She raced
to the hallway, Tommy on her heels.

TROY CHECKED HIS WATCH. He normally made
sure not to come to the condo in the evenings,
but he'd forgotten his dress shoes. He looked
ridiculous dressed in running shoes and a tux,
but he was on his way to a charity event and
just needed to grab the right footwear and run.
Surely, if he did see Michelle he could be cool.
Cool and aloof. He braced himself as the elevator doors pinged open.

Michelle and Tommy were standing in the
doorway. Their faces fell when they saw Troy,
and he felt anger stirring. Then he noticed that
Michelle looked haggard and panicked. Her
hands were gripping the doorway so tightly
he saw the whites of her knuckles. Tommy's
eyes were wide and his lips trembling. He was
as close to his mother as he could be.

Something was wrong.

The anger, the hurt, was all gone, replaced by concern. Michelle and the kids were in some kind of trouble, and he had to help them. It was that simple.

"What is it?" he asked.

"Angie's missing," she said in a tight voice.

The hallway seemed to spin, and Troy put a hand on the wall, trying to keep the sudden vertigo at bay.

"Missing? What happened?"

"She was supposed to get a ride with a friend to her interviews with Coach Albee. Instead, she seems to have gone on her own. She got to the rink okay, but no one's seen or heard from her since. Coach thought she was taking the subway home, but she's not here. There's no answer on her phone."

Troy forgot all about the benefit, and that he was wearing a tux with gym shoes. He steered Michelle and Troy into their condo.

"Okay, how long ago?"

Michelle bit her lip. "Almost four hours now."

"Was she upset about anything?"

Michelle shook her head. "From what her coach said, he gave her nothing but praise. She's been mostly good with me since she was out with you. I can't imagine anything that could have upset her after her interview."

"Have you called the police?"

Michelle trembled. "I was about to. Then we heard the elevator…"

Troy fought to keep his voice level. "You should probably do that. They can get eyes out there, let people know to look for her."

Michelle pulled in a shaky breath. "Right."

Troy looked at Tommy. "Hey, Tommy, why don't you come with me while I get some better clothes on and we'll let your mom make that call."

Michelle seemed to notice Troy's attire for the first time. "Oh, you have someplace to be—"

Troy shook his head. He had nowhere else to be while Angie was missing.

"It's okay, Mom. Troy said we could call him if we needed help," Tommy added.

Troy and Michelle froze. Then Troy shrugged. He glanced at Michelle.

"The kids were worried about something happening to you."

Michelle's brow creased. "But we have family…"

"Maybe they thought your family was too far away. I don't know. I told them I had no legal standing, but if they needed help, I'd do whatever I could."

Michelle glanced away, blinking quickly. Troy could have slapped himself. This was not the time.

He said quietly, "I'll change and be right back. I meant it. Anything I can do." He turned for his door.

Tommy followed him with a look over his shoulder at his mother. Troy thought Michelle wouldn't want Tommy listening to her call the police. Plus, he did need to change before he started searching.

Michelle was sitting with the phone in her hand when Troy and Tommy returned. "They're sending someone over," she said, sounding numb.

"Do you want me to stay while you talk to the police, or should I start searching right away?" Troy asked.

Michelle blinked. "I, uh..." She looked around as if the answer was lying around the apartment someplace.

"I'll stay till they get here," Troy said, taking the initiative. "Tommy, could you check the route she would have taken on my phone so I have a place to start searching?"

Troy passed his phone to Tommy and sat

down beside Michelle. He paused a moment and then wrapped his arms around her. She shuddered, leaning in to him. Beneath the worry, he felt a sense of rightness. This was where he belonged.

"It's my fault," Michelle said.

"No." Guilt would only make things worse. If they could get any worse.

"She had interviews and Tommy had his promotion ceremony at the same time. She insisted she could go on her own. She said she was getting a ride with Brittany, but she didn't. I shouldn't have—"

"Shhh," said Troy. "You couldn't be in two places at once. If she lied to you, that wasn't your fault."

"But why would she lie?"

"She's a kid. She believes she's old enough to do things herself—you know her. This isn't your fault."

If he'd been around…he could have gone with Angie. Angie would have liked that. If only… Troy realized he was doing the same as Michelle—trying to find a way to force some control on the situation. It wasn't helping.

"I keep imagining—" she started.

He tightened his grip. He saw her glance at Tommy and choke back the words.

Troy was having problems controlling his own fear and anxiety. He could only guess what was going through Michelle's mind. There were too many stories out there; too many girls who'd gone missing.

He wished he knew the right thing to do to help, but offering his presence was all he could think of. So he kept his arms wrapped around Michelle, trying to share the burden the best he could. He wanted to get out on the streets, hunt for Angie, do something active, but he could tell by the way Michelle was clinging to him that he was helping in some small measure where he was.

Two officers were buzzed up by security. Troy released Michelle, and she stood up to greet them. She went over the story from the time Angie had last been noticed at the rink to the present. Her voice was shaky, but she gave a concise account.

The officers recognized Troy. Troy recounted that during the same time frame, he'd been at Mike Reimer's, getting ready for the event he was no longer attending. He had no idea what had happened to Angie, or what was going to happen now, but he wanted to be sure he was not a person of interest so that he was free to help Michelle and Tommy.

The police were issuing an AMBER Alert. Troy said to Michelle, "I'm going to go out and search."

She took a moment and then nodded. He could read the indecision on her face. She wanted to be out looking, as well, doing something. Troy held her trembling hands in his.

He spoke gently. "You should be here in case she comes home. Call me right away if she does. I'll ask for all the help I can, but she knows me, so if I call out for her, she'll hopefully feel safe enough to answer. I'll keep in touch."

He turned to Tommy. "Thanks for that map. I realize you already checked, but it gives me a place to start."

Tommy gazed at him seriously. "Can I come with you?"

Troy could see the fear in Michelle's eyes.

"I think your mom needs you here. She shouldn't be alone. Can you help her?"

Troy wasn't sure how he'd respond, but after a moment the boy squared his shoulders and nodded. "Do you have a gun?" Tommy asked.

The cops turned, but Troy was already answering in the negative. "No, but if I find anyone has hurt her, I won't need a gun." He moved to give the cop a reassuring look. Right now the kid needed reassurance more than a lecture on leaving things to the proper authorities. Fortunately, they were too busy to notice, and probably sympathized enough not to say anything.

Four hours later Troy returned. His feet hurt, and his voice was hoarse from shouting. He'd sent Michelle messages every quarter hour. Still looking. But he was stumped. He'd taken every possible transit route Angie could have followed, but found nothing. He had run into people who recognized him, and they'd all wanted to help, but no one had noticed Angie.

Then he'd gotten into the truck and driven over the routes. Still nothing.

Once the police were satisfied that Troy was just a friend and that Michelle didn't have many financial resources, they concluded that ransom wasn't a factor. They'd left to search themselves, and Troy, Michelle and Tommy had sat to wait. All through the night.

The night was endless. The only communication they received was from people asking if Angie had been found. The concierge notified Michelle that a reporter was downstairs and wanted to speak to them. Troy's name had been connected to the story, and that, combined with the AMBER Alert, had attracted attention.

Troy sent down a refusal, and the family stopped answering any phone calls if the number wasn't Angie's. Michelle would sometimes get up and walk over to the windows, but mostly she sat holding Tommy, and Troy kept his arm around them both, offering what comfort he could.

He knew she was imagining what horrors could have taken place, could *be* taking place, but she didn't speak them because of Tommy, and because sharing them would do no good. She wasn't a person to reveal her pain. He wondered if she'd always been that way, or if the situation with her husband had made her like that. He wanted more than anything, more than another Cup, more than a guarantee of no cancer, to bring Angie home, but he was helpless again. The look in Michelle's eyes was killing him.

"Maybe I should tell you something," he said, breaking the tense silence.

Michelle focused, coming back from some horror-filled place in her head.

"What?"

"I confessed this that one night you went out with your friends, when I carried you into bed."

She nodded, confused.

"I thought you probably didn't hear me. I was the one who paid for Angie's hockey. Not the club."

He could see the information working its way slowly past the fear. For a moment she forgot the current situation.

"I knew something was up. I figured you'd made the coach take her on." Then her eyes filled with tears as Angie's present whereabouts came to the forefront of her mind again.

"Thank you, Troy. I should be mad, but she's loved hockey more than anything else this year." Her smile was more of a grimace.

He pulled her close again. He had wanted to take her mind off the present, just to give her a respite, but he'd failed. His fists clenched, wanting physical release in case the worst case was true.

This was why he didn't want responsibilities. They hurt. They messed up an easy, carefree existence. But if he could go back in time, take the option of not getting involved with this family? No. For better or worse, he was with them.

Tommy had dozed off, and the adults were careful not to disrupt his temporary oblivion.

Troy had told Michelle she should try to sleep, too, and she'd ordered him to do the same. Neither did.

Somewhere toward the end of that night of horror, Michelle turned to Troy and said, "I'm sorry."

Troy stayed still. He was fuzzy with lack of sleep and worry.

"It was never that you weren't good enough. Never. It's me. You've been nothing but great to us, and I'm sorry I let you feel that way."

A weight lifted off Troy's heart. It was a small weight, compared to what they were currently going through, but he had needed to know that. He pulled Michelle a little closer, and her head drooped onto his shoulder. It wasn't much, but it gave him a glimmer of hope.

Neither had moved. Daylight started to thrust its fingers through the windows when they heard the ping of the elevator again. They sat in disbelief for a moment, and then heard hesitant footsteps.

Michelle beat Troy by a head to the door. Angie was weaving on tired feet, with a tear-streaked face and disheveled hair toward the door.

"Mom?" she said in a tremulous voice.

Michelle grabbed her tightly, and Angie

clung to her, crying. Troy wrapped his arm around Tommy, who'd followed them to the door and was fighting tears himself. Angie was dirty, but her clothing wasn't torn, and she didn't appear harmed.

Michelle finally pulled back from Angie. "What happened? What? Why?"

"Let's go in and sit down," suggested Troy. They dragged themselves in. Michelle sat Angie down on the couch. Troy went to the kitchen to make some coffee and pour juice for the kids.

"I'm sorry, Mom," whimpered Angie. "I wanted to call but I dropped my phone and I was so scared I just hid…"

Michelle hugged her. "It's okay, honey, I'm not mad. I'm just so glad you're here now. Tell us what happened."

Angie had decided to prove that she could take care of things without her mom. She'd taken the subway to get to the rink, and things went well. But when she got to the bus stop to come home, she'd realized she was short the full amount of cash. She considered going back to the rink and borrowing some money, but she'd been the last interview, so she didn't think very many people would be around.

Plus, her mother might hear she hadn't handled everything on her own.

Then a car had stopped and asked if she needed help. She said she was missing a dollar for the bus, and the two men offered to give her a lift. She said no. They persisted, and she started to feel afraid. She walked away, but the car followed, so she ran, heading through a park where the car couldn't drive. One man got out to chase her, and she panicked.

She got away from him, but had dropped her phone. She found a hiding place, and stayed there till she got too cold. She finally started moving. She went back to the rink, but it was locked.

She avoided the bus stop and headed in what she thought was the direction of home. The only people she saw looked scary. She decided she should just walk home on her own.

It had been a long walk. By this time, most stores were closed, and she was afraid to approach people for help. She stayed in the shadows and walked as fast as she could.

Michelle reassured her that she'd done the right thing. She'd kept herself safe. When she could bear to part herself from Angie, Michelle called the police. They would come over to take Angie's statement.

Troy suggested he take Tommy to his room and see if he could get him to sleep. Michelle nodded, keeping close to her daughter.

Tommy had been quiet through the whole ordeal. Troy wasn't sure if that was a good thing or a bad thing.

"You okay, Tom?" he asked when they'd reached Tommy's room and were out of hearing.

"I want to go get those men," Tommy answered intently.

Troy was taken aback by the fervor in his voice.

"You and me both, bud."

Tommy sat for a moment, then gazed up at Troy.

"We should go now. You and me."

"Go?"

"Go get them. We could take them."

Troy paused. He couldn't imagine any circumstance in which he'd take Tommy with him on that mission. He was surprised that Tommy wanted to go on such a mission himself. He was just a kid, after all.

"Your mom would be pretty upset if you disappeared on her now," Troy said, feeling his way for the right answers.

Tommy sat, considering.

"Can we get them later? When Mom is better? Can you help me find them?"

"You don't want to leave that to the police?" Troy asked. He doubted most kids planned on being vigilantes, but maybe it came from all the superhero video games the kid played.

"It's my job," said Tommy as if this was obvious.

But it wasn't obvious to Troy. "Why do you say that?"

"That's what Dad said. He said if he wasn't around, it was my job to protect Mom and Angie. He said it was good that I was taking martial arts, because I'd be the man of the family and I have to take care of them."

Tommy said it matter-of-factly, but Troy felt ice shoot down his spine. Did this ten-year-old really believe he had to physically protect his mother and sister?

"I doubt he meant you should track down the bad guys and beat them up," Troy suggested.

Tommy nodded. "Oh, yes, he did. He showed me how to shoot his gun, but Mom got rid of it. All I've got are my hands and feet now." He swiped with his hands to show what he meant.

Oh boy, thought Troy. This was what the

kid had been grappling with ever since his father's death. And it was way above Troy's pay grade as a rookie father figure.

He stared down at Tommy's trusting face. What was he supposed to say? That a ten-year-old shouldn't have to take on that kind of responsibility? That his dad had been wrong to put that kind of burden on him? That his mom could probably beat up any bad guys better than Tommy could? Should he just play along until a professional stepped in to show Tommy how to put aside the load he'd taken on?

But Troy couldn't wait. Tommy was waiting for him to respond.

"You know, the police would be pretty upset if you shot someone. You might end up in trouble then, and that wouldn't help your mother. Why don't you let me take care of this one?"

Tommy considered. "Okay. I have my blue belt now, but until I'm bigger and get a black belt, I probably can't do it on my own."

Troy let out his breath.

"Good thinking. Meantime, we all need to catch up on some sleep. Are you okay to do that now?"

"Will you stay till I fall asleep?" Tommy asked, his tough facade slipping a bit.

"Absolutely," Troy said.

Tommy stripped down to his underwear and T-shirt, and Troy pulled the covers up over him.

"You rest—I'll take over the watch now."

It didn't take Tommy long to fall asleep, now that he'd passed his worries along. Troy took a few moments to consider what he'd heard. Tommy was going to need some help, and it was more than Troy or Michelle would be able to handle. But Troy was determined the boy would get the help he required.

He and Michelle were going to have a talk, and Troy was ready and determined to make his case this time.

MICHELLE THANKED THE officers for their help. They were going to put out an alert for the two men in the car, based on Angie's description, but everyone was aware that the chances of finding them were small. Still, they'd put out a warning to the schools and in the news. Michelle had her arm wrapped around Angie, and wasn't sure she would be able to let the girl out of her sight again.

Troy had come out of Tommy's room and

sat at the breakfast bar during the session with the police. He'd stayed in the background, quietly, as the officers wrapped up. Michelle could feel his support, even though he wasn't holding her any longer. He was the one who opened the door for the officers and shut and locked it behind them.

Angie had recovered enough to be hungry. Troy scrambled some eggs for them all. He said Tommy had gone to sleep.

Michelle felt a huge sense of gratitude to Troy. She had her daughter, here, eating eggs and starting to worry about missing practice. Her son was safe in his room. And Troy. He'd been a rock. Michelle apologized for how she'd treated him, but even before she'd done so, he'd stepped up, and done everything she could have asked for—only without her asking. She wasn't sure she'd have made it through the night without him. She watched him assuring Angie that he'd called her coach and let him know she was fine. He made Angie smile when he teased her about Nils being worried about her. Giving her something better to think about than her night in hiding, terrified and frozen.

He was big and kind and safe. Despite her reservations, her walls, her fears, he'd become a part of their family. They'd never really been his benefactors; he'd been theirs. She could see now that she'd been afraid that night, when he'd offered himself, and because of that she'd said no to something, no, someone, special. She wished she could go back and undo her decision. She couldn't live a life without risks. Last night had made that painfully obvious. And she wasn't sure she was strong enough to go it alone.

Troy looked up. Michelle wasn't sure what was showing on her face, but he took note.

Angie was yawning. The lack of sleep, the withdrawal of adrenaline, had all caught up with her.

"Come on, Angie," Michelle said. "And Troy, I don't think I've said thanks."

"Don't worry about it."

Angie made a token protest about not needing her mother to take her to bed, but she followed willingly enough.

"G'night, Troy. Will I see you—"

"You will," he replied.

Michelle's heart lifted a bit at his words. She'd be well served if Troy chose to disappear again after this, but thankfully he at least wanted to see Angie.

She'd been afraid that Angie might have a

hard time getting to sleep, but once Michelle crawled into bed beside her, she crashed almost before her head hit the pillow. Michelle gently brushed the hair back from her daughter's cheek and felt exhaustion wash over her. She'd been through lifetimes these past twelve hours. She should go out and properly thank Troy, but her eyes drifted closed…

TROY FINISHED CLEANING up what was left in the kitchen. He went down the hallway to see if Angie had been able to sleep. He smiled when he spotted Michelle curled up with her, both sleeping the slumber of the exhausted. He wanted to talk to Michelle—about Tommy, and more—but she needed her rest now. He wanted her awake and alert when he talked to her.

He took his phone out and noticed that it was almost dead. He found Angie's keys lying on the counter. He double-checked that the family was safe and sleeping, and then, reluctantly, went on to his place alone, locking up behind him. He plugged his phone in to charge, and made a couple of calls, then went to lie down himself.

He woke up early in the afternoon, a little disoriented. He had a quick shower and some coffee. There was a buzz from the main floor, and a few minutes later Bridget and Mike were at his door.

Troy invited them in and thanked them for coming. He noticed Bridget assessing his furniture, but she didn't comment, though he could imagine what she was thinking. He explained what had happened during the night, and how it had been resolved with Angie's return.

"I know Michelle won't want to leave the kids right now, but I have to tell her something I learned about Tommy, and it should be where we won't be overheard. That's why I wanted you to come and stay with the kids so we can talk privately."

Mike nodded. Bridget tilted her head.

"Just about Tommy?"

Troy shrugged. "I'll start with Tommy and see how it goes."

Bridget smiled back at him. "Believe it or not, I'm rooting for you, Troy."

Troy sent Michelle a text, and she responded that they were all awake. With an exhilarated, anxious tension similar to that of starting a playoff game, Troy led the way across the hall.

Michelle opened the door promptly, but was surprised to find Mike and Bridget.

Troy took the lead. "I need to talk to you, Michelle. Mike and Bridget will watch the kids. This isn't something they should hear."

She stilled, a strange expression on her face.

"It's about Tommy," Troy said in a low voice.

Worry crossed her face. He hated adding to her burden, but Tommy should get help as soon as possible. He also planned to alleviate some of that worry. He just hoped he had marshaled up sufficiently good arguments.

Michelle nodded, squaring her shoulders. She invited Mike and Bridget in. The kids were happy to see them and didn't put up a fuss about being left. Troy noticed Tommy checking that he was on hand, and that Angie settled in close to Mike and Bridget. It would take some time to overcome the effects of the past night.

MICHELLE FOLLOWED TROY over to his place, worry gnawing at her stomach. For a moment she'd indulged the hope that last night had bridged the gap she'd made between them, and that maybe Troy would give her another chance. But no, he wanted to discuss Tommy.

Troy had said he was attached to the kids, and he'd demonstrated that. If he thought there was a problem with Tommy, she needed to know what it was. She wouldn't have made it through last night without Troy, but she had to be prepared now to handle whatever was coming on her own.

Troy sat in his usual seat, and Michelle sat across from him. She examined his face carefully, not sure what to expect. He took a moment, and she clenched her fists.

"First, I just wanted to say that I think he mentioned it to me because I'm a man. It's something his dad told him."

Michelle felt those last words hit her in her gut. This was not going to be good.

Troy explained what Tommy had shared. Protecting the family, Tommy's belief that he had to go get these guys and deal with them somehow. His responsibility, at ten.

Michelle felt sick. How could she not have known her little boy was carrying this burden?

"Did you guys talk to someone after Mitch died?" Troy asked. His voice was gentle, inquiring, not accusing.

"Yes, we saw a counselor," Michelle said stiffly.

"Woman?"

Michelle nodded. Everyone had said a woman would be less threatening to the kids.

Troy leaned forward and grasped her hand.

He held it, carefully, between his two large hands. Strong hands that she so wanted to hold on to.

"I told him I'd take care of this particular problem, and that seemed to reassure him enough that he could sleep. But I think he's going to need help to deal with this one. Professional help, and probably with a guy, but I'm just guessing."

Michelle nodded. She'd start searching today for someone to help Tommy. Would it be covered? Would it be expensive if not? She fought the tears. She wasn't strong enough for this right now.

Troy gently tugged her hand. "Hey, look at me. I have a suggestion."

Michelle blinked. Was he going to offer to pay? How much more could she owe him?

He pulled their linked hands up till she could feel his chest beneath her cold fingers, bringing them closer. "First, I think Tommy will relax if I'm around, because I'm a man and can tell him I'm taking on that duty so he doesn't have to. That won't solve everything, but maybe it can give him space to work things out.

"And it's not just Tommy. I can also help Angie with hockey—I've got connections."

Michelle was confused. She wasn't sure

exactly what he meant. He hadn't offered money...did he want to go back to the friendship they'd had? When she didn't respond right away he continued, rushing his words now.

"I can't promise I won't get sick or hurt, but Michelle, you can't, either. Something could go wrong for any of us, including the kids. Like last night.

"I don't want to be another burden for you. I want to help. And if something does happen, well, it must be the same in the army as it is on a hockey team—having your team around is supposed to make things better. You don't have to do everything yourself.

"And I've got money. If we need help, we can get it. I promise, if it's the cancer or something else, we won't hide it. We'll do whatever it takes and you won't have to face it on your own."

Michelle bit her lip. What was Troy saying? Had he forgiven her for her rejection? Was he willing to give her a second chance?

"Michelle?" he asked. "Are you going to answer?" He sounded nervous.

She smiled a wavering smile. "I'm not sure what to I'm supposed to answer. I think I may be hallucinating. Are you really saying you haven't given up on me?"

"Given up on you?" He shook his head. "I'm not really an expert on these serious relationships, but it seems when you fall in love with someone, it doesn't just stop when you want it to. I know I've been angry, and I was trying to avoid you, but it wasn't because my feelings had changed. I was just trying to deal with them." He shrugged. "But last night I realized I didn't have to be a burden to you. I could help, make things better. I decided we are worth fighting for."

Michelle wondered if she was somehow living in a dream. Was it the aftereffects of last night? But no, this was beyond anything she could have imagined.

"After— After everything I—" she started.

He nodded. "Forever."

His arms were there and Michelle found herself enfolded against that strong chest, exactly where she wanted to be. She shuddered, wrapping her own arms around Troy, feeling safe and warm and protected and truly not alone for the first time in years.

"So is that a yes?" he asked against her hair.

"What am I saying yes to?" she asked, moving her face to see his.

"Well, with the kids and all, I think we probably should get married."

Her breath caught in her throat. "I'll say yes to that. I do love you, Troy. I have for a while, but I was scared. I'm not afraid now." And that was the truth.

Their lips met.

This time Michelle held nothing back. She'd been given a second chance: a second chance to share her life with a man she loved, and a second chance with Troy. She wanted him to feel the emotions she didn't always express easily.

Troy finally pulled away. "I'd like to keep this up, but I don't want any knowing glances from Bridget when we get back to your place. And maybe we should tell the kids."

Michelle smiled. Despite the horrors of last night, the lack of sleep and the certainty that she wasn't looking her best, she felt better than she had in years.

"They'll be thrilled," Michelle said. Troy grinned, a little smugly, and she poked his ribs.

"How much fuss do you want about a wedding?" Troy asked, pulling her in under his arm. Michelle leaned her head against his chest, hearing his heart beat beneath her. She made herself focus on what he'd said.

A wedding. Michelle blinked. She hadn't considered that. "I don't know. I hadn't thought that far ahead."

Troy tightened his embrace. "Because I was hoping we could arrange it as soon as possible. I don't want to give you a chance to change your mind. And I'm not sleeping in your bed till we're married. I won't give you the details now, but Angie has learned way too much about sex for a twelve-year-old."

Michelle wondered when that had come up, but she'd ask later. First, she was going to convince Troy that he had no need to worry about her changing her mind, and that she'd be happy to marry him as soon as possible. She planned to be very thorough about it.

EPILOGUE

TROY HELD HIS hand out to Michelle. The crowd was gathered around the dance floor—friends, family, everyone they'd invited to share their special day. All eyes were on them. This was their moment.

He was grinning, and she answered with her own smile. The circles were long gone from under her eyes, and she no longer looked worried. She was glowing, and gazing up at him with a warmth that still thrilled him.

She still sometimes gave him that look, the one with the narrowed eyes that said he was pushing things, but now it was a challenge for him.

They'd already had a quick, quiet wedding—just the two of them and the kids. Neither had wanted to wait to plan a big event, though she'd refused to do it on the Edge Walk. They'd gone on their honeymoon after the hockey season, and she'd been happy with that. Until he mentioned he was taking her to

Bora Bora. Then he'd gotten the look. But they had gone to Bora Bora.

Michelle finally had her spring break there, albeit more of a summer break by then. They'd had lazy days on the beach, danced until they were too tired to dance any more, and took the time to learn to be married. Troy thought they'd done pretty well.

When Troy suggested this big party in the summer to celebrate the wedding with family and friends, she'd been on board until he described how big a party he wanted. When he'd suggested they do this dance for their first dance, she'd definitely given him the look. But Troy loved to dance, and he knew they were both good at it. He'd seen videos of people doing choreographed dances at their weddings, and he was sure they could do even better. What had sold it, though, was adding Angie and Tommy in for the last bit of choreography. Once the kids were involved, he'd won.

The biggest look, though, had come when they'd discussed a prenuptial agreement.

Troy could hear his dad's voice, loud and clear, telling him to get that locked down and signed. Troy was ready to shake off both that voice and his lawyer's suggestion, but Michelle brought it up. He told her he didn't need one, but she set her chin and said she wouldn't marry him without a pre-nup.

He had a good lawyer, and the thought of that shark trying to batter down the value of his, Troy's, family to the smallest possible dollar amount made him angry, especially when he knew Michelle would probably offer to take even less.

So he'd come up with a clever way to get that pre-nup to work to his advantage so Michelle would never leave. He couldn't bear thinking about that.

He wanted to discuss the pre-nup in private, so he arranged for Mike and Bridget to take the kids to the O'Reillys'.

Michelle had taken some weeks to get over the anxiety the night Angie had been missing had caused her. Troy had bought them all new cell phones that could be tracked, to help her feel a little more relaxed. And the O'Reillys' was about the safest place for the kids to be. Michelle had agreed, and had even stopped checking her phone every five minutes.

They went out for a nice dinner, in a quiet booth in a restaurant that specialized in discreet and romantic. Troy felt nervous, much like he had when he proposed the deal for Angie's hockey, though this time he was going to be completely honest.

"I've been talking to a lawyer about a pre-nup, like you asked," he said.

Michelle nodded. "I'm glad you finally agreed to be sensible. After all, I'm not bringing anything in—"

Troy cut her off. He reached for her hands and locked their fingers together. "You're bringing in a lot. What you bring, though, is just not the kind of thing lawyers can write into a contract. I've come up with an amount for you to get every month, if ever—"

Michelle squeezed his hands. "I'm not leaving."

Troy grinned, never tiring of hearing that. "I'm not, either, but I have to write down something for the agreement. After all, you insisted." So he straightened his expression, and told her the figure he had in mind.

Her jaw dropped. "That's insane."

He held back another grin. "Well, yeah, but don't worry, that's just for you. There's also an amount for the kids, if they're still living with us." Giving her that figure didn't seem to help her come to terms with things at all.

Troy continued. "And of course, I'm setting up trusts for their education. I was wondering about putting aside an amount so they could have a down payment on a house at some point in the future, too. I mean, we don't want them to be spoiled, but it can be hard to break into that home-owner market. As well, you'd get to keep where we were living..."

Michelle drew her hands away.

"That's completely insane! This is all way too much money. I won't accept it!" She gripped the edge of the table and glared at him.

Troy reclaimed her hands. "I know." He smiled at her, looking all indignant on her side of the table.

"I know, without a doubt, that you're not in it for the money. That's why, I figure, if you sign this agreement, you'll never leave, because you wouldn't want to have that kind of money coming to you. It would be like a safety net for me, that you'll stay."

Michelle stared at him. She didn't look like she wanted to flip him to the floor, but she wasn't happy, either.

"You don't need a safety net, Troy. But this..." She shook her head. "That's a lot of money."

He nodded. "I have a lot."

Her expression froze. He'd assumed that

she'd have some trouble with the money once she realized how much there was. After all, she was still the woman who'd almost had a conniption over three jerseys he'd bought them. He'd actually been surprised she hadn't brought it up yet.

"How much?" she whispered.

"Enough that we can have name-brand tacos. Every night."

Now she looked ready to flip him.

"I'm serious," she said.

He gazed at her curiously. "You never looked it up? It's not exactly private."

She looked down. "I didn't really want to know."

Troy shook his head. Then he stated the figure.

She swallowed. "That much?"

"That much," he responded.

"How many years does that cover?"

"That's per year."

"Every year?" she questioned, disbelievingly.

He raised his eyebrows, pretending offense. "I'm good, you know."

She looked up apologetically. "Sorry, I didn't mean to imply you weren't. I just hadn't put the pieces together."

"There are more pieces," he warned. "Endorsements, appearances…"

She appeared even more troubled.

Troy squeezed her hand. "Michelle, I don't want to give up the money. It gives us some security. Can you learn to live with this?"

She took a deep breath. "Is there anything else?"

He shrugged. "Well, I own the condos."

"Where we live? You own that condo building?"

He shook his head. "No, I haven't got that much cash. I just own the penthouse floor. My place and Mrs. Epps's."

Her voice rose. "You own Mrs. Epps's condo? Our condo?"

"Well, it's in a holding company but yeah," he said, hoping she wasn't going to freak out.

Instead, she just sat there, head shaking. "I don't know what to say."

Troy was worried. "Say you'll marry me anyway?"

Michelle sighed, and for a worrisome moment he wondered if the money was going to be too much for her to handle. Then she smiled at him. "Okay. I guess I'll just have to learn how to live with money."

Troy sighed with relief. "I promise, it's not that hard."

And now here they were, married, pre-nup signed and celebrating in front of most everyone they knew. He'd gone shopping with Michelle to pick out a dress, sure that her frugal habits would torpedo his idea that she'd get the most gorgeous dress in the city. It had taken some convincing, but he still felt his breath catch every time he looked at her in that dress. It wasn't the dress, though. She was breathtaking.

He'd survived meeting her two brothers and her parents. Every male in her family had threatened him with dire consequences if he hurt her. It was a good thing that he was a tough hockey player, or he might have been a little scared. He'd never intentionally hurt her, and he was convinced he could make her life a little easier. They'd work out anything else. If not, he'd offer himself up for their beat down, if Michelle didn't take care of it herself first.

MICHELLE SMILED AT TROY. He was grinning like an idiot, and she was pretty sure she was doing the same. She was nervous, but only about the dance. She wasn't as comfortable in the spotlight as he was, but here, she just had to follow his lead.

So far, things had gone smoothly. She'd asked Troy for a chance to go back to Winnipeg and talk to Mitch's parents before they married. Troy had agreed immediately. Karen had volunteered to stay with the kids since Troy had games to play and Michelle was nervous about leaving them alone for any length of time, Angie especially. Angie hadn't fought the decision to have Karen stay over, so she had still been a little unsettled, as well.

It hadn't been an easy visit, but Michelle had decided to take the honest route. They'd had almost two years to come to terms with Mitch's death, so she decided it was time they understood exactly what he had been dealing with. There had been tears, but Michelle felt a weight had lifted off her. She told them that she was remarrying, a man Mitch would have approved of. Troy had already decided the kids could keep calling him by his first name, so Mitch would always be their dad.

Michelle had signed Troy's pre-nup, but under protest, and only because she never planned to claim it. Understanding how much money he had was intimidating. If she'd realized…but life was so much better now that she just couldn't let it get in her way.

It wasn't just that she didn't have to worry about how to pay for what they needed. Having a partner, one who was able to bear the responsibilities equally again, had eased so many of her worries. Troy had suggested she take a year off from school and work, just to figure out what she wanted to do without any pressure. It was a luxury that his money was providing her, and she appreciated it.

It was easier to deal with the money in the abstract than in reality. When he'd said they were going to Bora Bora, that had seemed as feasible as going to the moon. But they'd gone.

She'd been thoroughly spoiled, totally relaxed and felt like a new person was hatching inside her. A new person who had shrugged off some worries and shared some with the man beside her. This new person felt lighter and so much happier. She was frowning less, worrying less. She was more everything that was good. She sometimes had to pinch herself to make sure this was real.

Tommy was seeing a male counselor, but having Troy there to take the responsibility for the family had already helped her son. While she and Troy were in Bora Bora, Bridget had interested Tommy in swimming. He was good at it. Troy swore Bridget was doing it to get back at him, but Michelle was thrilled that Tommy had a nonviolent hobby to keep his interest. He'd started to shoot up in height, was spending less time playing video games and was making friends.

Angie had spent a month in a hockey camp during the summer. Troy had pulled strings for that one, and Michelle hadn't been able to do anything but frown. Angie appeared to have rebounded from her ordeal, although there were times she wanted to stay close to Michelle and Troy.

But there was going to be a break from hockey while they all went on a "family-moon" to Hawaii. After the trip Troy said he had to really concentrate on getting in shape for hockey again.

Michelle had been surprised by that. He had been maintaining his fitness all summer, Michelle thought, and she could definitely attest to how good he was looking. But he and Angie had planned to finish the summer getting into hockey shape.

There was something Michelle wanted to explore with the time she now had available.

She asked Troy how he would feel if she got involved in PTSD advocacy.

Troy thought it was a great idea.

"But maybe I should help with cancer awareness… I mean, that's your issue," Michelle had answered. She'd been afraid Troy might think she was choosing Mitch over him.

But Troy had pulled her close. "Hey, I do stuff for cancer all the time. You went through a lot with Mitch, and if you can help people with that, go for it." Michelle had to kiss him. She appreciated that he could be pushy, but he let her make her own decisions. Honestly, was it any wonder she was in love with this man?

So here they were, in front of a crowd of family and friends, about to do this complicated dance routine, bringing in the kids. Just like they were going to start a complicated life together, the four of them.

Michelle gave her hand to Troy, ready to follow his lead. For this dance, and forever.

* * * * *

HOME on the RANCH

YES! Please send me the **Home on the Ranch Collection** in Larger Print. This collection begins with 3 FREE books and 2 FREE gifts in the first shipment. Along with my 3 free books, I'll also get the next 4 books from the Home on the Ranch Collection, in LARGER PRINT, which I may either return and owe nothing, or keep for the low price of $5.24 U.S./ $5.89 CDN each plus $2.99 for shipping and handling per shipment*. If I decide to continue, about once a month for 8 months I will get 6 or 7 more books, but will only need to pay for 4. That means 2 or 3 books in every shipment will be FREE! If I decide to keep the entire collection, I'll have paid for only 32 books because 19 books are FREE! I understand that accepting the 3 free books and gifts places me under no obligation to buy anything. I can always return a shipment and cancel at any time. My free books and gifts are mine to keep no matter what I decide.

268 HCN 3760 468 HCN 3760

Name	(PLEASE PRINT)	
Address		Apt. #
City	State/Prov.	Zip/Postal Code

Signature (if under 18, a parent or guardian must sign)

Mail to the **Reader Service:**
IN U.S.A.: P.O. Box 1867, Buffalo, NY. 14240-1867
IN CANADA: P.O. Box 609, Fort Erie, Ontario L2A 5X3

* Terms and prices subject to change without notice. Prices do not include applicable taxes. Sales tax applicable in NY. Canadian residents will be charged applicable taxes. This offer is limited to one order per household. All orders subject to approval. Credit or debit balances in a customer's account(s) may be offset by any other outstanding balance owed by or to the customer. Please allow 3 to 4 weeks for delivery. Offer available while quantities last. Offer not available to Quebec residents.

Your Privacy—The Reader Service is committed to protecting your privacy. Our Privacy Policy is available online at www.ReaderService.com or upon request from the Reader Service.

We make a portion of our mailing list available to reputable third parties that offer products we believe may interest you. If you prefer that we not exchange your name with third parties, or if you wish to clarify or modify your communication preferences, please visit us at www.ReaderService.com/consumerchoice or write to us at Reader Service Preference Service, P.O. Box 9062, Buffalo, NY. 14240-9062. Include your complete name and address.

Get 4 FREE REWARDS!

We'll send you 2 FREE Books plus 2 FREE Mystery Gifts.

FREE
Value Over
$20

Both the **Romance** and **Suspense** collections feature compelling novels written by many of today's best-selling authors.

YES! Please send me 2 FREE novels from the Essential Romance or Essential Suspense Collection and my 2 FREE gifts (gifts are worth about $10 retail). After receiving them, if I don't wish to receive any more books, I can return the shipping statement marked "cancel." If I don't cancel, I will receive 4 brand-new novels every month and be billed just $6.74 each in the U.S. or $7.24 each in Canada. That's a savings of at least 16% off the cover price. It's quite a bargain! Shipping and handling is just 50¢ per book in the U.S. and 75¢ per book in Canada*. I understand that accepting the 2 free books and gifts places me under no obligation to buy anything. I can always return a shipment and cancel at any time. The free books and gifts are mine to keep no matter what I decide.

Choose one: ☐ **Essential Romance**
(194/394 MDN GMY7)

☐ **Essential Suspense**
(191/391 MDN GMY7)

Name (please print)

Address   Apt. #

City   State/Province   Zip/Postal Code

> Mail to the **Reader Service:**
> **IN U.S.A.:** P.O. Box 1341, Buffalo, NY 14240-8531
> **IN CANADA:** P.O. Box 603, Fort Erie, Ontario L2A 5X3

Want to try two free books from another series? Call 1-800-873-8635 or visit www.ReaderService.com.

STRS18

READERSERVICE.COM

Manage your account online!

- Review your order history
- Manage your payments
- Update your address

*We've designed the
Reader Service website
just for you.*

Enjoy all the features!

- Discover new series available to you,
  and read excerpts from any series.
- Respond to mailings and special
  monthly offers.
- Browse the Bonus Bucks catalog and
  online-only exculsives.
- Share your feedback.

Visit us at:
ReaderService.com